CW00496952

DARK HARVEST

DAVID J. GATWARD

WEIRDSTONE PUBLISHING

Dark Harvest
by
David J. Gatward

Copyright © 2023 by David J. Gatward
All rights reserved.

 Created with Vellum

To Louise, for making the best damned fruit cake on the planet (pass the cheese ...)

Grimm: nickname for a dour and forbidding individual, from Old High German grim [meaning] 'stern', 'severe'. From a Germanic personal name, Grima, [meaning] 'mask'. (*www.ancestory.co.uk*)

ONE

Darkness, thick as oil, had Amber wondering if she'd even opened her eyes. A cough sent a cold stab of pain through her body, and she screamed, only to cough again, and choke. The scream came back at her, the sound of it lonely and terrified and lost.

She was lying on her side, that much she knew. Her feet were cold, she noticed, and wriggled her toes. Her shoes were gone, but she had no recollection of taking them off. She tried to roll over, but as her back touched the ground beneath her it exploded it hot agony, her head swam, then waves of nausea made her gag. She tasted vomit in her throat, spat out blood and mud and grit. She blinked, squeezing her eyelids shut until sparks burst behind them, her thoughts a jumble, her memories a mess. Where the hell was she?

Once the nausea was gone, Amber went to rub her eyes with her hands, but they wouldn't move. They were tied fast, behind her back, and attached to something else away from her body. She tried again, tugging, yanking hard, felt something rough tighten around her wrists, then panic crashed into her out of the nothingness, burning away whatever grogginess she felt from waking up. And again, she screamed.

The sound bounced away into whatever space she was in,

chased away into hidden holes by some terror in the darkness she could sense but not see. The echo of her panic ricocheted back, and she heard in it her own desperation as it faded to nothing.

Far off, the sound of water dripping reached her, and she was shocked by how something so innocuous could sound so bloody terrifying.

Closing her eyes again, Amber forced herself to calm down, to trace a path back through what had happened, to discover somewhere in her aching head what had brought her to where she was right now.

Josh ...

The name flashed up in neon in her mind, and love and panic twisted together inside her, a maelstrom she couldn't control. There was no sense to it, no sense to any of this. Where was he? Where the hell was Josh? Where the bloody hell was her husband?

'Josh? Josh! Where are you? What's happened? I ... I can't ...'

Amber couldn't remember. She wanted to, needed to, tried to reach back in time, but all she could claw back were the shattered remnants of memories that had no link at all to where she now was, not that she knew where that was, or how she'd ended up there in the first place.

She called again into the dark.

'Josh!'

The stark sense of being utterly alone crushed Amber, reaching into her chest like the hand of a surgeon, its icy fingers slipping around her heart to squeeze it.

She gasped, coughed, spluttered out a cry, tried again to free her hands, but whatever they were tied to held fast. She followed the rope backwards, pulling herself clumsily along the damp rough ground, until her hands brushed against something cold, hard, unyielding, and fixed to a jagged wall of rock. Even in the blackness of the space she was in, her touch told her enough. The rope holding her was tied to a hard ring of iron, its surface rough with rust.

Amber twisted around, pivoting on her left hip, braced her

bare feet against the wall, and heaved. The rope stretched a little, gave out whispers of complaint, but didn't give. She tried again, pushing with her feet, pulling with her hands, her muscles soon on fire. She had no phone, remembered that she'd left it back at the campervan, not that it would be any use anyway wherever she was now.

'Josh! Please, where are you? Josh!'

Nothing.

Just the metronomic drip, drip, drip of water far off.

Amber tried again to free herself, only to have her hands slip on the slick, wet rope. She fell, rolled onto her back, crushing her arms, grazing her hands, and again the fire coursed through her, but somehow she held in the scream.

Her head cracked off something sharp and hard. A rock on the ground beside her, too large to shift. She shuffled up against it, forcing herself to ignore the pain, felt her nails scratch against the ground beneath her. She slid back to the ground, had another go, fell once more, kept going, until at last, she was upright.

The exertion of such a simple act left her breathless. Sweat beaded on her forehead, her neck, slipped into her eyes, stinging them, sending cold trails down her back.

The sound of her breathing was loud, almost bearlike. Her heart beat hard, the thump-thump-thump of a drum in her ears.

The campervan, she remembered that, clear as day. Rain, too, and lots of it. Josh had headed off on his bike, hadn't he? Yes, that was right, and she'd declined, deciding instead to snuggle up with the book she was reading. It was a good one, too, and she was just getting to the really good bit, didn't want to pull herself away from the story. She'd nibbled a few biscuits, some lovely sticks of buttery shortbread from that bakery they'd found in town. Washed them down with a small glass of red. A lovely afternoon by anyone's standards.

Then nothing.

A blank.

Amber found only a hole in her mind where whatever had

happened to bring her here, to darkness, to the cold, to silence broken only by dripping water, and her wrists tied behind her back.

Amber imagined the tap the water was falling from, realised how thirsty she was, then the nausea came again, and she retched. This time, she couldn't stop it, and she bucked forward, felt vomit burn its way up her throat to splash down onto the ground beside her, onto her feet. The warmth of it was almost welcome. She retched again, but nothing came, so she spat the taste of it from her mouth. The acid taste of wine lingered.

Josh had promised more wine ...

That was a memory, and a clear one, so she grabbed hold of it and held it close. But why? Amber knew she had been alone in the campervan, reading, all warm and cosy, then ... then Josh had returned, hadn't he? That was it; Josh had come back from his ride, all excited about something, desperate for her to come with him so that he could show her what it was he had found.

Amber smiled then, the memory of Josh's excitement, that grin on his face, the bright eyes lit with a wildness she adored.

But what the hell had it been? What?

Amber screamed, screamed again, let her cry rip from her, tearing her throat to shreds as she chased one echo with another, but the dripping water snatched them away.

Could this be the place Josh had wanted to show her? But how was that even possible? How had they even got here in the first place? And where the hell was he anyway?

'Josh! Please! Josh!'

The love of her life, her every waking moment, the part of her she hadn't even known had been missing.

'Josh!'

The man who she'd bumped into over the buffet at a party in a pub, spoken to about the inherent joy of a cold roast potato, ended up talking to all evening at the bar.

'Josh! Please ... Where are you?'

The man with whom she just seemed to fit, who loved her for who she was, didn't want her to change, and who sometimes looked at her with such hungry eyes that she would have no choice but to just fall into his arms.

'Josh!'

Drip ... drip ... drip ...

The bikes! That was it, she remembered now. Josh had been insistent she go with him, out into that god-awful rain, had fetched her bike for her, and she had followed. Reluctantly, yes, but still she'd gone, happy to just go with him and to trust that whatever was at the end of the journey would be more than worth it.

The rain had been so heavy that riding through it had been painful, stinging her face as she'd raced after him. They'd both been laughing, speeding through puddles, Josh unable to miss any opportunity to get his bike airborne, Amber declining to follow at first, only to end up soaring after him, chasing him with laughter.

Josh had fallen at one point. He'd hit a puddle too quickly, and it had snatched at his wheel away, sending him flying. She'd stopped, expecting the worst, dashed over to him, only to be dragged down by him for a roll in the grass, a kiss. And it would've turned into more if she'd let it, despite the weather. And then ...

And then what, exactly? What the hell had happened after that?

She spat again, took in a breath, good and deep, exhaled slowly to try and calm herself, to focus her mind.

The campervan ... the rain ... the bikes ... the trail ...

And now darkness.

They'd stopped, Amber remembered that much, as she somehow dredged the depths of her mind for memories like damp photographs from a still, grey pond, their colours fading, bleeding into each other.

Josh had been even more excited at that point, and closing her eyes she heard his laugh, saw him running ahead, but to where, Amber couldn't remember, couldn't see. And she needed to, had to force herself to look, to try and spy what lay hidden in the gloom, because the answer had to lie there.

Amber shook her head, tried to dislodge something more, something that made sense, something that would tie whatever that memory was to where she was right now, give her a path to follow from the heaven of that afternoon to the hell of right now.

There was no thread, though, just those last memories of Josh laughing, of her racing after him and laughing, too, the rain still coming down, footsteps in puddles, the landscape around them shrouded in thick, grey cloud.

Then, out of the tar-like blackness, a thought made itself known as it scratched weakly on the inside of her skull, a thin nail etching something else, something mean and dark and nasty, and the conclusion Amber then came to was so wrong, so terrifying, so crushing, that she heard her soul break in two.

Josh had brought her here. Josh had led her to this darkness. And now Josh was gone.

TWO

'I'm not sure what's worse, Harry,' said Dave Calvert, unable to hide his smile. 'Your face, or this weather.'

Harry was standing outside the main entrance to Hawes Auction Mart, with Dave Calvert and Jim Metcalf. Dave had recently qualified as a Police Community Support Officer and was now the newest member of the team. He was also giving Constable Jadyn Okri a run for his money for being the keenest.

Which was no small achievement in itself, Harry thought.

To help Dave get to grips with the role as quickly as possible, he was shadowing the team's other two PCSOs, Jim and Liz, for the next couple of months. As Liz was away up the other end of the dale, today it was just Jim, and the look Harry saw on the young PCSO's face at what Dave had just said was one of shock.

As for his face being as bad as the weather, Harry suspected that he wasn't doing all that well at hiding his feelings. And that was saying something, because it wasn't as though he was the proud owner of a world-winning, smiling visage. He'd never been all sunbeams and toothy grins, that was for sure.

Quite the opposite, truth be told.

The almost permanent scowl his battle scars had gifted him all those years ago in Afghanistan had served him well as a barrier between himself and the people around him, generally guaranteeing that they never got wind of whatever was going on in his head, no matter how traumatic. And considering how things were with Grace right now, that was the way he wanted to keep it, though perhaps to describe it as "traumatic" was over-seasoning it a little, Harry thought.

Still, it was on his mind and vying for attention with the other thing bothering him, that being everything that was going on with Gordy and Anna. All in all, now was not the time to let his mind wander, so he pulled himself back out of his thoughts and into the moment as best he could.

'Would you prefer it if I looked like this?' he asked and broke his scowl with a grin. He could feel the scars complain as he forced them to stretch, the skin going taut, his lips baring his teeth in a snarl.

Dave stepped back in horror.

'What the bloody hell are you doing?' he asked, recoiling, lifting a hand to point at Harry's face. 'What *is* that?'

'This is me smiling,' Harry said, and kept it hanging there for a little longer, seeing Jim turn away to hide a smile and a roll of his eyes. 'Not something I do much.'

'I can see why.'

A low rumble of thunder rolled through the black, roiling clouds above them, as thick rain fell, and Harry was glad of both the waterproof jacket he was wearing and his Wellington boots. What he wasn't so glad about was how much those items had cost him back when he'd bought them in those very early days in the Dales, but there was no doubting their effectiveness.

After a quick Monday morning team meeting at the office in the Hawes Community Centre, to go through the Action Book and check on things for the week ahead, Harry had walked to the auction mart with Dave and Jim. Jen had been the only one missing from the meeting, having had to stop on the way over from Middleham to deal with a driver who'd split a tyre on a pothole in the road.

Harry had suggested they drive, but Dave had marched off into the rain. He was keen that people would get to see him in his shiny new uniform, and regard him as someone who would be out in all weathers doing his duty, and utterly oblivious to the rain, and to the lightning that lit up the angry sky.

Leaving his Rav4 in the marketplace, Harry had chased after him, with Jim by his side, and Fly and Smudge coming along for the stroll. Harry had expected Smudge to resist, but the bond with Fly was strong, and no sooner were they outside, than the dogs had started play fighting, quickly getting their leads into a tangle as they found the nearest puddle to roll in. They were neither of them bothered by the thunder.

By the time they'd all arrived at the auction mart, Dave must have said good morning to at least half the population of Hawes, Harry thought, the inhabitants of the small market town at the top end of the dale going about their business regardless of the weather.

'Just a reminder,' said Jim, turning to stare at Dave. Harry noticed that the young PCSO's chest was puffed out a little. 'Harry's a Detective Chief Inspector.'

'I know that, lad,' said Dave, slapping his hand on Jim's shoulder. 'What's your point?'

'My point,' said Jim, 'is that I generally avoid commenting on his face, or on anything personal at all, if I can. It's not my place, if you catch what I'm saying.'

Harry watched as Dave's brow furrowed into a deep frown, the man pondering for a second or two on what Jim had just said.

'You know, that's a fair point,' he agreed, then looked at Harry. 'Sorry about that. Just need to get used to us moving all of this on from being mates, to us working together.'

'We're still mates,' Harry said.

'Which is why I'm concerned,' said Dave.

'Why? There's nothing for you to be concerned about. It's not that unusual for people to like the people they work with.' Harry realised then what he had just said. 'Though, if I'm honest, it's a first for me, too.'

Jim laughed at that.

'What? You can't be serious.'

'When is he ever anything else?' said Dave.

'It's this place,' Harry said. 'It does something to you, doesn't it? Makes you break the rules you live by.'

'You have rules about friends at work?' Jim asked.

'Used to,' Harry said.

'Like what?'

'Like the people I work with are not my friends.'

Dave narrowed his eyes and leaned in towards Harry.

'And there's the problem right there,' he said.

'What problem?'

'We're your friends, aren't we?' said Dave, dropping an arm over Jim's shoulders, like two young boys ganging up in a playground. He then tapped the side of his nose with a finger before pointing at Harry. 'Which means we can tell something's up. We can smell it.'

'That's the auction mart,' said Jim.

Harry said, 'Fun though this all is, standing here in the rain and waiting to get struck by lightning as we discuss my face, I think we'd be better off getting on with the real reason we're here, don't you?'

'Crime survey, wasn't it?' Dave asked, turning his attention to Jim. 'What's that when it's at home, then?'

'Bit of a grand term for you and me walking around and chatting to folk,' said Jim. 'If people get funny about seeing you asking questions, that kind of thing, just fox them with a bit of jargon.'

Harry said, 'We've decided that it makes sense for us to do a bit of intensive intelligence gathering. Most of what we learn is through meeting people, chatting to them, but this is just a little more focused, that's all. So many farmers in one place; it's good to make use of it. We'd be foolish not to.'

'Rural communities have their own issues to be dealing with,' said Jim. 'Obviously, there's theft—'

'Livestock?' Dave asked.

'Yes, but machinery is more common,' said Jim. 'Easier to make a quick profit by nicking a vehicle then stripping and flogging the parts, or throwing a quad bike onto a trailer, than trying to shift a few head of stock. Then there's vandalism, hare coursing, fly-tipping, trespassing ...'

'We're looking to see if we can spot any patterns, that kind of thing,' said Harry.

'And to see if we can do anything more to help,' Jim added. 'There's not many of us on the team, and we cover a huge area, which is a bit of a problem, to say the least. But the more we're seen, the better a deterrent we are.'

Harry stared at Jim for a moment, very aware of the wry smile now on his face, though he made sure it didn't go any further and stray into the recently revealed awfulness of his smile.

'You know, sometimes you sound more like a constable than a PCSO,' he said.

'Do I bollocks,' said Jim, then caught himself, realising what he'd just said, and to whom. 'I mean, I'm not about to move jobs, am I, if that's what you're thinking? Just because Dave here's a PCSO now, doesn't mean I'm about to head off to some police college and get badged.'

'Why not?' Dave asked. 'You're young, bright; you'd be brilliant.'

'He's got a point,' said Harry, but as he spoke, a yell split the moment and he looked up to see half a dozen sheep making a run for it, racing hell for leather down the concrete road that led up into the mart. They were heading straight for them, and after that, there was nothing but the open main road. And despite the weather, it was busy, with traffic thundering past, and vehicles pulling hefty stock trailers turning in.

Before Harry could react, Jim unleashed Fly, and at the same time let out a piercing whistle. Fly raced off towards the sheep, and Jim followed him at a calm jog, sending out another whistle. Fly, head down, his eyes focused on the escaping animals, whipped around and cut off their escape, corralling them off to the left, towards where Jim was now standing. There was another whistle from Jim, and Fly responded, man and dog working as one, and soon they had the sheep turned, and walking calmly back up into the auction mart and their waiting owner.

'I think that answers your question,' Harry said, standing with Dave and watching Jim and Fly as they helped get the sheep back to where they were supposed to be, under cover and in a pen, before heading back down to stand with them once again.

'What question?' Dave asked.

'Why Jim will never be a constable,' Harry said. 'And believe me, it's not that he wouldn't be good at it. He would. I've even suggested as much myself numerous times, but there's something else that runs stronger in his veins, I think, don't you?'

'The family farm?'

'The farm, the Dales, all of it,' said Harry, looking around and breathing in the rich, peaty air. 'It's part of his DNA. There's no escaping it, not now.'

'And why would he want to?' added Dave. 'He's lost to the place, isn't he?'

'There are worse places,' said Harry.

Jim came to a stop in front of them and dropped down to give Fly's head a scratch.

'Good lad,' he said. 'Well done.' He then stood back up, shaking his head. 'Hobby farmers,' he said. 'Don't get me wrong, I admire anyone who wants to have a go at farming, but it's not something you can do just because you've got a lot of money and fancy a break from city life, is it? Some of them are absolutely clueless. You know, I think they even see sheep as pets, and they're not, are they?'

'That was impressive,' said Harry.

'Was it?' said Jim, then he shook his head, clearly disagreeing with Harry. 'Sheep are good at two things: dying for no reason at all and escaping. Not much I can do about the first, but escaping? Fly and I have become dab hands at thwarting it.'

'I can tell.'

Jim laughed, then patted Fly's head again, the dog's tail tapping gently in the stream of water running down from the mart to the road below.

'Dad never thought he'd come to much, back when I first got him. Mind you, he was an idiot, wasn't he? But you've proved him wrong, haven't you, lad?'

Fly's tail tapped a little harder.

'Still is, if you ask me,' said Harry, as Fly swiped a paw at Smudge, then flopped onto his back, paws in the air, tail now wagging excitedly.

Jim and Dave laughed.

'Who were they, then, these hobby farmers?' Harry asked.

'Not a clue,' said Jim. 'I think this was their first time here. They'd just bought the sheep and were a little excited by it all by the sound of things. I've said I'll give them a hand in a bit to get them into their stock trailer. And as they're new, I was thinking that Dave and I could head over to their place later in the week, give it a look over, see if there's anything we can advise on with security, that kind of thing.'

'Very sensible,' said Harry, then noticed someone running towards them, shoulders hunched against the rain.

'That's Elsa,' said Jim. 'Works at the mart office.'

'What's she want, then?' Harry asked.

'Now then, Jim,' Elsa said, then looked up at Harry, her face tucked beneath a hefty bobble hat. 'There's a call for you from Constable Okri.'

'Jadyn? Where?'

'In the office,' Elsa said, then turned on her heel and jogged back up the way she'd come.

Harry went to pull his phone out of his pocket, baffled as to why Jadyn hadn't called him on that instead. Except it wasn't there.

'You'd best head off,' said Dave. 'Whatever it is, it'll be important.'

'It had bloody well better be,' said Harry, and followed Elsa through the rain, Smudge at his side.

THREE

Detective Sergeant Matt Dinsdale was in the office down at the community centre, nursing a pint mug of tea, and flicking through photos on his phone. Every single one of them was of his daughter, Mary-Anne. He knew he was smiling, could feel his face beam with every captured moment in his hand. Jadyn was sitting at the other side of the office, phone to his ear. Matt lifted his phone and turned it around so that the young constable could see the screen.

'Have I shown you this one?' Matt asked. 'This was when she woke herself up from a nap with a massive burp. Puked all down my jumper, too. Funniest thing ever! I mean, it was revolting, like, obviously, but I couldn't stop laughing.'

Jadyn leaned forward for a closer look, narrowing his eyes.

Matt flicked through to another photo.

'What about this one? Isn't she beautiful? The most amazing eyes, just like her mum's.'

Jen walked into the office, shaking off the rain from her jacket as she unzipped it, then hung it on a hook on the wall.

'How is Joan?' she asked, stealing the quickest of kisses from Jadyn before heading over to the small kitchen area.

That made Matt smile. Neither Jen nor Jadyn was for showing much in the way of affection at work, which was fair enough, he thought, and sensible, too. Indeed, they'd done well to keep their clearly deepening private life separate from work. But the old romantic in him couldn't help but smile a little at seeing it, and the resultant grin on Jadyn's face, which he failed utterly in trying to hide.

'Not seen her for ages,' added Jen. 'We should have a team night out sometime, book a table at The Fountain.'

Matt saw a faint look of relief on Jadyn's face that he didn't have to try and think of something to say about the photos.

Jen looked down at the carpet. 'And what's with all these muddy footprints?' she asked.

'Joan's grand,' said Matt. 'She's taken Mary-Anne to baby yoga or something this morning over in Leyburn. The footprints were here when I arrived. Jadyn had a visitor, which is why he's now on the phone to Harry.'

'Baby what now?' Jadyn asked, talking over Matt. 'Yoga? You mean like all that stretching and the lotus position? How does a baby do that?'

Matt wasn't entirely sure himself.

'It's very good, apparently,' he said, attempting to sound like he really knew, which he really didn't. 'Don't knock it till you try it, right?'

'And you've tried it, then have you?' Jadyn asked.

Matt shook his head.

'No, of course I bloody well haven't,' he said, unable to hide the laugh. He'd done a good number of activities with his daughter, but the yoga was new. 'Not sure anyone should see me trying to do any of that, particularly my own flesh and blood.'

'Who was this muddy visitor, then?' asked Jen, glancing over at Jadyn. 'And why do we need to speak to Harry about them?'

Jadyn went to answer, when his attention was hooked in by the crackle of a voice on the phone.

'That'll be Harry now,' he said, as Jen sat down next to Matt, and he went back to the phone.

Matt saw a confused frown appear on Jen's forehead.

'Isn't Harry up at the auction mart with Jim and Dave?' she asked.

'He is,' Matt answered, 'but thanks to the owner of those muddy footprints, we've had something come up and figured we should let him know what it's about. You know how he gets if we keep things from him.'

'Which we don't,' said Jen.

'And that's exactly what we want him to think, isn't it?' winked Matt. 'Though right now, with the mood he's in, it's probably best to not keep anything from him at all, isn't it?'

Jen frowned.

'How was he?'

'Bear with a sore head,' said Matt. 'Only worse.'

'So, what's happened, then?' Jen asked. 'What's come up?'

'The owner of those footprints is a biker,' explained Matt, pointing at the mucky marks on the carpet. 'One of those off-road types. There was more mud on his face than on his boots, so God knows what he's been up to.'

'His leathers were a proper mess, too,' Jadyn said, cupping his hand over the receiver.

'Leathers?' said Jen. 'Must be some old dude then; most folk you see on the lanes wear modern all-weather gear now; leather's more your road bike user, or Harley owner.'

'He came in off the fells about an hour ago,' continued Matt. 'Wearing half a peat bog on his boots, it seemed, and he blessed us with depositing half of it in here.'

'Why?'

Jadyn chucked his mobile phone over to Jen.

'It's a campervan up on Cam Road,' Matt said, as Jen flipped Jadyn's phone over in her hand to look at the image on the screen.

'You mean that track that leads out the back of Hawes? If you follow it for long enough, you end up over Horton-in-Ribblesdale way. I've run up there loads of times, and you can tag on a trip up Pen-y-ghent, too, if you want.'

'Which I don't, and never will,' said Matt, leaning over to swipe through the rest of the photos. 'There's a few more, see? Looks like the van's been there for a couple of days. The awning looks like it's taken a fair battering from the storm, and there's various bits and bobs laid out inside the van itself, a meal, bottle of wine, that kind of thing.'

'That's a bit weird, isn't it?'

'It is,' Matt agreed. 'Very.'

Jen was quiet for a moment, flicking back through the photos.

'Could the owners just be in Hawes out of the weather?' she suggested.

'They could,' said Matt, 'but we need the numberplate to check on the owners so we can do a ring round to try and find them, which means we need to head out there ourselves. The biker took a photo of it, but it's not great, as you can see ...'

He flicked through to the last photo.

'It's half covered in mud,' said Jen.

'Exactly,' said Matt. 'Can't read it at all. Which is why we need to go up and have a look for ourselves.'

'And that's why you're calling Harry.'

'Exactly that,' said Matt. 'Don't want him thinking we're out on a jolly.'

That made Jen laugh.

'In this weather? You think it's been abandoned, then?'

'Possibly.'

'That doesn't make sense though, does it? Why would anyone do that?'

'Why indeed?' said Matt. 'Which is why we thought it best to tell Harry about it. We're going to head up for a look as soon as Jadyn's finished talking to him.'

Matt looked over at Jadyn, who was now listening more than talking. He could hear the rough-edged grumbling of the DCI's voice at the other end of the call. Didn't sound like his mood had improved any, he thought.

'He's really not himself at the moment, is he?' Jen said, clearly having heard Harry's tone herself.

'Hasn't been for a week or two,' said Matt, scratching his chin.

'Any idea what's going on?'

'I've asked, but he wasn't exactly forthcoming.'

Jen laughed.

'He told you to bugger off and to stop being so bloody nosy, didn't he?'

'Something like that, though a little less polite and with considerably more growling,' said Matt. 'I reckon if I'd asked again, a bloody nose is what I'd have been risking.'

'It could be Gordy,' suggested Jen.

Matt shook his head.

'What Gordy and Anna are doing, that's their business, and we'll be fine, I'm sure. Reckon it'll do them a world of good, myself, moving somewhere new. Warranted, it's down south, but to each their own. No, it's more than that, isn't it? Has to be.'

'Does it?'

'Of course it does! And that's what worries me, though hopefully more than it should. Not sure I'm all that enamoured of Harry being even grimmer than his name and general demeanour would suggest.'

Jadyn put the phone down and released a heavy sigh.

'What did he say?' Jen asked.

'Probably best I give you the censored version,' Jadyn replied.

'And what's that, then?' said Matt.

'He's on his way.'

'Come on, he must've said more than that,' said Jen. 'That's only four words.'

'Oh, he did,' said Jadyn. 'A lot more. That's why I was on the phone for so long. And you'll have noticed that I didn't exactly do much speaking. But like I said, I censored it. I got the impression he's not best pleased to be called out to an abandoned campervan. He thinks it's going to be nothing more than a wild goose chase.'

'He's got a point,' said Matt. 'Chances are the owners are lying in a warm, comfortable bed somewhere after a night or two on the beers, and don't exactly fancy the walk back out to where they've parked, what with the weather being so close to apocalyptic as to make no difference. How many days of solid rain have we had now, four?'

'At least,' said Jen. 'And it's not been solid, has it? I distinctly remember that yesterday there was a full half an hour when the rain stopped.'

'The roads are a nightmare,' Matt said. 'River's up, so the road over to Appersett is flooded, as is the one over to Hardraw.'

'Any idiots tried driving through it yet today?' Jen asked.

Matt said, 'I'm hoping word got round after the three we had to rescue yesterday that unless you're in a four-by-four, then you have to detour via Bainbridge.'

'Remind me why we decided to tell Harry about this?' asked Jadyn.

If Harry is in a bad mood, then there is no way that any of this is going to improve it, Matt thought, but there was nothing he could do about that right now.

'Because it's weird, that's why,' he said. 'You've seen the photos, with the table all set out for a meal, that half-drunk bottle of wine, and whatnot. Something's not right, and I'd rather know than not what's happened to the owners, even if they are just holed up somewhere half-cut.'

'And you're sure it's up on the Cam Road?' Jen asked. 'Not exactly a road you'd take a campervan up, is it?'

'It's a popular route for off-roaders, mountain bikers, but that's about it,' said Matt. Then he looked at Jadyn and asked, 'Remember that track we ended up on when we were out looking for that lad who'd run away from his family over Marsett way?'

'That the one who does a bit of work for Grace now?' said Jadyn. 'How could I forget?'

'That's another popular route as well. There's a good number of tracks like that, around and about, like. They're good fun, so long as you're careful. Joan and I camped out on one years ago, back when we were courting. Had a lovely evening watching the sun set over the fells. Those lanes, they're ancient. Makes it feel like a bit of an adventure, like you're off exploring.'

Jen rested a hand on Matt's leg.

'You old romantic, you,' she said.

'Nowt wrong with that,' said Matt. 'In fact, I'd actively encourage it.' He glanced at the clock on the wall. 'It'll be another ten minutes before Harry gets here.'

'Not much we can get done in that time,' said Jen.

Matt lifted his mug and drained it, then lifted it into the air.

'Oh, I wouldn't be so sure about that,' he said. 'Who's for another?'

FOUR

When Harry arrived at the community centre with Smudge, his mood had soured even more, no small thanks to the rain he'd just tramped through. The weather had been promising sunshine for days, only to then change its mind completely, darkening at the tail end of Thursday, to then welcome everyone in the Dales that Friday morning with a deluge. And it had rained ever since, with all but the occasional break, though even those scant few were but a lessening of the rain, rather than a desperately needed pause. The rivers were up, the roads flooded, fields were shimmering lakes, and the fellsides were lit with the bright white of raging streams, which threw themselves down the steep flanks of green with wild abandon.

Harry pushed through the front doors, and they swung shut behind him, only to be stopped halfway by a violent gust of wind, the storm clearly intent on not letting him get away from it that easily.

Leaning against the doors, he forced them closed, then turned around to make his way over to the office, only to find Smudge in front of him, shivering. He crouched down to give the dog a rub and a chin scratch.

'You poor little bugger,' he said, his dark mood brightening for a moment in the glint of the hound's kind eyes. 'Have to get you a coat for weather like this, won't I? Think we best find you a towel.'

Smudge's tail thudded against the floor in agreement, and she shuffled in closer to Harry to steal his warmth, tucking herself between his legs.

The door to the office opened and out walked Matt.

'There you are,' he said, handing Harry a towel.

'I'm not exactly hard to miss,' said Harry.

'You're soaked.'

'Putting those detective skills to good use there, I see.'

'Just call me Matt Sherlock Dinsdale.'

'No.'

'Fair enough.'

Harry gave Smudge a last rub with the towel and stood up. Smudge, tail still wagging, padded over to Matt for a head scratch, which he duly provided.

'How's Dave doing, then?' Matt asked.

'One thing he's not lacking in is enthusiasm,' said Harry. 'I'm sure Jim will have a lot of fun with him up at the mart.'

'He'll certainly make an impression.' Matt smiled. 'A lot of folk know him, and about his goats, but they'll not be used to seeing him in uniform. He'll be in for a bit of a ribbing, no doubt.'

'He can look after himself,' said Harry. 'So, this campervan, then; what do we know about it?'

'Bugger all,' answered Matt, turning to lead Harry and Smudge into the office, where he saw Jen and Jadyn.

'Succinct.'

'I thought so.'

Once in the office, Harry peeled off his jacket and hung it up. He noticed a faint, sweet smell in the air, like an open fire, and it reminded him of an old officer he'd served under who always smelled of expensive tobacco.

'You taken up cigars or something?' he asked, looking at Matt.

'Probably the biker,' said Matt, then added, 'You'll be wanting a brew.'

'No, I'm fine for now,' he said.

Matt leaned in, eyes narrowed.

'Didn't ask how you were,' he said, his voice a low whisper. 'But at some point, you're going to have to tell me what's going on; you know that, don't you?'

'Like I said, I'm fine.'

'Anyone who turns down a mug of tea in the morning is very much not fine,' said Matt, voice a little louder now, and Harry saw that Jen and Jadyn were doing their level best to make it look like they couldn't hear what he was saying, despite the fact they were obviously listening to every word. 'I know something's up, Harry, in fact, we all do. You can't hide it. Well, you can try, but you'd be wasting your time.'

'There's nothing to worry about,' Harry said, trying to sound convincing. 'I just don't want tea, that's all. Not a crime, is it? I mean, it is possible to go for more than two hours without a brew.'

Matt lifted a hand and pointed a finger directly at Harry's nose.

'Then why that face?'

Harry couldn't help himself and laughed, rather enjoying the feel of it in his belly.

'Not sure there's much I can do about this,' he said, jabbing one of his own fingers at his face.

'You know what I mean,' said Matt. 'You can only hide so much behind those scars, and Lord knows we all respect you for it. But don't you go thinking we can't see beyond that, not now that you've been here as long as you have. We know you better than you realise, I think.'

'He's right,' said Jadyn.

Harry glanced over at the police constable, who immediately looked as though he wished he'd kept his mouth shut.

'Here,' said Jen, holding out a steaming mug of tea.

'I said I didn't want one.'

'There's want and there's need,' Jen smiled. 'And I think you need a mug of tea.' She lifted her other hand. 'And I also think you'll want a biscuit,' she added, shaking the packet.

'You don't usually encourage me to eat those.'

'You're still running, aren't you?'

'Three times a week, and no one's more surprised by that than me.'

'Then take a biscuit.'

Harry sucked in a deep breath, then exhaled through his nose, the noise that of a cantankerous bull.

'Thanks,' he said, giving in at last and taking the tea and a biscuit from Jen. He sat down, then looked again at Matt. 'But I'm fine, really. There's nothing to be worried about.'

'And we'll leave it at that,' said Matt. 'For now.'

Harry took a sip of the tea and nibbled the biscuit.

'That's a relief,' he said. 'Now, about this campervan ...'

Matt quickly explained where the van had been found, and Harry listened to what little detail they had on it. He then had a flick through the photos on Jadyn's phone, all the while enjoying the mug of tea Jen had made him and the biscuit. Not that he was about to admit it, though.

'Right then,' he said, deciding to take charge of what they would do next. 'Usual process is one we all know, but probably best we do a quick reminder, just in case.'

'Do I need the board, Boss?' Jadyn asked.

'No, you very much don't need the board,' Harry said. 'But if it'll make you feel useful ...'

Jadyn was already on his feet and at the board with a pen at the ready.

Harry held up a hand, three fingers raised. 'Three things to cover,' he said, then proceeded to count down on his fingers as he spoke. 'One, we need an initial inspection of the vehicle to check its condition, make sure it doesn't pose a hazard to the public, and to try and ascertain if it's been stolen and dumped, or maybe even involved in some kind of criminal activity.'

'Like what?' Jadyn asked, jotting notes on the board.

'Stolen vehicles are used in all kinds of dodgy stuff,' said Matt.

'Theft, drugs, whatever, really. Nick a vehicle, swap out the plates, do the job, dump the vehicle.'

'What if someone spots the fake plates, though?'

'Slim chance of that,' said Harry. 'I've seen only one vehicle tax spot check in the last ten years, plus they don't chase after you right there and then if your vehicle is pinged. So, it's a risk most criminals are happy to take.'

'Anyway, this vehicle is probably a bit obvious for anything too dodgy though, isn't it?' said Matt. 'Might have just been dumped. Someone spotted keys in the ignition, took it for a joy ride.'

'Up a dirt track into the hills?' said Jen.

'There's nowt so strange as folk,' said Matt, with deliberately more gravitas than was needed, noticed Harry, who ignored him, and moved on to point two.

'Two, we need to check for obvious clues as to what could've happened.'

'You mean documents, number plate, personal belongings, that kind of thing, right?' said Jen.

'Exactly that,' nodded Harry. 'Anything that can point us in the direction of the owner. We'll give the registration number to the Driver and Vehicle Licensing Agency.'

'You've one point left,' said Jadyn.

'And there was me thinking I couldn't count to three,' said Harry. 'This one, well, it's not something we check as such, but it's definitely something we might do,' he explained. 'Though seeing as it's out in the middle of nowhere, there's probably bugger all point, but always best to be thorough.'

'And what's that?' Jadyn asked.

'Public notice,' said Matt. 'We put up a few signs round and about, asking for the owner to come forward, and to contact us here at the office.'

Harry asked, 'This biker, then; we've their contact details if we need another chat?'

'Right here,' said Jadyn, and pointed at a post-it note on the wall on which Harry saw a roughly scrawled number. 'He jotted that down for us.'

'No name?' Harry asked and saw Jadyn's eyes widen at having missed a detail.

'No,' the constable said, shaking his head. 'I don't think he … No, wait, he did; he said his name was Jeff.'

'Jeff …'

'Yes.'

'Jeff what?'

'Just Jeff.'

'Jeff Goldblum? Jeff Bridges?'

'Jeff Beck?' added Matt. 'Now there was someone who could play.'

'So, just Jeff, then,' said Harry, and getting nothing else from Jadyn, decided to leave that point for now. 'I'm assuming you've been in touch with the DVLA?'

'The photo of the number plate we have from the biker is no good, we can't read it at all,' said Jadyn.

'Covered in mud,' said Matt.

Harry finished his tea. Outside, the weather, which had only got worse since he'd escaped out of it, was throwing itself all over the place, the rain slapping against the office windows, wind howling around like wolves chasing deer.

Harry pushed himself to his feet. 'No point sitting here, is there? Won't get anything done.' He pointed out the window at the weather. 'Not that I'm desperate to go back out in that, but we've no choice.'

Jen stood up.

'Is there anything else you should be on with?' Harry asked.

'There is, yes,' said Jen, 'but only if you're absolutely sure I'm not needed.'

'What is it?'

'Had a call-in last week from a farmer who thinks someone is leaving his gates open on purpose and letting his sheep out.'

Harry looked at Matt.

'That wasn't in the Action Book.'

'My fault,' said Jen.

Harry decided to let that go for now.

'On purpose, though?' he said. 'Why the hell would anyone do that? Is it not just walkers and ramblers forgetting the countryside code because they're too busy taking photographs and dropping clingfilm and crisp wrappers everywhere?'

'Says it keeps happening,' said Jen. 'I gave him a call after I'd sorted out the car with the blown tyre. Said I'd be over at some point today to have a chat with him and see if there's anything we can do to help investigate it.'

'Why's he not bothered to call us about it before?'

'That's something I'll be asking him.'

'Then you're better heading off to deal with that than coming with us,' instructed Harry, then turned his attention to Jadyn. 'I want you to stay here for now, as well, Constable. No reason for us all to get drenched, is there? I'll send you a photo of the number plate when we get to the van. I want you to get onto the DVLA as soon as I do. And, assuming you're able to get the details of the owner, see if you can find out as much about them as you can, family, address, contact details, start ringing around the pubs, then B&Bs. Also, we've no idea what might happen with Dave let loose at the mart, so it's probably best to have you on standby, just in case.'

'Just in case of what?'

'Exactly,' said Harry, but couldn't fail to notice the disappointed look on Jadyn's face. 'I'll be leaving Smudge here to keep an eye on you, though,' he added.

A smile creased the corners of Jadyn's eyes, and having heard her name, Smudge went over and sat with him, leaning in against his legs, tail wagging gently.

'You sure you don't want to take her?' Jadyn asked, resting a hand on her head.

'No point,' said Harry, grabbing his coat. 'She's wet enough as it is, and I don't want her covered in half the fellside as well. She's a bugger to get clean as it is, without most of Wensleydale clinging to her paws. She loves jumping in and out of rivers and mud puddles, but throw her in the shower to clean her off and you'd think I was trying to spray her with acid.'

With a quick farewell, Harry led Matt out of the office, leaving Jadyn with Smudge, and Jen to get herself off to see the farmer she'd mentioned. At the community centre's main door, he hesitated.

'How can there be this much rain?' he asked. 'I mean, it just keeps coming, doesn't it?'

'What's the problem?' Matt asked. 'There's nowt to worry about, is there?'

'Is there not?'

'No, of course there isn't; this is Yorkshire rain, Harry!'

'And what's that got to do with anything?'

'It's good for you!'

As if to emphasise just how good, Matt pushed through the door, then leaned his head back and took the rain fully in the face, eyes closed as though the good Lord himself was baptizing him from above.

Harry pulled his hood up and joined him.

'The worrying thing about that statement,' he said, 'is that you genuinely believe it to be true, don't you?'

Matt wiped his face, then rattled a set of keys in the air. 'We'll take the old Land Rover,' he said.

Harry jogged behind Matt, down towards the marketplace and over to the Land Rover that Gordy had somehow managed to procure for them a few months back. It was a little tired, a little worn, with ripped seats crisscrossed with gaffer tape, scratched and dented bodywork, and a heater that seemed to be louder than the turbo diesel engine under the bonnet, but it excelled when it came to navigating rutted tracks, flooded roads, and muddy fields.

Harry climbed into the passenger seat, heaving the door shut with a clang, then clipped himself in.

'Hold on,' said Matt, and started the engine.

'I've never been much of a fan of vehicles where the first thing the driver says is that,' said Harry.

The vehicle shuddered and shook.

'Sometimes, I think this thing's just going to rattle itself to pieces,' he added.

'That's the charm of it,' said Matt.

'Charm? I've driven these things for years, in the Army, and in the police, and I've never described one as charming. Uncomfortable, noisy, smelly, yes, but never charming.'

Matt tapped the dashboard.

'Don't you listen to him,' he said, before spending a few seconds waggling the gear lever around as he tried to find first, releasing the hand brake, then sending them off into the rain.

The storm was so loud against the roof, Harry wondered if he would be completely deaf by the time they arrived at their destination. Soon, though, the sound became hypnotic, melding in with the drone of the tyres on the road, and he had to fight to keep his eyes open and not simply drift off to sleep. But he couldn't, even if he wanted to, not with so much on his mind.

Leaving Smudge with Jadyn had shone a light on at least a part of it. Usually, Grace would've usually taken her, with Jess, her own dog, loving the company. But that wasn't possible right now, thanks to them being on, what was it? A break? Yes, that was it. Apparently, it was different to breaking up, not that Harry was convinced. It was to give them time to have a think, a bit of space to work out what they each wanted.

Well, he knew what he wanted, or at least he'd thought he did, but now he wasn't so sure. Or was it that he was sure, but just didn't know how to express it? Whatever it was or wasn't, the result had been a dark cloud he couldn't shift.

It had happened a couple of weeks ago, and Harry was still not dealing well with it, or why it had happened in the first place. He'd thought everything was fine, but clearly, he'd been wrong. They were due to meet later that week, to chat things through, and that was good, but the thought of it twisted his gut something terrible.

He wasn't surprised the team had picked up on his mood; he'd have to work harder at bottling things up. There was no way he was going to start sharing anything personal like that with any of them, because that just wasn't professional, was it? No, it was definitely better this way, he thought, to keep it inside for now and work it out on his own. But then there was the other thing, wasn't there, with Gordy? He still had time to change her mind, but he doubted it would do any good.

Harry rubbed his eyes, weariness in his bones, and he shivered a little from the damp and the cold. Ahead, he saw the road bank right, and directly in front of them, a rough track leading off the road and up into the hills.

FIVE

'It's been a good while since I was last up here,' said Matt, as he steered them along the lane, the Land Rover thumping and bumping as it crept along, the wheels chewing their way forward through loose gravel and mud, and puddles growing ever deeper with the rain. 'A group of lads were up in Hawes on a stag do, all with mountain bikes, if you could even call them that, because it didn't look like any of them had been designed to tackle anything more mountainous than a quick shortcut to the supermarket, if you know what I mean. They thought they could just throw themselves down the hillside with wild abandon and zero experience.'

'I'm going to assume they thought wrong,' said Harry, as Matt navigated a section of the track which narrowed while taking a sharp dip into a gully, then out again.

Around them, Harry noticed how the fells faded beneath the cloud, the horizon a soft-edged sheet laid on green fields and grey stone, their summits hidden from sight.

'To be honest, credit where credit's due, that's exactly what they did,' said Matt. 'No helmets, all of them with hangovers from the night before. They were up here puffing and panting, until one of them, the groom would you believe, decides to take a shortcut back to town.'

'But there isn't a shortcut.'

'Exactly,' said Matt, deftly steering the Land Rover up out of the gully to carefully navigate a section of the track that seemed to be little more than huge ruts and puddles. 'Don't ask me how, but on a lane that you simply can't get lost on, they got lost. They had no idea where they were, no map, which didn't help, though I doubt they'd have been able to use one anyway. No decent gear, no food or water, and the groom, who'd clearly had enough and just wanted to be back in the pub, heads off on his own.'

'What happened?'

'He didn't get far, though he got further than expected, I have to say. Mountain Rescue were called out. It wasn't difficult to find them, and the rest of the group were fine, just cold and hungry and in need of a damned good talking to, which we gave them, once we had them all safe and sound.

'The groom, though, he was in a bit of a state. Lost control of his bike, somehow ended up halfway down the fellside in a gully with a broken leg and shattered wrist, face all smashed up, and up to his waist in water. By the time we got to him, he was hyperthermic. It was touch and go. He was bloody lucky to survive. He could've just as easily knocked himself out and drowned, never mind frozen to death in the beck. Must've looked a picture for the wedding photos.'

'Young men, they're a law unto themselves,' said Harry. 'And I should know; I certainly was.'

'Same here,' said Matt. 'But then what's the point in being old and wise if you don't spend a good bit of your life being young and stupid? That's my excuse anyway, and I'm sticking to it.'

'Taking up philosophy now, are you?'

'I've hidden depths, Harry,' Matt said, lowering his voice to a whisper. 'Hidden depths ...'

'Best you keep those to yourself and Joan,' Harry laughed, then through the water being smeared across the windscreen by the not entirely effective wipers, spotted a dark and boxy silhouette just ahead. 'There it is.'

Matt rolled the Land Rover on and pulled them to a stop a short walk away from the campervan, switched off the engine. With the power plant silent, and the vehicle still, the sound of the rain grew even louder, the rattle of ball bearings being tipped relentlessly onto the roof from above.

'Nice of the weather to ease off for our arrival,' he said.

'Thought you said it was good for us?' said Harry.

'You can have too much of a good thing, though, can't you?'

Harry unclipped his seat belt, checked his jacket was zipped up, pulled his hood up again, then pushed out into the rain. Wind grabbed at him immediately, snapping the hood from his head, and sending a spray of chill water down his neck.

Harry swore as Matt jogged around the front of the Land Rover to join him.

'You need your hood up, Harry, or you'll catch your death,' he said.

Harry stared at Matt just long enough to get across his appreciation for the observation, then pulled his hood back up without saying a word.

'They did well to get that thing up here,' said Matt, as they set off towards the campervan, unable to avoid the deep puddles in their way. 'My money's still on them just leaving it here because the weather's so bloody awful. Probably couldn't get it started or something. Maybe the heater gave up. Knowing there's a warm pub just a couple of miles' walk away would be difficult to ignore.'

'Maybe,' Harry muttered, but from the moment he'd stepped out into the rain and seen the other vehicle with his own eyes, he'd sensed something.

Not that he was one for reading anything into odd feelings and strange sensations or anything like that. Quite the opposite, in fact. Although he'd never admit it to anyone, and certainly not to Matt, after so many years on the force, and so many crime scenes that he'd attended, sometimes he just knew when what was in front of him wasn't quite right. And this was one of those times. He just didn't know why.

Stuffing his hands into his pockets, Harry closed the distance between him and the campervan, trudging through mud and water, once again thankful for the Wellington boots he was wearing. Water was still finding its way inside them, but that was more from the fact that his trousers were sopping wet than any potential holes in the rubber soles.

The van was a pale green Volkswagen, but not one of the smart, shiny-looking ones Harry was used to seeing racing around the roads rammed full of children and their parents, or couples keen to show the world just how adventurous they are by covering the thing in bike racks and SUP boards. It was squarer in design, resting on large, off-road tyres, with a hefty roof rack on top, which was filled with various crates and boxes and bags, all held in place by ratchet straps. Attached to the side of the campervan was a small and sorry-looking awning, the open door flapping in the wind like the broken wing of a dead bird.

Harry could tell that the body of the vehicle had been lifted to give it extra ground clearance and guessed that it was four-wheel drive. It was the kind of campervan he could see himself driving were he ever to consider buying one, which he knew for sure he never would. The idea of spending a night in something so cramped, cold, and undoubtedly uncomfortable was not one that lit a fire of enthusiasm within him. His days of roughing it were long behind him. Which is no bad thing, he thought, pushing away the memory of too many nights in scrapes in the desert wondering if he was going to wake up in the middle of a firefight and have to survive it just to get the chance to try and enjoy a breakfast of cold burger and beans eaten out of a foil bag.

'Anything jump out at you?' Matt asked.

Harry shook his head.

'Nowt yet,' he said, a bit of Yorkshire straying into his reply. His west country twang would never leave him, he was sure of that, but he'd spent so long now in the company of those with a broad Yorkshire accent that flickers of it would light up his sentences from time to time. 'Right now, it looks like the owners have just buggered off somewhere, like you said. I mean, that's odd, but it's hardly suspicion of foul play, is it?'

'Not really, no,' agreed Matt.

After a quick walk around the vehicle, during which Harry wiped the numberplate clean and quickly sent a photo of it through to Jadyn at the office to try and trace, he pulled on a pair of disposable rubber gloves and went to step inside the awning, but something made him pause.

'Something up?' Matt asked. 'What've you seen?'

Harry wasn't sure. He stepped back away from the vehicle, looked up and down the lane, then back at where it was resting.

'Does it look odd to you?' he asked.

Matt came to stand beside him.

'Does what look odd to me?'

'The van,' Harry said. 'Where it's parked, I mean.'

Matt said nothing for a moment, then shook his head.

'Can't say that it does, no; why?'

Harry circled left until he was at the back of the van.

'Not exactly level, is it?' he asked.

'You've lost me,' said Matt.

Harry walked over to the van and rested a hand on it, peering inside.

'You have these so you can sleep in them, don't you?' he said. 'That's the whole point; head off on a little adventure, park where you want, have a kip, carry on. Then why park like this?'

Matt scratched his head.

'I'm still lost,' he said.

Harry held his right arm out horizontally in front of him.

'That's flat, right? My arm, I mean. And last time I went to sleep, so was my bed. Now look at the angle this thing's parked at; must be what, twenty or thirty degrees? You can't sleep in a bed like that, can you? You'll end up rolling to the side and up against this window here.'

He pointed to the window on the driver's side of the van.

'If it was leaning the other way, you'd roll out.'

'Maybe they were just desperate to get parked up with the weather like it is,' suggested Matt.

'Maybe,' Harry said. 'Maybe.'

He stood back for another look at the van, then headed back around to the front and in through the awning door, and beckoned for Matt to follow.

'Let's see if we can't find something that helps us find the owners,' he said.

SIX

'Eerie, isn't it?' Matt said, stepping in behind Harry.

There was an odd silence now that they were out of the rain, but Harry wasn't about to read anything into it.

Inside the awning were two low chairs, both of which were constructed from thin aluminium tubing and a canvas-like material, allowing them to be collapsed and folded away. They were lying in the corner as though just tossed there, their legs caught up together like they'd spent a few minutes chasing and trying to trip each other up.

There was a table as well, made in the same way. It was on its legs and sitting on it was a plate of biscuits, now very soggy thanks to the pool of water they rested in, and a couple of plastic mugs. Across the floor, soggy and ruined by the mud, was a scattered pile of leaflets.

Harry knelt on the ground for a closer look and saw that they were about various tourist sites across the Dales, and for further afield in the Lake District. Perhaps that's where they were planning to head next, he thought, as he snapped photos on his phone of what he and Matt were looking at.

Hanging from several hooks attached to the awning frame were climbing ropes and harnesses and various other bits of gear for scaling a crag, a couple of wetsuits on hangers, and what looked like an air pump.

Probably for inflating a Stand-Up Paddleboard, Harry guessed, thinking he'd spotted one in its bag on the roof rack when they'd arrived. Harry had seen plenty of people using them, especially over on Lake Semerwater. Never had a go himself though and was happy for it to stay that way.

Ben had gone and bought himself one though and seemed to regard the use of the thing as a religious experience. His enthusiasm was infectious, but not so much as to persuade Harry to join in. Not yet anyway, and he had a feeling that might end up with him having to have a go anyway, if only to shut Ben up.

'Must be something in here with a name or an address,' Harry said.

The silence was torn apart by the wind snapping the sides of the awning with the sound of a whip crack, and he noticed that one of the plastic windows of the awning was ripped.

'How do you think that happened?' he asked.

'Wind must've caught it,' Matt said, peering past Harry to look around the awning, then over through the open door of the campervan itself. Which was something else that struck Harry as odd.

'Why would they leave that open?' he asked, nodding towards the door. 'If you were leaving this up here to head to a pub, or to go for a walk, you'd lock up, wouldn't you?'

'I guess so, yes,' said Matt. 'Maybe they thought they were coming back but got caught by the weather.'

'You still wouldn't leave it open, though, would you?' said Harry. 'Doesn't make any sense at all.' He gestured around the awning with a wave of his arm. 'And there's all this, too. None of it's cheap, is it? And it's just left here, either hanging up in an awning that frankly feels like it could blow away at any moment, or just thrown in the corner. Why leave it open like this and risk getting stuff nicked? Makes no sense.'

'The table's still standing,' said Matt.

'It is,' Harry agreed. 'Can't say I know what that tells us, though.'

For a few moments, neither Harry nor Matt spoke, and Harry was grateful for the time to just try and get his head around what they were seeing. But no matter what he did, he couldn't make sense of it.

'It's almost like they've just disappeared,' Matt said, interrupting Harry's thoughts. 'Everything's all laid out, like, isn't it, like they were here enjoying themselves one minute, then the next minute they weren't?'

'People don't just disappear,' said Harry, though he wondered if that was strictly true, thinking back to all the missing persons cases still unsolved up and down the country, never mind further afield. He'd seen files and files of them back down south, an ever-increasing mountain of people just slipping through the cracks, faces blurring together until he couldn't place even one of them.

'You know what this reminds me of?' Matt said. 'That ghost ship, the Mary Celeste,' said Matt.

Harry narrowed his eyes at Matt.

'I'm supposed to know what that is, am I?'

'Did you ever watch those Arthur C. Clarke programmes on the telly, back in the eighties?'

'Can't say that I did,' Harry replied, wondering what on earth Matt was rambling on about.

'It was all about unsolved mysteries, like the Bermuda Triangle, aliens, that kind of thing.'

'No mystery there,' said Harry. 'It's all a load of bollocks.'

'You're firmly on the sceptic side, then, I see.'

'I'm firmly on the aliens don't exist, and neither does the Bermuda Triangle side, that's where,' said Harry.

Matt folded his arms.

'Then why do so many ships and planes disappear?'

'Just like people, they don't,' said Harry. 'Bad weather, freak storms, nothing more mysterious than that.'

'Know that for sure, do you?'

Harry gave his answer with nothing more than a narrowing of his eyes and hoped that would be enough to quieten Matt's musings.

It wasn't.

'Well,' Matt continued, unperturbed by Harry's grizzled stare, 'the Mary Celeste was this ship found adrift and deserted in the Atlantic, back in the eighteen hundreds. Can't remember the date exactly, but the weird thing about it was how when it was found it was still seaworthy and under sail, with all of her cargo intact and the crew's belongings undisturbed. No one aboard, though, and the lifeboat was gone.'

'Just because no one's come up with a rational explanation doesn't mean that there isn't one or that the only alternative is aliens or whatever other nonsense those conspiracy nutjobs try and suggest,' said Harry.

'Oh, there's plenty of rational explanations for it,' said Matt. 'But I still like the mystery of it, the what if ...'

Harry said no more, instead trying to direct his attention to the job in hand, but barely a minute later, Matt called him over.

'Look at this,' the detective sergeant said, and Harry turned around to see him standing at the open side door to the campervan.

'Look at what?' asked Harry, peering past Matt's shoulder for a closer look. 'You found something?'

'What you were saying a few minutes ago about the door being open?' Matt said. 'You're right.'

'Thank you for the confirmation,' said Harry.

'No, that's not what I mean,' said Matt. 'If this camper's been like this for a couple of days, who knows how many people have walked past?'

'Not many with the weather like this,' said Harry.

'We don't know that though, do we?' said Matt. 'For all we know, maybe some of them ducked their heads inside, not to just get out of the rain but to help themselves to a bite to eat or something shiny?'

'Doesn't look like anything's been taken though, has it?' said

Harry. 'I know we don't have a kit list, and everything's a bit of a mess, but for all we know nothing's missing.'

'Something else, then,' said Matt. 'The rain's got in, hasn't it? The awning's a mess, as we've seen for ourselves, the window's ripped, everything's soaking wet. You wouldn't want to come back here and find it like this, would you? It's not going to provide you with somewhere nice and warm and dry out of the wind and rain to get a good night's sleep, is it?'

'Anything else?' Harry asked, catching onto the fact that Matt was on a bit of a roll now, one that didn't contain half a pound of bacon for a change, so figured it was best to just give him a shove to speed things up a bit.

'The table inside the van looks like it's all set for two people to sit down and eat,' Matt said. 'I know there were photos of this from that biker chap, but it's a hell of a lot odder seeing it firsthand.'

'How do you mean?'

'Well, there's stuff here for two, isn't there? Two plates, a couple of glasses, half a bottle of wine, right? But it's all just piled up, isn't it? Like it's just been chucked in the corner.'

'Well, there's no way anyone could sit and eat at the table with it being at that angle,' added Harry.

Matt pointed over at two gas burners set into the cupboards built into the van.

'And see over on the stove? That's a pan with beans in it, though they're looking none too appetising now, even to me; they've clearly been there a while. Easily a couple of days.'

'About as long as it's been raining, then,' said Harry.

Matt leaned over and opened the small fridge, standing back to allow Harry a view of what was inside.

'And look at this,' he said, staring into the thing for the first time himself 'It's fully stocked. This just doesn't make sense, Harry, it really doesn't. And it's not even on.'

'Battery must've died.'

Matt shook his head.

'Something like this, it'll have a leisure battery on it for sure.

Would last a bit longer than a couple of days, even without getting a recharge from driving around.'

'It is a bit of a head-scratcher, I'll give you that,' agreed Harry.

Matt pointed a finger at the ceiling.

'Check those out,' he said.

Harry twisted his head to see what Matt was looking at. The ceiling was covered in a patchwork of neatly placed photographs, some of them Polaroids, all of them showing two very young, very healthy faces.

'Well, they didn't hit any of the ugly branches when they fell out of the tree, did they?' Harry said. 'The owners, I'm guessing.'

'Don't half look happy,' said Matt. 'Why would they have just gone off and left this up here? There's no reason for them to do that at all.'

'Well, there is,' said Harry. 'We don't know why yet. We also don't even know that there's a reason beyond wanting to enjoy a warm room, a cosy bed, and each other while the rain lasts.'

Harry flicked his eyes from photo to photo, quickly taking himself on a guided tour of this young couple's adventures. There were photos of them swimming in rivers and lakes, surfing in the sea, climbing and mountain biking, in woodlands and cafés, and in the van itself. He saw laughter around campfires, happiness on the hills, and a love of adrenaline as much as of each other in the activities they shared. He took a few photos of the happy young couple held as they were in a tableau of healthy young happiness, and one of the display as a whole.

'That's Semerwater, isn't it?' he asked, jabbing a finger at one of the photos.

'Looks that way,' said Matt.

'Recognise anything in any of the others?'

Matt had a closer look.

'Looks like Swaledale,' he said. 'There's plenty of places over there to go exploring on a bike. Good bike shop, too, down in Grinton, with a café serving some of the best cakes you've ever had.'

'Anywhere specific?'

Matt narrowed his eyes.

'I could be wrong, but there's an old track that runs along behind Reeth, over to Langthwaite, and I think it might be that.'

'So, they've been here a while then?' said Harry, and ducked back out of the campervan, only to pause on the way and double back to have another look at the photographs.

'Something up?' Matt asked. 'What have you seen?'

Harry stared at the photos again, not entirely sure.

'I don't know,' he said. 'You notice anything?'

Matt leaned in for another look, shook his head.

'Just two kids clearly having the time of their lives,' he said.

'Maybe it's just me, then,' said Harry, hesitating for a few seconds more as he tried to work out what was niggling him. Then it hit him. 'What about this?' he asked, lifting a finger to a gap in the display, then pointing to another. 'And this?'

'There's nowt there.'

'Exactly,' said Harry, and saw confusion in Matt's eyes.

'Exactly what?' the DS asked.

Harry pulled out his phone, took a couple of photographs.

'Those gaps look like they used to contain photos,' he said. 'Which makes me wonder—'

'Where they are,' finished Matt.

'And who took them, and why?' said Harry.

'Could be the owners,' said Matt.

'And it could be one of those passersby you mentioned, popping in for a look at the van and taking a fancy to them,' said Harry.

'But why would someone do that?' Matt asked. 'You're jumping to conclusions there a bit, aren't you?'

'Just asking questions, that's all,' said Harry, and saw a smile on Matt's face.

'What?'

'This is where you say that thing,' said Matt.

'What thing?'

Matt stood back, shaking his head.

'Come on,' he said. 'Say it. You know you want to.'

'Say what?'

'The thing you always say. It's your thing. Well, one of them, anyway. There's that other one about a pineapple, but that's for when you're feeling especially grouchy and someone's being a right idiot.'

Then the words fell into place in Harry's mind.

'Detective, remember?'

'There we go,' said Matt, clapping his hands together. 'Do I know you, or do I know you? But it doesn't make much sense, does it?'

'Spaces where photographs should be, in what looks for all intents and purposes like a vehicle abandoned by its currently missing owners, makes bugger all sense and has me asking questions,' said Harry.

'It's not much, but it is suspicious, isn't it?' Matt agreed.

'Nothing here points to anything specific,' continued Harry, 'and there's no way a few missing photographs are having me leap to the conclusion that this is in any way, shape, or form criminal. Still, though, I can't see anything here that points to why they'd leave, and do so with their van looking like this.' He glanced at Matt. 'What you said earlier about that stag do ... a good number of these photos have our young couple on mountain bikes, right? Expensive ones, too, by the looks of things.'

'Never been one for biking myself,' said Matt. 'I'm a liability.'

'That I can believe,' said Harry. 'But there are no bikes outside, are there? I didn't spot any, did you?'

Harry made his way back outside into the rain, Matt following. The DS was right, he thought; the camper was like a ghost ship. And they'd found nothing during their search to help them find the owners, just the number plate.

'What are you thinking?' Matt asked.

'The worst, as usual, though I'm trying not to,' Harry said. He gestured at the moorland in front of them, sodden now from days of rain, and cut through by streams and rivers swollen into violent torrents by the storm.

'Like what?'

'Like what if they're out there in all of this? What if they're injured, like that lad you were talking about on his stag do?'

'But all of this makes it look like this camper's been here for a couple of days at least,' said Matt. 'If they're out there in this ...'

'Then we need to find them sharpish,' said Harry. 'I'm seeing zero signs in there of a struggle or violence or that they were forced to leave under duress. They left, they never came back, and between where we're standing now, and wherever they are, is a hell of a lot of moorland, and we've no clue where they might have headed or ended up.'

'Needle in a haystack.'

'It is.'

'Want me to call it in?'

'Yes.'

'If we can somehow get hold of their mobile phone numbers, that would be useful,' said Matt. 'Location data is a lifesaver.'

'Hopefully, Jadyn will have some news on that.'

'Didn't spot a mobile phone anywhere here, did we?'

Harry shook his head.

'So, hopefully, they had them with them. Who goes anywhere now without a mobile phone attached to their hand like it's glued there?'

Harry checked his watch. They'd left the office just after midmorning and now lunch had already shot past without them even realising.

'We need Mountain Rescue up here to conduct a search right now.'

Harry's phone buzzed.

'Boss, it's Jadyn ...'

'You've found the owners? Contact details?'

'The van belongs to a young couple, Josh and Amber Hill,' said

Jadyn. 'Recently married by all accounts. But I've a little bit more than that as well.'

Harry noticed a hesitancy in the constable's voice, like he didn't want to tell him something. Also, information like being recently married wasn't what he had expected Jadyn to come back to him with.

'A little bit more of what, exactly? What do you mean? You've managed to trace their family, then? And you said *but,* which to me implies that, whatever it is you're about to tell me, I'm not going to like it.'

'We have another problem, Boss,' Jadyn said.

Harry wanted to drop-kick his phone over the nearest wall.

'Get to the point, Constable, if you'd be so kind; Detective Sergeant Dinsdale and I are currently taking bets on which happens first: we freeze to death, or drown!'

'Their, er, fans are here,' said Jadyn. 'That's how I know about the being married thing.'

That wasn't quite the answer Harry had been expecting. Fans? What the hell was Jadyn on about?

'Whose fans are where?' he asked. 'And more to the point, why should I even care?'

'Josh and Amber's fans,' Jadyn answered, 'that's whose. They're the owners of the campervan, right? But it turns out they have a following thanks to being, well, celebrities, I guess.'

'Celebrities? How do you mean?'

'I mean that they're celebrities and they're famous,' said Jadyn. 'Not like film or pop stars or anything like that, but yes, they are, they're famous.'

Harry could feel a headache coming on, but ignored it.

'How? For what? No, let me guess, it's some reality TV nonsense, right? Bloody hell, what's wrong with the world? Why would anyone care? More to the point, Constable, why should I?'

Jadyn said, 'I've just checked their socials, and they've hundreds of thousands of followers.'

'Socials?'

'Social media, Boss,' said Jadyn.

'Lucky them,' Harry said, not at all impressed. 'Just so long as they're not all in Hawes, then right now it's not my or yours or anyone else's problem, is it?'

'But some are here,' Jadyn said. 'In Hawes. And that's the problem.'

'Some? How many exactly?'

'Three.'

Harry dropped the phone from his face, swore loudly into the rain, then lifted it back up again.

'I think you can handle three,' he said. 'Anything else?'

Jadyn said, 'Do you remember that massive lottery jackpot a few months ago?'

'What, you mean that huge one everyone was talking about? The one in the papers and on the news?'

'Yes.'

'Of course I bloody well don't!' Harry snapped back, a little sharper than he perhaps meant to. 'Why would I ever care about that, and why are you mentioning it now?'

'It was millions, Boss,' said Jadyn. 'I can't remember how many, but lots of them.'

'And your point is?'

'Josh and Amber? They won it.'

'So, they're millionaires?'

'Yes, Boss. And then some.'

Harry looked at Matt, then over at the abandoned campervan, and that suspicion inside him twisted his gut just a little tighter.

'Bollocks,' he said. 'I'm on my way.'

SEVEN

Back in the office, Jadyn hung up the phone, then swung around in his chair to look over at Smudge, glancing over at the door on the way. Behind it were the three individuals who had turned up unannounced just moments after he had received the details of the van owners, Josh and Amber Hill. Like Harry, he didn't believe in coincidences, so had excused himself from dealing with them to call his boss. Smudge stared back from where she was curled up on the floor beneath a radiator and thumped her tail on the floor.

'I don't think he was very happy with what I told him,' he said, briefly wishing he had a life as easy as Smudge's. 'But then, I don't think he's happy with much at all at the moment, is he?'

Smudge pushed herself up onto her paws and padded over to rest her head on Jadyn's lap, and he couldn't help but smile as he gave her head a scratch.

'Do you have any idea what's going on with him?' he asked. 'Is he grumpy at home as well?'

Smudge nuzzled into Jadyn's hand.

'Not sure that's an answer.'

A knock at the door made Jadyn jump.

'Hello? Mr Policeman? Are you there? Can we talk, please?'

Yes, I am, and no we can't, Jadyn thought, and was sorely

tempted to take a feather out of Harry's hat, open the door, and roar at the small gathering to bugger off. And who calls anyone Mr Policeman, anyway? What the hell was that about?

Another knock, this time louder and more impatient.

'We know you're in there, remember? You have to talk to us. We're worried and we need to know what's happened to them. You can't withhold information from us.'

Another voice then chimed in with, 'We have a right to know!'

Jadyn shook his head and sighed. Rights? To what, exactly? He wasn't withholding information, he was just doing his job. And anyway, the mere thought that someone might even suggest he had given out information he shouldn't, and then Harry finding out, was enough to make him consider changing his name and moving abroad.

The door resonated again to the sound of a rapid tap-tap-tap.

'We're streaming this right now, you know?' the first voice said. 'You can't ignore us.'

Jadyn didn't care what they were doing, but he also knew that they kind of had a point. No matter how much he wanted to, he couldn't simply hide out in the office and hope that they would go away. And it was more than obvious that they weren't about to do that at all.

After Jadyn had told him about the three who were now standing outside the office, Harry had said that Matt would drop him off at the office to speak to them himself, so that was something. And Jadyn didn't fancy handling this completely on his own, so perhaps it was better to just wait until Harry turned up?

The door erupted in another flurry of knocks, the crescendo of taps like a shambolic military tattoo on the wood, a rolling, drunken drum solo which sped up and only stopped when Jadyn stood up, gripped the door handle, and having steadied himself with a calming breath, given it a twist.

On the other side of door, three faces stared back, one man and two women all in their early twenties.

The young man stepped forward, his phone up in front of his face.

'And here he is at last, everyone! Didn't catch your name last time, Officer ...?'

The unspoken question was clear.

'Okri,' said Jadyn. 'Perhaps we could go through to our interview room for a chat so that I can take some details?'

'We've already told you, they're missing,' said one of the others, a woman with long, brown hair, wearing a bright pink waterproof jacket covered in Japanese cartoon characters. The other woman was in a blue waterproof, hood still up, her eyes half hidden behind wet strands of a black fringe. The man wasn't wearing a waterproof and was utterly soaked. Jadyn noticed then that he was shivering a little, though clearly trying to ignore it.

'You're here to report a MISPER,' said Jadyn. 'A missing persons, yes?'

'Missing people,' said the man. 'Josh and Amber—'

'We call them Jamber!' said the woman in the pink jacket, a little too excited about what she'd just said. 'Cute or what?'

With nothing to say to that, Jadyn pointed down the hall.

'If you could follow me?'

He set off, hearing footsteps follow, then stopped at the door to the small interview room to find only the young man was with him, still with the phone up in front of his face.

'You have to turn that off,' Jadyn said, his voice calm but stern, though he was unable to hide the hint of disdain just at the back of it.

'Why?'

'Because if you're here to report that two people are missing, then I need you to focus on that, and not your social media profile,' Jadyn said, finding it hard to believe he was speaking to a grown adult, and not a teenager.

The phone sank.

'There,' the man said, showing Jadyn the phone in his hand as he switched it off. 'Happy now?'

Not really, no, Jadyn thought, but asked, 'What about the other two?'

'They're busy.'

'With what?'

'Social media stuff. Jamber have a lot of followers so we're keeping them up to date.'

Jadyn opened the door to the interview room and let the young man in, gesturing for him to sit at the table. He then took out his notebook.

'Right then, your details first ... Name and address, please, and telephone number.'

'Colin Hampton,' the man replied, then provided the other details Jadyn had requested, his address jumping out at Jadyn right away.

'You're from Ingleton? That's not too far away, is it?'

Jadyn had never been over that way, but he knew of it, not least because the name of the place was on a road sign at the top of Hawes.

'That's why I'm here, really,' said Colin. 'Didn't take long to head over, and we were worried. The other two are Karen Wallace, she's the one in the Manga jacket, and Helen Cartwright. They're local, too, I mean they live over Ingleton way.'

'And you're here about Jamb— I mean, Josh and Amber Hill, yes? Can I ask how you know that they're missing? Are you close friends, family?'

Colin shook his head.

'We've been tracking them,' he said. 'They've kept their location secret for a while now, but we've managed to work out where they are. Which is here. Except they're not, are they?'

Jadyn didn't understand what Colin was saying exactly.

'Tracking them?'

'Not in a creepy way,' Colin replied, jumping in, then he pulled out a map of the whole country, unfolding it on the table between them.

Jadyn saw that it was annotated with various lines and squiggles in black and red pen.

'What's this, then?' he asked, wondering how on earth this wasn't creepy.

'Where they've been and where they are,' Colin replied, dropping a finger onto the map to trace a line. 'See, they've been all over the place. Down in Cornwall, surfing, over in Wales, across to the Peak District, then they headed to the coast, over to Skegness, and now they're here. The stuff they posted about Skeggy was brilliant, really funny! You should watch it. There's this one bit where they're in the arcades, right, and—'

Jadyn cut Colin off mid-flow, fairly confident that whatever Josh and Amber had been doing in an arcade in Skegness wasn't relevant to finding them right now. 'Why is it you think they're missing?' he asked

'It happened after they left the Peak District,' Colin said. 'Before that, they were posting all the time, keeping everyone up to date. But then, after they'd been up that way, they started leaving a gap of a few days between when they'd done something or been somewhere, and when they'd throw it up on Instagram and their blog, that kind of thing.'

'What are you saying exactly?' Jadyn asked, a little confused.

'I'm not saying anything,' said Colin. 'I just think something happened in the Peak District that made them want to try and keep things a little more private, I guess. But that didn't stop their fans following their route.'

'This is beginning to sound like stalking,' said Jadyn, and saw a flash of shock widen Colin's eyes.

'What? Stalking? You mean you think we …? No, it's not like that at all, I promise!'

Jadyn said nothing, just waited for Colin to continue.

'Look, what I mean is, we were expecting to see a post from them a few days ago, right? But there wasn't one,' Colin said. 'There was no post at all. Nothing.'

'You mean a video?'

Colin shook his head.

'Not a video, no. They do blog posts first, with a few photos, but never anything that can give away their location. Videos come later once they've moved on.'

'But you found them.'

'Yes.'

'How?'

Colin said nothing, just focused on his phone for a few seconds, then turned it around for Jadyn to see the screen.

'This photo,' he said. 'They weren't as careful. Look ...'

Jadyn brought his face closer to the screen to stare at a close-up photo of Josh and Amber. Behind them he could just make out some green and grey scenery, but nothing else, nothing that to him gave any sense of where they were when it had been taken.

'What am I trying to see?' he asked.

Colin placed his fingers on the screen and zoomed in.

'That,' he said. 'Recognise it?'

'Should I?'

'It's the Buttertubs Pass,' Colin said. 'I've already checked the photo with the location. Went up there for a look around before we came here, just to make sure. It's a definite match, I'm sure of it.'

'You must know the area well then, to spot that.'

'I'm a keen cyclist.'

Jadyn couldn't quite see the relevance of that statement.

'And ...?'

'The Buttertubs Pass is a killer on the legs, but it's good training,' said Colin. 'I do a long route from home, over to Hawes, out the back, and over the Buttertubs Pass, then round through Thwaite, Nateby, and back down to Sedbergh, then home again.'

Jadyn was impressed.

'That's quite a route,' he said. 'I'm not a cyclist myself; more a gym person.'

'You should try it,' Colin suggested.

'No, I shouldn't,' said Jadyn. 'Trust me.'

He was about to drag the conversation back to what they were talking about when there was a knock at the door. He got up to open it and found Harry on the other side, staring back at him, Smudge sitting at his heels.

'Matt needs you,' Harry said. 'We're calling in the Mountain Rescue Team. Shift it.'

Jadyn ignored that Harry was even more brusque than usual and quickly went through what he had learned from Colin. He saw the DCI's expression grow darker as he spoke, then he stepped into the room and sat down in front of Colin, Smudge flopping down on the floor.

'DCI Grimm,' Harry said, his eyes close to burning a scorch mark on Colin's forehead. 'I'm afraid that Constable Okri will have to leave us rather urgently, so how about you run through everything you've told him again, only this time with me?'

EIGHT

With Jadyn off to meet up with Matt and the rest of the Mountain Rescue Team, and having listened to everything Colin had just told him, Harry wouldn't have been at all surprised if the weather decided that what it really needed to do was move to new pastures by pushing its way through the community centre's doors and making it rain inside as well as out; it was turning into that kind of day.

He was also very hungry; the job doing what it always did, and showing scant regard for a police officer's need for nutrition if they were to have any chance of keeping up with what was going on around them. Midafternoon had now flown by and Harry was resigned to the fact he probably wouldn't get a bite to eat before the evening.

As to what was happening with trying to locate Amber and Josh Hill, Harry knew all too well that things could get very messy very quickly, and Harry didn't do messy. A MISPER was a complex and demanding thing to deal with, especially when friends and family decided that they wanted to be involved, sometimes going so far as conducting their own searches, sometimes even armed with dogs and roping in help from local volunteers. That he was now dealing with a missing couple who not only had some kind of clearly misplaced celebrity status, but also a substantial fanbase? Well, that was one huge steaming pile of stupid he could rightly do without.

As Colin had talked, Harry's mind had filled with images of Hawes awash with Josh and Amber's followers, all traipsing across the fells, searching for their favourite lottery-winning couple and getting in the way while they were doing it. Then no doubt getting into trouble themselves, falling into gullies, twisting ankles, ending up lost, and generally causing a massive problem not just for him, but for all arms of the emergency services. Nipping all of that in the bud before everything went south was, he realised, as urgent as it was going to be problematic.

Harry knew he had to step lightly if he was going to get Colin onside to try and avoid things getting out of hand. With his clasped hands on the table, he stared at Colin.

'I'm going to need your help,' he said.

Colin's eyes lit up. 'Really? That's great because I was going to offer that anyway and I've already—'

Harry held up a hand to stop him from continuing.

'And the best way you can help both me and the rest of the team right now is by keeping this to yourself.'

'What?'

'To put it plainly,' Harry said, 'what no one needs is this being splashed all over social media. Not that I've a clue what any of that actually is, or why anyone cares, or indeed why being famous just for being famous seems to be an actual career these days. But I do know that if you start shouting off on there about what's going on, I'm not going to be very happy. And believe you me, you don't want that.'

'That sounds like a threat,' said Colin.

Harry shook his head.

'Not a threat, a reality,' he said, his voice still managing to cling to being almost calm. 'Josh and Amber Hill are missing, and I aim to find them. To do that effectively, I will have a team of professionals doing what they're trained to do. Now, if you go telling everyone what's going on, as sure as my face looks like a bear took a fancy to it as a midmorning snack, we'll be swimming in idiots.'

'Idiots? Wait, what do you—'

'I've dealt with this kind of thing before,' Harry said, talking over Colin's attempted protest. He was remembering a case not too long ago, where some local girls had decided that filming a crime scene and posting it on TikTok would be a bit of fun. It had been anything but. 'I've seen how something posted on social media can end up putting an investigation in jeopardy. Stuff like that, it doesn't just get in the way, it can be dangerous. I don't think anyone wants that, do they?'

'But—'

'No buts,' Harry said, holding a finger up to shush Colin. 'What I need, is for you to hear me loud and clear, understood?'

He waited for Colin to give him a nod.

'I do not want you telling anyone beyond these walls what is going on, and I very much do not want any of this being posted anywhere on social media. And don't go thinking I won't find out, either. Let us do what we do and find Josh and Amber first, then go for your life, but right now? Zip it.'

For a second or two, Colin was quiet.

'So, you don't want me to say anything, then?'

'Not a thing.'

A faint smile dared to find its way onto Colin's face. Harry resisted the temptation to reach over and smack it off.

Colin asked. 'You really don't understand social media at all, do you?'

'What?'

'It's already out there,' Colin said, leaning forward and waving an arm around in the air like he was trying to catch something. 'And really there's not much I can do about it.'

'What do you mean, it's already out there? Who have you told and what have you told them?'

'I mean,' said Colin, 'I'll do what you've said, but that it won't matter. Once information is out, there's nothing anyone can do to get it back.'

'Well, try!' said Harry, not liking where this was going.

'Try? How? What do you expect me to say?'

'I expect you to say that you'll make sure no one else comes here trying to take selfies in the middle of a planned, coordinated search, that's what!'

Colin sat back, folded his arms, and laughed, a sound that put Harry even more on edge than he already was.

'And that wouldn't be suspicious at all, would it?' Colin said. 'People would know. They'd see through it, because I'd be lying, and I'm not going to lie. The truth, that's what people want; you can't deny them that.'

Harry was on his feet before he knew what he was doing and brought his hands down hard on the table as he leaned over, bringing his face within inches of Colin's own. So much for being careful ...

'Truth? Really? And you know a lot about that, do you, Mr Hampton?'

'I know that the elites lie to us, that the truth is kept from the masses, that—'

Once again Harry cut Colin's sentence in two.

'The only truth here, in fact the only truth that matters at all, is that two people are missing, and I have to find them,' he said. 'If you or anyone else gets in the way of that, I'll throw the book at you so hard you'll be able to read it on the inside of your skull. Do I make myself clear?'

'That's another threat.'

'I said, do I make myself clear?' Harry repeated, fully aware now that the bellowing of his voice was loud enough to shake the window.

At last, Colin gave a nod.

'I'm sorry, but I didn't hear that,' said Harry. 'Loud and clear, please. Imagine I'm not in this room at all. Imagine I'm outside in the rain wondering why it is, on a day such as this, I have to explain myself to someone whose grasp on reality is clearly less than secure.'

'Yes,' said Colin, his voice louder, clearer, and pinched with irritation. 'You've made yourself clear.'

'Give the lad a coconut.'

'What?'

'A prize,' Harry said, smiling briefly as he remembered something Matt had said earlier about phrases he liked to say. That one had come from his old mentor, DCI Jameson, and somehow had stuck. 'For listening, and for understanding.'

'Bit condescending, isn't it?'

Harry pushed away from the table and walked over to open the door, pointing out into the empty hallway beyond. 'Now, if you don't mind?'

Colin stood up and slouched past Harry, pausing as though he was about to say something, but a twitch from Harry's head had him continuing on his way.

Harry watched as Colin shuffled through the main door of the community centre and out into the rain, then spotted Liz jogging up the lane from the marketplace and into the building once he'd gone. Harry was fairly sure he'd made himself clear. He was also sure that this wasn't the last he was going to see of Colin.

'Who's that, then?' Liz asked. 'Doesn't look exactly happy.'

'That makes two of us,' Harry said, then asked, 'How are you with social media?'

'I'm that rare animal who doesn't have a Facebook account,' answered Liz. 'Never saw the point of it. Why would I want to go posting things about my life to a bunch of people I either hardly know or don't know at all? And anyway, if I did know them, I'd tell them, wouldn't I, so why would I need Facebook?'

Harry didn't explain further, and instead led Liz into the office, Smudge following along behind. Once inside, he quickly told her what was going on, about the campervan and the owners and their apparent fame.

'I need you to see if you can find out as much as you can,' he said. 'Not only about Josh and Amber, because we need to contact their family yesterday, if you get my meaning, but also to keep an eye on whatever social media stuff is going on.'

'I'll get right on it,' said Liz. 'Their feeds will be easy enough to find, especially with that lottery win. I remember something about that, I think. Won a tenner myself the same day, which was nice.'

'What did you spend it on?'

'Put it towards a takeaway with Ben.'

'How is he?' Harry asked, having not seen his younger brother for a while. But then his life was busy, not just with his job at Mike's garage, but with Liz and, alarmingly, motorbikes.

'Enjoying his new bike,' Liz said. 'He's got his test in a few months, so we're out whenever we can.'

'I'm going to be very, very disappointed if he ends up wrapping himself round a telegraph pole on that thing,' said Harry.

'You worry too much.'

'Detective, remember? Worrying is my job.'

Harry opened the office door.

'I'll leave all that social media stuff with you, then,' he said. 'And if you're able to find out any family details, then it would be good if you could contact them. They might know something we don't. But regardless, they need to be informed. Amber and Josh's mobile numbers are what we need, though. If we can get some location data from them, we might at least be able to narrow down their movements, up to the point where their batteries died.'

'Assuming they had their trackers on,' said Liz. 'If they didn't, then geolocation isn't going to work.' Then she asked, 'Where are you off to?'

'Back out to join the search,' Harry said. 'Mind looking after Smudge?'

'Of course not,' said Liz. 'Seeing her a lot more at the moment, aren't we? Though it must be difficult for Grace to have her sometimes, what with the shooting season in full flow now. I've lost count of the number of near-misses I've had on the roads with pheasants with a death wish.'

Harry said nothing, and with a nod left the room, hushing the door shut behind him.

Outside, the rain seemed even harder, and as he pushed on through it to make his way to his vehicle, he tried to not think about Grace. Trouble was, the more he tried to not think about her, the more she floated to the top of his mind, and soon enough, she was all he could think of.

Once in the driver's seat, the door quickly shut to block out the storm, Harry pulled out his phone and quickly typed Grace a message, then deleted it immediately. What was he trying to say anyway? He hadn't a clue. And right there was the problem, he thought, keying the ignition and heading back up into the hills.

NINE

Back at the campervan, after dropping Harry back in town to speak with Jadyn, Matt had put in the relevant calls to the Mountain Rescue Team. He'd had another quick scout around the area just in case he spotted something out of the ordinary, but soon concluded that the wind and the rain would have erased anything like that anyway. And it didn't look as though that was about to abate anytime soon.

Sitting out of the rain in the Police Land Rover, which was now the designated rendezvous point for the search, he was waiting for everyone to arrive for the team briefing. While he waited, he was having another scroll through photos of Mary-Anne when a shadow appeared at the window.

'Bloody hell!'

Matt dropped his phone into the footwell as on the other side of the glass, a middle-aged bearded face stared back.

'Now then,' the face said. 'You alright in there, like?'

Matt said nothing for a moment and picked up his phone, before turning to look at the beard, the owner of which, who Matt guessed to be in his late forties, early fifties, was now smiling broadly. The beard itself was as far removed from being hipster as it was possible to be, a thick bush of black wire, a tangled mass of springs bursting from the man's smiling face, cut here and there by flashes of white.

'Oh, I'm just fine and dandy,' Matt said. 'Just give me a minute while I check my vitals and make sure I don't need to head back home to change my pants.'

The smile turned into a laugh, and Matt opened the window. Wind threw rain in at him and he quickly closed it again, wiping his face in the process.

'Can I help?' he asked, shouting through the glass.

Matt recognised the face but couldn't put a name to it. The Dales were small enough to know most people if you lived there long enough, that was true, but remembering who was called what was a little more difficult.

'He found you then, did he, that biker?' the man asked. 'That's why you're here, isn't it? Must be. Can't think of any other reason you'd be out here in this. Not exactly sightseeing weather, is it? Not much to see, what with visibility being not much further than the end of my nose.'

The man's words grabbed Matt's interest immediately.

'You saw him?'

The man gave a short nod, then pointed away behind him, over towards Cotterdale and Shunner Fell.

'I farm over at Fairfield, over there, like,' he said. 'One of our dogs buggered off after a rabbit a few hours ago. Been looking everywhere and I know he's been up here before. He's getting old, you see. Lovely old Lab, used to be good with the gun, but can't hear a bloody thing now, and he's half blind. Once he gets a scent, he just keeps going until he drops on his arse and falls asleep.'

Matt was struggling with trying to lipread the words he couldn't quite hear above the howling gale and constant rattle of rain as it tried to drill its way into the cabin.

'Come round t' other side,' he said, gesturing at the passenger seat with his thumb. 'Jump in.'

The man did as Matt said, and a moment later was sitting

beside him. From a jacket pocket, he pulled out a pipe with a metal stem and a small leather pouch.

Matt watched as the man stuffed tobacco from the pouch into the pipe, then shoved the pipe stem into his mouth and, from another pocket, removed a lighter.

'Don't see many of those around nowadays,' said Matt, especially with anyone under the age of seventy, he thought.

'This?' the man said, taking the pipe from his mouth to hold it out in front of his face. 'No, I suppose not. I don't smoke it much, but on a day like this, it just works.'

'I'm sure it does,' said Matt, as the man stuffed the pipe back in his mouth and flicked a flame into life on the lighter, 'but it'll have to work somewhere else; can't have you smoking it in here.'

The flame danced across the tobacco for a moment, then the man cut it off.

'Fair enough,' he said, stuffing the pipe, lighter, and pouch back in their respective pockets. 'Now, where were we? Oh yes, that's right ...' He held out a hand for Matt to shake. 'Pete Fawcett,' he said. 'You're Dinsdale, right? Seen you about, but I don't think we've ever met.'

'Matt Dinsdale,' Matt said, shaking Pete's hand. 'Detective Sergeant.'

Pete blew on his hands, then rubbed them together.

'Nippy out, isn't it?' he said. 'You here to tow it back, then? The campervan, I mean. Shouldn't really be parked up here anyway. It's one thing to be using these old roads for a bit of adventurous driving, but if folk start parking up out here for days on end, next thing we know the Dales will be covered in pop-up campsites, won't they?'

'My guess is that you don't want that,' said Matt.

Pete shook his head.

'No one wants that,' he said. 'But the Dales need tourists, of course it does. Trouble is, there's always a small number of them who turn up and cause a problem. Shame really, but that's just the way of things, isn't it?'

'Did you know the van was up here, then?' Matt asked.

'First time I've seen it,' said Pete.

Matt glanced outside. 'How did you get up here? You didn't walk, not in this.'

'Got myself one of those little Polaris four-by-fours,' said Pete, pointing out through the windscreen at a small vehicle barely visible through the low cloud. 'Surprised you didn't hear it.'

'Can't hear anything with this rain,' said Matt.

'It's basically a quad bike with a roll cage,' Pete explained. 'Mine's got a covered cab, though, which I'm rather thankful for when the weather's like this, I can tell you.'

Matt pulled out his notebook. 'Now, this biker; I don't suppose you've a description, have you?'

'Leathers, helmet, that kind of thing,' said Pete. 'Mentioned something about what I'm guessing is that campervan you're parked in front of, so I sent him down to the community centre; figured it best if he spoke to your lot.'

'Don't suppose you've seen anyone else up here?'

Pete shook his head.

'There's no one out in this except yourself, and me looking for my daft dog,' he said. 'Farming's not a job for those who can't be doing with the bad weather, is it? It's in your blood, isn't it, if you know what I mean?'

'I do,' said Matt, remembering numerous conversations with Jim about his family's farm.

'Wasn't as though I was going to do anything else anyway,' Pete continued. 'I just followed my dad into it. Seemed as natural as breathing.'

'You farm together, then?'

'We run the place together. He's getting on a bit now, but not showing any signs of slowing down, the stubborn old bugger. Any road, it's just the two of us, like, with my mum not being around anymore.'

'Sorry to hear that,' said Matt.

'Don't be,' said Pete. 'It was years ago, back when I was a kid. I was only seven. She wandered off into the moors one night, never came back.'

'Really? And she was never found?'

'There was a search by the fell rescue team, right enough. I think that's what it was called back then, wasn't it? But no, they never found her.'

Matt wondered what had happened.

'That's terrible,' he said.

'It was, but Dad worked even harder without her around. I was young, but that didn't matter. I still joined in. Soon as I could walk, I was out with him, fetching the sheep. Got my first dog when I was eight.' He looked at Matt, eyes serious, distant. 'Aye, there's blood in it, that's for sure, like you said.' Pete's face broke into a smile. 'Anyway, why are you sitting up here all on your tod?'

'I'm actually waiting for the Mountain Rescue Team,' Matt said, then checked his watch. 'Should be here in ten, fifteen minutes, I should think. I could find out what happened in that search for your mum if you wanted? Mountain Rescue keeps a detailed record of every call-out. It would take a while, but I'm happy to have a look for you.'

'No,' said Pete. 'The past is the past. Best leave it there. What's the rescue team on with?'

'Finding the owners of the campervan,' Matt said.

'You don't think they're out in this, do you?' Pete asked, frowning. 'It's chucking it down.'

'The camper looks like it's been there a few days,' Matt said. 'Doesn't make sense. We've someone back at the office ringing around to local pubs and B&Bs to see if they've checked in anywhere, but if that comes to nowt, then there's a chance they've got themselves into trouble somehow. Better to start looking now, and find they're warm and cosy in a pub, than leave it till we find they're not in a pub at all and injured and half frozen to death out in that.'

Matt jabbed a finger at the weather.

'Even so,' said Pete. 'Who'd be daft enough?'

'You've met people, right?' Matt said. 'They do daft things.'

'That they do, right enough. Worse than sheep,' Pete agreed, then opened the door. 'Anyway, sitting here won't find my dog, will it? I'd best get on.'

'Hope you find it,' said Matt. Then, as he was thinking back over what Pete had told him, something scratched at the back of his mind, something the man had said about seeing the campervan, but as he turned to ask him about it, movement caught his eye, off to his left. 'Wait, what's that?'

Pete turned to see what Matt was looking at.

'I don't see anything.'

Matt leaned forward, narrowing his eyes.

'There,' he said, pointing a finger. 'Behind that wall ...'

Through the rain, the movement had been just enough to grab his attention. His first thought was that it was the dog Pete was out looking for, but he soon realised it was far too big for that. A deer perhaps? No, it wasn't that.

He kept staring, saw the shape twist and turn in the rain, a blurred shadow smudged by the weather like paint on a canvas.

Matt climbed out of the Land Rover, walked around the bonnet, and lifted his left hand to shield his face from the weather, spotting Pete's Polaris just a few metres away down the track.

Pete joined him.

'What is it you've seen, then?' he asked, shielding his face from the rain with a raised hand.

Matt didn't reply, just pointed.

No, not a deer, he realised, because he was fairly sure they didn't walk around on their back legs.

'Hey!' he shouted, raising an arm into the air to wave.

The figure was motionless.

Matt waved his hand more vigorously, then called out once again.

The figure responded by breaking into a run.

'Oh, you didn't just ...' he said.

Whoever it was, running away was beyond suspicious. Matt's

only conclusion was that they knew something, otherwise, why would they run away?

Matt quickly checked his watch. Chasing after whoever it was on foot wasn't going to work, not with the weather the way it was, the headstart they had, and his own less than adequate running speed. He could take the Police Land Rover, but it was a heavy beast and could easily get bogged down. What he needed was something lightweight and nimble.

'Pete,' Matt said, pointing at the farmer's own vehicle. 'Don't suppose you'd mind giving me a lift, would you?'

TEN

Up at the auction mart, Jim was relishing being in a world he'd known for as long as he could remember. He was standing beneath the sheet metal roof of one of the main buildings and leaning against the gate of one of the numerous pens which stretched out before him. Fly was sitting at his heel, quiet and still.

Jim reached out into the pen, his fingers pushing through the thick fleece on the back of one of the Swaledale sheep it contained and gave a squeeze. The sheep turned its head and regarded him with a look that somehow managed to mix both trust and vengeance in a single stare, as though it was more than happy for him to give it the once over, but that at any moment, it would happily turn on him and stamp him into the ground to escape.

Jim removed his hand and gave the animal's head a quick scratch. It knocked back against it, stamped a foot.

'These'll go for a few quid,' he said. 'Best here by a country mile.'

Dave Calvert was standing beside him, arms folded across his broad chest.

'I've never quite seen the attraction myself,' he said. 'Working with sheep, it just seems to be a quick way to poverty and an early grave.'

'Says the man who keeps goats,' Jim laughed.

'Goats are different,' said Dave. 'They've got character.'

Jim stared at Dave for a moment, stunned by what the man had just said.

'Character's what you call it, is it?' he said. 'An animal that will eat its way through a wall, kick you up the arse then head butt you, before buggering off into a neighbour's field to knock down a wall or two and scoff whatever they can find?'

'They're endearing.'

'They're insane.'

'Their cheese is delicious.'

'Their cheese tastes exactly like they smell: rank. Goats stink, Dave, they reek to high Heaven.'

Dave rolled his eyes, shook his head.

'You just don't understand them, that's all,' he said.

'No, you're right, I don't,' said Jim. 'And I don't want to, either. Sheep, though? They're beautiful animals, aren't they? I mean, look at these in front of us. Aren't they something?'

'They look like sheep,' said Dave, then waved a hand to gesture at the hundreds of other animals in pens around them. 'They all just look like sheep.'

Jim rested a hand on Dave's shoulder.

'You've a lot to learn.'

Dave laughed.

'How long are we staying here for, anyway?' he asked. 'It's already gone lunchtime. Are we popping into the café on the way out? We've had a good chat with plenty of folk, haven't we?'

The auction mart café had been there for years. Jim remembered being taken in there as a young lad by his dad as a treat, sitting down at the simple tables to attempt to eat his way through the better part of a full English.

Jim said, 'We've a few to pop out and see over the next few days as well, so that's good. Seems like fly-tipping is on the increase, so we should find out what we can.'

'The café, then?'

The look in Dave's eyes reminded Jim a little of Matt standing outside the window of Cockett's.

'Seems like a good idea,' he said. 'And as it's your first time up here in uniform, it can be my treat.'

'You don't need to do that,' said Dave.

'Need's got nowt to do with it,' said Jim. 'Come on.'

Jim stepped away from the sheep pen, and with Fly to heel, led Dave out into the rain and down towards the café. Once inside, he ordered them both a good-sized plate of food, a mug of tea, then sat down. Dave joined him and Fly slunk under the table and flopped down onto the floor.

'My brother loved it here,' he said, a memory coming at him so suddenly it filled his mind completely, pushing out everything else. Then he realised why. He tapped the table. 'Always used to sit here with him and Dad. Good times.'

Dave was quiet for a moment, stretching back in his chair. Then he leaned forward, his hands clasped together on the table.

'Tell me about him,' he said.

'My brother?'

Dave gave a nod, but Jim shook his head.

'No, you don't want to be hearing that,' he said.

'I know what happened,' said Dave. 'It was awful for you all. I'm not asking you about that. I'm asking about him; what he was like, what he was into, what he wanted to do with his life, what he did that really got on your nerves ...?'

Jim realised that he was laughing.

'You know, no one's ever asked me that,' he said. 'In fact, people don't ask me about him at all.'

'Well, I'm asking now, aren't I?' Dave said, and opened his hands to Jim, as he relaxed back into his chair again. 'And this seems like the perfect place to do that.'

For a moment, Jim wasn't quite sure what to do or say. Part of him wanted nothing to do with what Dave was asking. What business was it of his, anyway? All those memories—he only took them out to look at them in private. Hell, he didn't even talk about stuff like that with his parents. But then, as he scratched at the table with a scuffed nail, he heard his brother's voice. It was distant, an echo of something years back, a moment they'd shared while out in the hills fetching the sheep for their dad, and it was so real, so clear, that he almost turned around, expecting to find his brother standing behind him.

The food was brought over, and Dave handed Jim a knife and fork wrapped in a pale blue paper napkin.

'The last thing we did together,' he said, 'was also the best ...' And as he spoke, recounting first one story, then another, each one tumbling after the other, chasing it, the urgency of the memories charging the air around him, his words punctuated by mouthfuls of food, Jim smiled and laughed more than he had done in years.

When the meal was over, Dave dabbed and wiped his mouth with the napkin.

'Thanks for that,' he said.

'No bother,' said Jim. 'You can buy the next one.'

'I don't just mean the meal,' said Dave, 'but for telling me about your brother. He meant a lot to you. And it sounds to me like you still look up to him a little.'

'I guess,' said Jim.

'And Harry's right, isn't he?'

'What about?'

'Farming—your family farm to be more accurate, I think—it's part of your DNA, and there's no escaping it.'

'Maybe.'

'Then why are you trying to?'

Dave's question took Jim by surprise.

'I'm not,' he said.

'You wear a PCSO's uniform,' said Dave. 'And you're bloody good at what you do, don't get me wrong, but you're young, Jim. You can't do it forever, can you?'

'Never said I would.'

'Then what next?' Dave asked, but didn't give Jim a chance to answer. 'You know you're different here, don't you? In this place, in the world of farming, there's something else about you that gets a chance to stretch its legs, like, to breathe, if that makes sense.'

'Not sure that it does, Dave.'

Dave gave a shrug.

'You'll have to forgive me my metaphors,' he said. 'But you know what I'm getting at.'

'My brother was supposed to be the one to take on the farm,' Jim said, standing up to head over to the counter and pay for the food. 'And my parents have never pushed me into that life, always left me to make my own decisions. Anyway, I love my job.'

'That you do,' Dave said, rising to his feet. 'But I reckon you've a lot to be thinking about. Now then, what are we on with next?'

Jim was still a little shaken by what had just happened, the memories of his brother real enough to think he might bump into him outside in the mart at any moment. He was just about to suggest that they take another walk around the pens, perhaps have a look in the auction room, when a small group of farmers came into the café, momentarily blocking their exit.

'Now then, Jim,' said one of the farmers, his gnarled, windworn face betraying a long life spent out on the fells farming sheep. 'You've got some new help, I see?'

He glanced at Dave, then stepped forward and held out a hand to Jim. 'This is our new PCSO, Dave Calvert,' Jim said, shaking the man's hand, and introducing Dave to the farmer. 'Dave, this is Mr Fawcett. Farms over Cotterdale way.'

The farmer laughed.

'Mr Fawcett, is it? Come on, Jim, you know me better than that.' He looked at Dave. 'I'm William,' he said. Turning his attention back to Jim, he added, 'Saw you looking at my animals earlier.'

'Thought they might be yours,' said Jim. 'Lovely looking sheep.'

'Of course they are,' William beamed.

Jim smiled.

'Won a good few prizes has William,' he said to Dave. 'My dad's managed to knock him off the top spot a couple of times, but that's all. We'll keep trying, though.'

'Best you do,' said William. 'No point making it easy for me, is there?'

William went to head into the café, then turned back to look at Jim.

'Don't suppose you know what's going on up Cam Road, do you?' he asked. 'Our lad's just sent me a message. He's supposed to be finding one of our dogs that's run off, but sounds like one of your lot's had him on a wild goose chase after some idiot. And they must be an idiot to be out on the fells in weather like this.'

Jim knew of the van but hadn't spoken to the rest of the team since he'd been at the mart.

'I've heard nowt about that,' he said. 'Anyway, best be off.'

Leaving the café, Jim headed outside with Fly and Dave. The rain had eased a little, but he noticed that the sky was still a dark thing, bubbling with anger.

'I reckon my dad would give his eye teeth to have our farm do even half as well as William's,' he said.

'How do you mean?' Dave asked.

'Let's just say that business is booming at Fairfield Farm,' Jim replied. 'They've bought up a few other farms since the seventies, hire in professional shepherds, run a shoot. Done very well over the years.'

'All right for some,' said Dave. 'Back up to the pens, then, to look at even more sheep?'

Jim shook his head.

'No, I think we're good. And after what William's just told us, I'm wondering if we're going to be needed.'

'Back to the office, then?'

'Looks that way,' said Jim.

With Fly to heel, he led them out of the mart and back down into Hawes, wondering what Matt had been up to, but simultaneously finding his mind drifting back to the family farm.

ELEVEN

The darkness was absolute. Eyes open or closed, it made no difference. And time had vanished, or at least Josh's understanding and grasp of it had. He had no idea how long he had been there; hours, days, weeks. Though it couldn't be weeks, that much he was sure about because he hadn't been fed, and though he was hungry and thirsty, he knew that he was some way off from being starved. Though whether that was a good or bad sign, or no sign at all, he didn't know, didn't dare think.

The scent was sweet. It reminded him a little of the iced vanilla latte he liked to order from the coffee shop he and Amber hung out in for an hour or two on a Saturday morning.

Amber ...

The face of the woman he loved flashed bright in his mind. He screamed, the sound bursting out of him with such force that he choked, snarling the end of it into a shard of cracked, broken glass. His guttural roar exploded in the thick darkness, racing off in all directions, bouncing around him, then when the echo returned it brought with it something else, something worse.

A laugh.

There was no warmth to it, Josh noticed, and he tried to move away from it, pushing himself hard against a rock wall at his back, wishing he could hide, slip into some crack and disappear.

Josh remembered having a rucksack. It had torches, a GoPro, his phone, but where was it now?

Shuffling footsteps, a splash of water.

'Please,' Josh said, scrabbling around to find the bag, convinced it had to be close by, shocked to hear how broken his voice sounded. 'Please, just let me go ... please ...'

The laughter came again, closer this time. And it brought with it another sound of metal scraping against metal.

Josh yanked at the rope around his wrists, the thick, rough twine cutting into him, scraping away at his skin, the end of it wrapped around a metal hoop in the floor. The pain of it had numbed now, probably because of the cold, the shock, the fear.

'Where am I? Where's Amber? What do you want? Who are you?'

Metal against metal, shuffling footsteps closer still.

Josh couldn't remember what had happened exactly, but he'd managed to piece together the broken flashbacks just enough to know he still couldn't make any bloody sense of it.

He remembered returning to the campervan on his bike to fetch Amber. With the van itself being so cosy, especially with the weather as it was, she hadn't exactly been all that keen about following him. But after a little bit of gentle persuasion, and the promise of a couple good bottles of wine later on, she had agreed. He'd grabbed her bike and off they'd rode, down the track and through the deepest of puddles.

He'd dicked around a little too much, he knew that, grabbing more air than he'd expected over an impromptu ramp formed by a rise in a grass verge at the track's side, landed badly and hit the deck. Amber had rushed over, concerned, yes, but also pissed at his stupidity. They'd kissed and made up, and she'd sensibly put a dampener on any more of his advances, and so they had continued on their way. But to where? It wasn't where he was now. It couldn't be.

A rough hand grabbed Josh around the throat and pinned him to the rock at his back, scraping his head on rough stone, obliterating the memories. He would've cried out, but the hand squeezed, and he was silent except for the struggle of his legs kicking out, his hog-tied heels trying to find purchase on something, anything that would help him ease the pressure, allow him to breathe.

That sweet smell came again, this time on hot breath so close to his cheek that Josh felt its dampness on his skin.

A light sparked in the dark, became an orange tongue flickering in front of Josh's face, close enough to briefly set fire to his hair, which hung long and limp around his neck and over his face. It gave off just enough of a glow to show a pair of eyes inches away from his own. Mean eyes, and cold.

The hand around his throat eased a little, but still had him pinned, as a body's weight pressed into him.

'Please ... don't ...' said Josh, his voice a thin whisper forced through a crushed throat.

He knew what was coming because those eyes had visited him twice before. Each time they had brought with them agony like nothing else.

'Please ...'

Pain, hot and sharp and angry, exploded in Josh's chest as something cut into him, slicing through his shirt and into his skin. He tried to scream, to wriggle free, but the hand at his throat held him fast, and his voice was no more than the weak bleat of a lamb. Then warmth washed over his chest as his blood ran fast and free.

In seconds which lasted years, as the pain set fire to every cell in his body, Josh drifted out of himself, lost to the impossibility of what was being done to him. He was swimming with Amber, diving and splashing through watery jewels caught bright in a high sun pinned to an azure sky; he was dancing with her, spinning her around, grass at their feet, a moon dipping its chin to the horizon, the scattered gems of the night all around; he was placing a ring on her fi—

The hand at Josh's throat released him. He sagged, felt the weight of the body against him start to lift.

'Please ...'

Laughter, louder this time, smug and satisfied.

In desperation, in frustration, in anger and rage and fear, Josh kicked out, launching his legs into the nothingness around him so violently his knees cracked. And somehow, in that god-awful darkness, lit still by that solitary flickering orange light, his feet connected, bare heels ramming into he knew not what, but he heard a cry, and it was enough.

Adrenaline surged through Josh like wildfire. Blinded by desperate rage he scrabbled in the dark, kicked out once again, found only thin air, rolled left, rolled right, thumped into something soft but unyielding with his shoulder, kept rolling, pushing himself up on his elbows quickly enough to bring him onto his assailant's chest. His only weapon was his head, and he brought it down like a hammer, felt it smash against something hard, sending it to slam into the solid rock beneath with a dull, hollow thwack.

Josh lifted his head, ready to bring it down once again, but something sharp caught his leg and he hissed with the pain of it. Something deep inside him, the instinct of an animal caught in a trap, had him reach out and yank it free. He turned it on the ropes around his ankles, hacking and slicing and cutting and chopping until the rope fell loose.

Josh rolled onto his knees, forced himself to stand. Cramps and cold tore at his muscles and he dropped to the ground, landing on the one who had brought him here in the first place, tied him up, cut him. He tried again, gritting his teeth as he stood up, only realising then that he had, in falling, dropped the thing he had used to cut his feet free.

With wrists still tied, Josh padded the ground for it, desperate to find it before *they* came to.

He brushed against something, heard it skitter across the ground, caught it before it went too far for him to find again. His touch was enough to tell him what it was. Not the blade that had set him free, no, but something else.

With a flick of his thumb, light burst in his hand and a flame appeared, the simple lighter enough to show him where he was and who was at his feet.

'You sick bastard ...'

His voice was a rattlesnake hiss spat from broken teeth and a bleeding mouth.

Josh kicked hard, launching a foot at their torso, then went in again, this time bringing it down in a violent stamp hard enough to crack ribs, ready and willing to break every bone, cave in a skull, to kill.

A hand swept out, knocking his foot to one side.

Laughter.

And Josh, as best as he could in bare feet cold and deeply cut by rough rock, with his hands still tied together at the wrist, and with only a cigarette lighter to show him the way, ran.

TWELVE

Arriving back at the campervan, Harry found the old Police Land Rover surrounded by half a dozen other off-road vehicles of varying shapes, sizes, and conditions. Front and centre, however, was the Mountain Rescue vehicle. Yet another Land Rover it may have been, but it was also considerably newer and in much better condition than the one his team used. It was also laden with numerous bits of expensive rescue equipment, and judging by the mug Matt was clasping as he strolled over to meet him, a flask or two of tea to boot.

A gathering of people all clothed in all-weather mountain gear, hefty boots, and rucksacks were standing in a half circle around another figure who was obviously in charge and giving them instructions. Jadyn was with them, and Harry saw a look of intense concentration on the constable's face.

'No luck with the pubs, then?' Matt asked.

'Liz is on with that,' said Harry, 'and seeing what else she can find out through Amber and Josh's social media stuff, but nothing yet, no.'

'Does more harm than good if you ask me, all of that,' Matt said.

'I'm inclined to agree,' said Harry. 'But it's not really our generation, is it? What's happening, then?'

'Team briefing at the moment, then we'll be off.' Matt studied Harry. 'You think they're out here, don't you?'

'I do,' Harry said, and looked over at the campervan. 'That wasn't left in that state by a couple heading off to the pub for a few pints, then deciding it would be best to stay in the warmth and wait it out.'

'No, you're probably right,' Matt said. 'Worryingly so, if I'm honest.'

'So, what do we know?' Harry asked.

Matt lifted his mug to his lips.

'Want one? It'll warm you up a bit if nowt else.'

Harry shook his head.

'It's not tea I want,' he said, 'it's food.'

'You're not telling me you've not eaten?'

'Not since breakfast.'

Matt spluttered.

'What? But it's gone five!'

'You think I don't know that?' said Harry.

'You'll be fading away if you're not careful. Here.'

Harry watched as Matt reached into a pocket and pulled out a paper bag dotted with grease.

'And what's that?'

'What do you think it is?'

Harry opened the bag.

'Two of Cockett's finest,' Matt said. 'Best pork pies in the world, if you ask me.'

'Is there ever a time in your life when you're not carrying a pie in your pocket?'

'That's what pockets are for,' said Matt.

'I don't think they are.'

'Stop talking and get one of those down your neck.'

'Right now, I'm so hungry I'd even eat one of Phil's,' said Harry, remembering the truly inedible thing he'd been given a good while ago by an old friend of Grace's dad.

'No, you wouldn't,' said Matt.

'No, you're right, I wouldn't,' agreed Harry, and quickly devoured the first pie.

'Better?' Matt asked.

Harry wrapped up the other pie and stuffed it into a pocket.

'I'll save that for later,' he said, as Matt took another slurp of tea.

'I'm trying to think of the last time I saw you without a mug of tea in your hand.'

'Last week, at the Fountain,' said Matt.

'You were drinking beer.'

'There we are then,' said Matt.

The DS led Harry over to the crowd gathered by the Mountain Rescue Land Rover.

A woman stepped forward and held out a hand. Behind her, the rescue team set off to start the search for Amber and Josh.

Harry shook the woman's hand.

'Helen Dinsdale,' she said.

'DCI Harry—'

'Oh, I know who you are,' Helen said. 'Had the pleasure of driving that young constable of yours out on a search back during that winter's storm at the start of the year. Lovely young man.'

'Was that the lad who went missing from Marsett?'

'That was it,' said Helen.

'Where are we, then?' Harry asked.

'Out in the rain and staring a cold, wet night hard in the face,' Helen said.

'No change there, then,' said Matt.

Harry waited for one of them to say something sensible.

'We've already sent a team up the lane,' Helen said, gesturing away from the van and up into the fells. The tops were still hidden by thick cloud, the skies darkening by the minute. 'If they're on bikes, then the obvious place to start the search is there. It's a popular route, goes a fair way, too, and there are plenty of little lefts and rights to explore. Our hope is that we'll find them somewhere out there, huddled in a barn, with a broken ankle and a phone that's run out of charge.'

'What else?' Harry asked.

'We've put a call out for some other teams to come and join us,' Helen said. 'We've a couple of dogs of our own, but we've also been in touch with the Search and Rescue Dog Association, to see if there's anyone who can lend a paw.' Helen laughed at that, though Harry didn't join in. 'We've also a drone to send up if the weather improves. Right now, it'd get smashed around too much by the wind and rain. Impressive piece of kit, too. You know, a while back when we had it out one night, we had reports in of people thinking a UFO was flying about.'

'It's not going to be an easy search, is it?' said Harry.

Helen shook her head.

'They never are. If they're up the lane, or close by to it, then we've a good chance of finding them sooner rather than later. If they're not, then we have one hell of a task ahead of us. You'll have noticed that the Dales aren't exactly small.'

'No, they're not,' said Harry, 'but it's not all wilderness and the wilds, is it? Most of the area's farmed, and there's lanes and paths and bridleways all over the place.'

'You'd be amazed how easy it is for someone to get lost here,' Helen said.

Harry shook his head.

'No, I wouldn't,' he said. 'And that's what worries me.'

'It's going to be a long night, isn't it?' said Matt.

'It is,' said Harry. 'And a cold and wet one, too.'

Helen said, 'We've one lead, though, so that's something.'

Harry jumped at this, his eyes on Matt.

'Lead? What lead?'

'Did I not say?'

'No, you didn't say,' growled Harry. 'What've you found?'

'It was while I was talking with Pete,' Matt said. 'That's when I saw them.'

'Saw who?' Harry asked. 'Do you think it might have been Josh or Amber? Why didn't you tell me this when I arrived? And who's Pete?'

Harry could feel his temperature rising. He didn't usually berate Matt like this, but he was annoyed, unduly so perhaps, but he still should've been informed about this new piece of information.

'He's a local farmer,' Matt said.

'And this figure you saw that you didn't tell me about?'

'I'm telling you now,' Matt replied, and Harry heard the faintest note of irritation in the DS's voice. 'Pete was out looking for one of his dogs, which had run off. He mentioned the biker because he was the one who sent him down to the office to tell us about the camper.'

'Who was it you saw, then?' Harry asked.

'Not a clue,' said Matt, then pointed across the fields. 'Whoever it was, I spotted them over there. No idea if it was a man or a woman because they were too far away to tell. Pete was up here in this nifty little four-by-four he has; you'll have seen them all over the Dales I'm sure, very popular they are with farmers, now. Reminds me of when everyone had those little Subaru pickups, but that's a while ago now, like.'

'Matt ...' Harry said, working hard to stop himself from just grabbing the DS and giving him a good shake to get the information out of him.

'Pete gave me a lift, and we raced off in that direction, but they were gone.' Matt glanced over to where the search team were sorting themselves out into smaller teams as they headed off into the hills. 'If you want to speak with Pete, he's joined the search.'

'This person who ran off, then,' said Harry, getting them back on track. 'They were acting suspicious?'

'They were standing in a field in the rain staring at us and this here campervan,' said Matt. 'In anyone's book, that's a bit odd, isn't it? Especially when you add in the fact that they bolted like a scared rabbit.'

Harry frowned.

'Description?'

'Too far away to see anything. Though, whoever it was, it looked to me like they were all dressed up in green. Not like Robin Hood's Merry Men, obviously, more like a soldier.'

'How do you mean?'

Matt gestured to what he was wearing himself.

'Weather like this, we're all wearing decent gear, aren't we? And none of it blends in with our surroundings, which is kind of the point; makes it a little easier to be seen if things go south and someone needs to come and find you. Anyway, whoever it was, they looked to me like they'd had a fun time with a credit card in an army surplus store; combat trousers, army jacket, all that stuff you probably got sick of wearing back in the Paras. And I found this ...'

Matt pulled something from a jacket pocket and handed it to Harry. It was an evidence bag and inside it was something that looked like a scrunched-up ball of thin, green string or thread.

'Recognise it?' Matt asked.

'It's a scrim scarf,' said Harry. 'Actually, these are bloody useful; they keep your neck warm in cold weather, and you can use them as a makeshift camo net if you need to, wrap them around your personal weapon, that kind of thing.'

'Well, whoever it was, they dropped it. That's all we've found, though, I'm afraid.'

Harry held the evidence bag for a moment, his fingers squeezing the scrim net.

'It's not much, but it's something,' he said. 'Give the office a call. Liz is busy, but I want the rest of the team out looking for whoever this is. I know there's a good chance they won't find them, but they'll be easy to spot if they're dressed like you say.'

'I'll do that now,' Matt said.

Harry turned to Helen.

'Need an extra pair of hands?'

'Your feet and legs would be a little more useful,' Helen said.

'Best you point me in the right direction, then,' said Harry, and followed Helen to join in with the rest of the search team.

THIRTEEN

The night had been long, and all Harry had to show for it were weary legs, a body temperature close to hypothermic, and still no sign of the missing couple. And even though he'd consumed both pies gifted to him by Matt, his belly was still empty.

Liz had called him to say that she'd learned little from the social media stuff she'd looked at, but that in her ringing around of the pubs, a few had mentioned seeing them on Friday night, and that they had been in Hawes on their mountain bikes. It wasn't much, but at least they were able to put a time on when they were last seen.

The trouble was, that was a good few days ago now, and they had no idea when, exactly, that Amber and Josh had left their camper to never return. It could've been Saturday, could've been Monday. There was just no way of knowing. She'd also managed to get the contact details for both Amber and Josh's parents. She had spoken with Amber's, and they were already on their way, and she had left a number of messages with Josh's parents, too, and would try again come morning.

Amber's parents had also provided them with both Amber's and Josh's mobile numbers, but nothing had come from that. Their network provider confirmed what Harry had suspected but hoped wasn't the case, that as Liz had pointed out the day before, the trackers were switched off. He guessed that was because of their status as celebrities and not wanting their location to be easily pinpointed by fans or the press.

Harry had been a long way from being happy at many points in his life, but right then he couldn't recall one where he'd been so drenched, and after years in the Paras, spending too many days and nights in various sopping wet moors and marshlands across the country, that was saying something. Waterproof, his jacket may well have been, but after ten hours on the fells in a constant downpour, the rain had made its way in and soaked him to the skin. Add in the sweat from the exertion of all the walking, and Harry wasn't so sure he would even bother with washing his clothes once he got home; burning seemed to be the more sensible option.

He had joined up with two members of the mountain rescue team, a man called Bob Peacock, and a woman called Barbara Caygill. Harry had thought Bob aptly named, if only because of the ludicrous bobble hat the man had stuffed his head into.

'I can knit you one if you want,' Bob had said, when Harry had set out with them both across the fields, heading for moorland further on. They were all carrying head torches and plenty of spare batteries, with Bob and Barbara also carrying a rucksack each, containing first aid, survival blankets, even high-energy snacks and a flask of hot chocolate. 'I've made them for all the team.'

'He has indeed,' said Barbara, pulling her own bobble hat from a jacket pocket to slip onto her head. 'What do you think? Everyone wants to get their hands on Bob's Bobbles!'

'Good job the wife didn't hear you say that.' Bob laughed.

Barbara's hat was bright yellow, the bobble blue run through with flecks of silver, and was nearly the size of her head. Bob's hat was a Jackson Pollock affair, Harry had thought, as though the man had simply stuffed his hand into a random selection of wool and cracked on until finished. The bobble, equally as large as Barbara's, was red and had eyes stuck on the front.

'Not sure what I'm supposed to say, if I'm honest,' Harry said. 'It's certainly striking.'

'Everyone on the team has one,' said Bob. 'Makes it easier for us to spot each other when we're out on the fells, like.'

'Everyone?' said Harry, then looked around and for the first time noticed the sea of bobble hats now making their way out across the fields and fells.

'I reckon you'd suit purple,' Bob said. 'I've a good pile of purple back home. I'll knit you one when I get back.'

'You really don't have to.'

'What colour do you think for the bobble?'

Barbara said, 'Well, if the hat's purple, then the bobble has to be yellow, doesn't it?'

'It does,' said Bob. 'But you know what? Why don't I do the hat and the bobble with both purple *and* yellow? I can do a stripe or a zigzag, anything really.' He looked at Harry. 'Any preference?'

'I don't want a bobble hat.'

Barbara laughed. 'No one wants a bobble hat,' she said. 'But they do need one, I can promise you that.'

'I'll have it done by the weekend,' said Bob. 'Something to do when I've my feet up and I'm watching some bollocks on TV.'

Harry said nothing more about the hat, hoping that, come the end of the search, it would be forgotten. Trouble was, when morning forced its grey face across the horizon, the end had yet to come. The search was still ongoing, with no leads other than the scrim scarf Matt had found, and the sinking feeling in Harry's stomach was only growing.

Knowing that he needed to have enough sleep to make sure he was useful the following day, Harry left the search team in the early hours of Wednesday, sending a message to Matt that he didn't expect to see him or Jadyn in the morning.

A short drive back down Cam Road he parked up on the main street in Gayle, then stumbled along to his cottage. Which was when he realised that the last time he'd seen Smudge was back in the office with Liz. He assumed Liz had taken the dog home, and that Smudge had spent the evening being made a fuss over by both her and Ben. Harry, though, would have preferred to have her with him.

Stepping into the cottage and kicking off his boots at the door, he found the place to be quiet, still, and above all, cold. There was no point putting the heating on, and certainly no point lighting a fire, so he shuffled through to the kitchen and hung his jacket over the back of a dining chair.

With the rest of his clothes equally wet through and stinking, Harry could think of no reason to take them upstairs, knowing that in the morning he would only have to bring them down again and throw them in the wash. So, he stripped off where he was, threw everything in the washing machine, then headed upstairs. That he was butt-naked didn't bother him at all; it wasn't as though there was anyone else around to terrify with the naked reality of those scars on his face being joined by others that stretched themselves angrily over the rest of his body. The only thing Harry took upstairs with him was his phone, and as he lay down, he knew that it wasn't just Smudge that he missed, but Grace. He couldn't text the dog, but at least he could reach out to Grace.

Text sent, and too tired to care whether doing so had been a good idea or not, Harry pulled the duvet up over his head and let what was left of the night take him.

WHEN MORNING CAME, it did not arrive gently. Harry's first indication that it was a new day was his phone ringing.

'Grimm,' he croaked, eventually tracking it down to where it had somehow managed to sneak under the bed.

'Harry? It's Matt. How are you doing?'

Harry pushed himself up on one elbow and tried to rub the sleep from his eyes.

'Oh, I'm just tickety-boo,' he said. 'A ray of sunshine, you know me.'

'That's good,' said Matt, 'because you're needed.'

Harry was out of bed in a beat and noticed his breath condensing in the chill air.

'Why? What's happened? What've you found? Is it Amber and Josh? What?'

'It's not Amber and Josh, no,' Matt said, 'but I think you need to come see it for yourself in any case.'

'You're being mysterious.'

'That's because this is a proper bloody mystery, Har—' Matt's voice was cut off by a lengthy yawn. 'We've got some kind of camp set up here, about half a kilometre from Josh and Amber's camper. The search party didn't spot it on account of it being nigh on invisible. One of the dogs did, though.'

'A hidden camp?' Harry said, stumbling through to the bathroom to get the shower running. 'How's that relevant?'

'Like I said, you need to see this for yourself.'

Harry remembered then the scrim scarf Matt had found having given chase to someone he'd seen near the camper, who had then run off and, as far as he knew, not yet been brought in for a little chat.

'I'll be there as soon as I can,' Harry said. 'That yawn just then,' he added. 'Have you not been home yourself?'

'Oh, I've been home,' Matt said. 'Wasn't long behind you after you'd left. Couldn't sleep though, so figured I'd be more useful here. Plus, there was a risk of me waking little Mary up. So, I came back here at about six.'

'What time's it now, then?' Harry didn't wait for an answer and checked his phone. 'Nine? How the hell is it nine? Bloody hell!'

'No rush,' Matt said. 'Get some food inside you first, and make sure you sort yourself something to eat for the rest of the day, because it's going to be another long one, isn't it? And we don't want any of what happened yesterday, now, do we?'

Harry caught the faint mocking tone in Matt's voice.

'And what's that?' he asked.

'You being hungry. And when you get hungry, you get grumpy.'

'I'm always grumpy.'

'Grumpier, then, if that's at all possible,' said Matt, then went to say something else, but Harry had already killed the call.

With a quick message sent to both Liz and Ben to check on Smudge, who had apparently spent the whole evening lying on their sofa, and to see if Liz had heard anything from Josh's parents, which she hadn't, Harry finished getting showered and dressed.

It was only when he was downstairs and, having made a generous pile of marmite and banana sandwiches—a recipe he'd picked up back in the Paras and one he still fell back on in an emergency—was then pushing lots of toast into his face, that he noticed there was a text waiting for him on his phone. It was from Grace.

Harry clicked through to the message, half dreading opening it, but unable to stop himself from doing so.

'Ditto,' it said

For the first time in days, Harry smiled.

FOURTEEN

With a final piece of toast hanging out of his mouth, Harry opened his front door to find Jadyn staring back at him, knuckles raised, mouth frozen wide in a yawn.

'What the hell are you doing here?' Harry spluttered, the toast falling from his mouth. He managed to catch it before it hit the ground.

'Sorry about that,' said Jadyn, forcing the yawn to end. 'I was just about to knock. The Sarge told me to come and pick you up, said he'd told you.'

Harry wondered if that was what Matt had been saying when he'd cut him off.

'But I don't need picking up,' he said. 'I have my vehicle, and as far as I'm aware, I even know how to drive it. In fact, I've been driving longer than you've been alive!'

Harry stood under Jadyn's confused stare for a moment.

'Come on, then,' he said at last. 'Let's get going, shall we?'

At Jadyn's vehicle, Harry climbed into the passenger seat to be presented with a coffee.

'Thought you might need this,' Jadyn said, yawning again. 'Popped into that little café in the marketplace, The Folly; got one for myself as well.'

'Can I ask why you're not back home getting some rest?' Harry asked.

'I've only just got up,' said Jadyn. 'I'm picking you up on my way back out to join the search team.'

Harry wasn't entirely convinced.

'How much sleep did you get?' he asked.

'Enough,' Jadyn answered, the word stretched out on top of another yawn.

'Define enough.'

'Five hours.'

'That's not enough, and I should know,' Harry said, yawning them himself. 'I managed four.'

'Going to be a long day, then.'

Harry took a deep slug from the coffee.

'This'll help a bit,' he said.

As Jadyn drove them to Cam Road, he said, 'Sorry about earlier.'

'Sorry?' said Harry. 'For what? And how can you have already done anything worth apologising for? You've only just picked me up!'

Jadyn was quiet for a moment.

'No, it wasn't earlier, wasn't it?' he said. 'Well, it was, but it was yesterday, and that's more than earlier, isn't it? I think it is. Anyway, sorry.'

'I'm still no clearer as to what for.'

'Calling you about those three fans who turned up at the office,' Jadyn said. 'You had plenty to be going on with.'

Harry took another gulp of coffee as Jadyn slowed down, then eased the vehicle off the main road and onto the rough track leading into the hills above.

'Did you tell Colin and his two friends to come over and get in the way?' he asked.

Jadyn shook his head.

'Didn't think so.'

'That's not what I meant,' said Jadyn. 'I should've dealt with it myself. Which reminds me, they mentioned the Peak District for some reason.'

'They did?'

'Said that Amber and Josh started leaving a gap between when they'd been somewhere and when they'd put it up on social media.'

'Sounds to me like they were learning fame isn't all that it's cracked up to be,' said Harry. 'Can't think of anything worse myself; people always wanting to know your business, where you are, what you're up to. Who wants that?'

'Fair point,' said Jadyn.

'Anyway,' said Harry, 'back to what you were saying: you don't need to apologise for doing your job. I'd always rather you ask for my help than not. It's the only way anyone learns. Understood?'

'Didn't like to add to your day, though, that's all.'

'We're police officers,' Harry said, as Jadyn navigated up the lane, grey cloud still hiding the tops from view. 'It's our job to have things added to our day and more often the not, those things get progressively worse as the day goes on. Can't hide from it. And I don't want you ever thinking you should hide things from me or not tell me something.'

'Okay, Boss,' said Jadyn, but Harry heard a tone of reservation in the constable's voice.

'I know I'm a grumpy old bugger at times,' he said. 'And I also know that I don't exactly walk around with a smile on this knackered face of mine, or spend my days spotting half-full glasses, if you know what I mean.'

'Not sure that I do,' Jadyn muttered, but Harry continued anyway.

'Always tell me what's going on,' he said. 'Your job as a police officer is to uphold the law, isn't it? That's what you do; it's what we all do, as a team. Don't let this'—Harry pointed at his own face—'go putting you off doing exactly that because you're worried what I might say.'

Jadyn pulled up in front of the Police Land Rover, which was still sitting where Matt had parked it earlier.

'Your bark's worse than your bite, you mean?' he said, switching off the engine.

Harry raised an eyebrow, smiled.

'Where the hell have you heard that from? No, don't tell me ...'

He pointed over at Matt, who he'd just spotted standing over at the rear of the Mountain Rescue Team Land Rover with Helen.

Jadyn gave a nod.

'Just keep on doing what you're doing,' Harry said, 'and you'll be fine.'

Opening the passenger door, Harry heaved himself out into the chill air of the fells, thankful that the rain had softened to a relentless drizzle. But as he made to shut the door and head over to see Matt, he dipped his head back in and said, 'As a point of note, though, Constable, he's wrong.'

'The bark?'

'The bite. It's a lot worse,' Harry said, and shut the door.

Walking over to meet Matt, Harry zipped up his jacket, aware that the pockets were stuffed with sandwiches and that even though he'd eaten enough toast for breakfast to last him a week, he was sorely tempted to crack them open. But then Matt turned and waved at him with a packet of biscuits.

Harry took two.

Matt shook the packet.

'Grab a couple more,' he said. 'Can't ever have too many ginger nuts.'

Harry said, 'So, where is it, then, this camp you got me out of bed to see?'

Matt didn't respond, mainly because his mouth was full of biscuit. Instead, he just turned on his heels and headed off across the lane and through a gate into the fields beyond. Harry followed Matt across a large, empty field. The rain had turned the ground into a sponge. Every step he took came with a sucking squelch as he heaved his boots out of the grip of the mud. The grass was long and soon his trousers were sopping.

'This a long walk, then, is it?' he asked.

Matt pointed away from the vehicles and over the fields.

'Just over there,' he said, crumbs launching into the air.

Harry followed silently, doing his best to ignore the chill of the wind, doing its best to use his rain-soaked trousers to give him hypothermia. He was also rather wishing he was wearing one of Bob's lurid bobble hats.

'Here we are,' Matt said, stopping by a small copse of trees, all of them bent and twisted by their years spent exposed to the elements. They were hunched over the banks of a small gully, which ran full and angry down the side of the fell, their bent forms like old anglers discussing the best flies to use and where to cast.

'Here we are, where?' Harry asked, looking around a little baffled. 'There's nowt here, Matt, not a damned thing! Except the weather, obviously. And that's everywhere right now; you didn't need to bring me here to show me even more of it.'

Matt pointed over into the crooked trees.

'There,' he said. 'It's pretty well camouflaged, but if you look closely, you'll spot it soon enough.'

It took a moment or two for Harry to finally spot it, and when he did, he was stunned.

'Bloody hell, that's a hammock!'

Matt led him in for a closer look, and Harry followed, threading himself between bent bow and branch, knocking water from the leaves to race down his neck.

'Not what you were expecting, was it?' Matt said. 'I couldn't believe it myself when I first saw it.'

Harry saw that the hammock in which a sleeping bag was lying was dark green and lashed between two trees by dark green webbing and black karabiners. Above the hammock, a sheet of green plastic had been tied that reminded Harry of the makeshift shelters he'd grown used to calling home back in the Paras. Also hanging from the tree was a small rucksack, similar to the ones he had used out on patrol.

'Any idea what they were doing here?' he asked, stepping in for a closer look.

Matt pulled on a pair of disposable rubber gloves, then reached over to the rucksack. He lifted it down from the broken branch it was attached to. He held it for Harry.

'I left everything here as it was found,' he said. 'Figured best to check it all through with you.'

'You've had a peek, though, haven't you?' Harry said, slipping on a pair of gloves too, before taking the rucksack from Matt.

'Of course I have,' said Matt.

Harry opened the rucksack. Inside was a small gas stove and a collection of boil-in-the-bag meals, neither of which got him very excited.

'Looks like we've got ourselves someone who likes to do a bit of solo camping,' he said. 'It's weird to be doing it in weather like this, that's for sure, but I can't say I know why you brought me over here. There's no reason to think all of this is anything other than someone out here on their own who doesn't like company, which is something I can relate to.'

Matt kicked at the ground, dislodging a small pile of branches to reveal a pile of vodka bottles.

Harry gave a shrug.

'And that only supports what I've just said. Whoever this belongs to, they're out here on their own and drowning their sorrows, and whatever they are, I'm not interested.'

'Why don't you have a bit more of a dig around in that bag,' Matt said.

'It's just a stove and boil-in-the-bags,' said Harry. 'I've eaten plenty of those in my time, trust me, and though they're tasty when you're bootstrapped, I'm not looking to add whatever's left to my kitchen cupboards.'

Matt simply stared back, so Harry opened the bag again and had a rummage. At the bottom of the bag he spotted something, reached in, and pulled it out for them both to see.

'Binos,' he said.

The binoculars were pocket-sized, so nice and portable, but they had a higher magnification than Harry had expected. And they looked expensive, too, not just a cheap pair of rubber-cased ones bought on the high street.

He shrugged.

'As far as I know, hammocks, booze, and binoculars aren't illegal. In fact, nothing here is. Maybe this is just a birdwatcher. Last time I looked, spotting whatever wildlife manages to exist out here isn't against the law.'

Matt reached into a jacket pocket and removed an evidence bag.

'This was on top of everything when I opened the rucksack,' he said. 'Bagged it instinctively but left everything else as is.'

He handed it over to Harry.

'A camera lens?' Harry said, staring at the object. 'Looks like a telephoto or zoom kind of thing. Photography's not really my thing.' He lifted the binoculars in his other hand. 'Like these, it looks expensive. Obvious question: where's the rest of the camera, then?'

'That I don't know,' said Matt. 'However ...'

Harry was about to say something not exactly polite about Matt wasting his time and not getting to the point when the detective sergeant reached into another pocket and pulled out another evidence bag.

'Who do you think you are?' Harry asked. 'Paul sodding Daniels? Is this the Matt Dinsdale Magic Show? Because if it is, it's rubbish.'

Matt laughed at that and handed the evidence bag over to Harry.

'Well, you'll like this; not a lot, but you'll like it.'

'And these were in that bag?' Harry asked, examining what he was now holding.

'They were,' said Matt, his face grave, voice solemn. 'Three photographs, that's all. It's not much, I know, but I reckon it's more than enough, don't you?'

The photographs were of Josh and Amber Hill. In each one, their young, healthy, smiling faces stared back at Harry, almost as though they were laughing at him, enjoying a joke he wasn't party to, a joke about him.

'These are from the camper,' he said. 'Have to be, don't they?'

'From those spaces you spotted, I reckon,' Matt agreed. 'Which means—'

'Whoever was camping out here in this hammock is very much a person of interest.'

Harry took another look at the photographs before handing them back to Matt. He then stepped back to take in the makeshift campsite, glancing back over to the campervan in the distance, only its roof visible over the top of the old drystone wall lining the lane.

'That camper being abandoned is odd enough on its own,' he said. 'But this as well? It's a weird bloody coincidence, isn't it?'

'And you don't believe in coincidences, do you, Boss?' said Matt.

'No, I don't,' said Harry, shaking his head. 'Maybe they were here anyway, saw the camper, went over for a nosy ... But then again ...'

That was too easy an explanation, and he knew it.

Having not had a chance to do so the day before, due to the search being well underway when he had returned to the rendezvous point, Harry quickly went through with Matt what he had learned from Jadyn, and then from Colin Hampton during their nice little chat in the interview room.

'You think it's a fan, then?'

'What I think,' Harry said, 'is that whatever this is we're dealing with isn't just a young couple who've gone missing.'

'But what else could it be?'

'I don't know, but I do know it's not right.' Harry pointed at the hammock. 'And I also know we really need to speak to whoever set this up. I've had the rest of the team out looking, asking around, but there's been no word of a sighting of anyone matching your description, vague though that was. What's worrying me is that they'll be long gone by now, won't they? Leaving us with bugger all chance of finding out who they are.'

'I wouldn't be so sure about that,' said Matt, and reached into a trouser pocket.

'About what?' Harry asked, then heard the soft jangling of metal and plastic and saw a set of keys hanging from Matt's fingers. He reached over and took them from him, flipping through them to the one that had immediately caught his eye, a black fob with a button set in the centre.

'They're not the keys to the campervan, are they?' breathed Harry.

'No,' Matt replied. 'I reckon our friend here has left his own car somewhere round here'.

'Well, well, well,' Harry said, then turned and led Matt back towards the campervan.

FIFTEEN

Walking back across the field with Matt, Harry had wondered aloud where the owner might have parked. Matt's initial answer of, *anywhere,* hadn't been exactly helpful, so Harry had ignored it and suggested that he come up with something a little better. By the time they had arrived at the campervan, they had decided that the best course of action was to continue up Cam Road to a junction Matt was sure Harry couldn't miss, a hard left turn which would then have him heading back down the dale.

If the vehicle was a 4x4, then there was a chance it was parked along the lanes somewhere, suggested Matt, so it was best to check. And, if not, Harry could then roll on into Gayle and Hawes, to search there. The fob itself gave no clue as to the vehicle's make, which was a little frustrating, but there was nothing Harry could do about that, so he didn't dwell on the fact.

Jumping into the old Police Land Rover and unzipping his jacket to stop it from riding up in an uncomfortable bunch at his waist, Harry dropped the keys to the hammock owner's car on the passenger seat. Time to go treasure hunting, he thought, because that's what this was going to be; somewhere there was a vehicle those keys would open, and he was going to find it.

Leaving Matt and Jadyn to rejoin the search for Amber and

Josh, and instead of heading back down the way he had come, Harry swung the vehicle around and headed away from Hawes, sitting behind him in the valley below.

The lane was a thin, grey line of grit, dirt, and muddy puddles, disappearing far off in the low cloud, heavy with rain. He wondered about Josh and Amber Hill, where the hell they were, and hoped to God that they weren't out in all of this somewhere.

As Harry drove, visibility quickly grew worse, the cloud thick as porridge, which wasn't helped by the windscreen wipers not working properly. Eventually, he ended up leaning his head out of the window to see if that was any easier, which, to his surprise, it actually was. So, for a while, Harry drove on, head sticking out of the driver's door, face and hair getting more and more wet, as he slowly navigated the track, crawling through rut and muck and puddles brown and deep.

Keeping a lookout for the mystery vehicle he was searching for, Harry thought back to what they knew so far of the campervan and Amber and Josh. In and of itself, a vehicle like that, parked up on a remote lane, wasn't hugely suspicious. Maybe Josh and Amber had headed out camping somewhere? Perhaps they'd set off before the rain hit, got caught in it, and just decided it was safer to wait it out than try and make their way back through it. But even as he thought that through, Harry found himself dismissing it almost immediately. If one of them was hurt, then the other would likely head off to look for help. If neither of them were injured, then this was hardly the Himalayas, was it? The walk back would be carefully taken, but there was little risk of falling into a chasm or being attacked by a marauding yeti. So, where were they? And surely, if that was what had happened, the search team would have found them by now.

Then there was the mystery of the hammock and the person Matt had chased. If there was a list of ways to make the police suspicious, then running away from them was number one, Harry mused.

The discovery of the binoculars and the camera lens, but especially the photographs of Amber and Josh, which most certainly looked as though they had been taken from their campervan at some point, gave a clear connection between all of those things and the person he now very much wanted to find. Whether they had anything to do with the disappearance of the young couple or not was unknown, and that only made finding them all the more urgent.

A corner loomed ahead, and Harry hooked the steering wheel around, directing the Land Rover into a sharp left bend, the tyres clawing at the road and sending grit and stone and curtains of water slimy with peat into the moss-covered drystone walls lining the lane.

Heading on, Harry was careful to navigate his way across a couple of streams, both of which had breached their banks to send deep scars across the lane. At one point, the power of the water surprised him, snatching at the wheels and tugging the vehicle to his right, but he managed to stay on course, and further down the lane had to stop to get out and open a gate or two, making sure they were firmly closed behind him before continuing. Doing so made him smile, remembering a morning a few months ago, clay shooting with Grace and her dad, Arthur. They'd been interrupted by someone who had marched across a field to complain to them about the noise. Arthur had put a fly in their ear, not least because they'd left a gate open in their haste to voice their anger.

By the time Harry had reached the end of the lane, and found himself in the top end of Gayle, he was beginning to think that this was a wild goose chase. For all he knew, the key next to him was only a spare, and the owner had already bolted with their other key and was well on their way home. But there was only one way to find out, and if it took him all day, then he would explore every lane, every possible place a car could be parked, and find the thing.

At least this wasn't Bristol, Harry thought, because this task would've been next to impossible in that warren of streets, threaded as they were in and out of each other as they wound their way across one of the hilliest cities he'd ever had been in. Here though, he knew the way around, and had soon covered over half of the village.

Driving around painfully slowly, his sopping-wet arm hanging out of the window as he pointed the key at every parked car he passed, put him on the receiving end of a good number of strange looks.

With little left of Gayle to explore, Harry pointed himself in the direction of the small yard area just over on the south side of the ford over Gayle Beck, and at the foot of Beggerman's Road. He'd already driven past it on his way to check out the rest of Gayle. Seeing it made him smile as he remembered Jadyn turning up at the office a few months ago, still damp and covered in green slime from when he'd managed to fall in, and all while doing his best to prevent two walkers from doing the same.

Harry nosed his way down into the yard. Though not an official car park as such, it was certainly used as one, and he spied a small collection of vehicles, a couple of which looked ratty enough to probably be road-worthy. A number of trucks of varying sizes were also parked around the edge, along with a tractor and a couple of old farm trailers, but as Harry drove around, tapping the button on the key fob, he saw no lights flash, no indication that the car he was looking for was in front of him.

Having reached the far end of the parking area, and with nothing in front of him bar field and fell, Harry swung the vehicle around to head on into Hawes. He swore in frustration and hurled the key fob onto the passenger seat a little harder than he'd meant to. It bounced off the seat, then down into the footwell. Harry clenched his jaw, sucked in a deep breath through his nose, then stopped, exhaled, and leaned over to scrabble around for it with an outstretched hand, but couldn't find it.

Swearing and muttering to himself, Harry turned off the engine and climbed out. No sooner had he done so than a blast of wind and rain crashed into him, whipping at his face, and ripping at his jacket zip as he struggled to pull it up. Walking around to the passenger door, he heaved it open and leaned in.

Just when he had been resolved to the notion that the key had somehow completely disappeared, and would no doubt turn up in a few days somewhere random, such as behind the fridge back at the office, Harry found it. The key had somehow managed to bounce itself into a tight corner, pinning itself in between the braces holding the seat in place and the cubby box where various mechanical things happened, none of which Harry had ever had the slightest bit of interest in understanding. He reached in, his fingertips finding the key. After a bit of a struggle, he finally managed to hook them around it enough to give it a sharp yank. The key came away, albeit it too sharply, and shot over his shoulder and out into the rain.

'Bloody hell!' Harry roared, pulling himself out of the Land Rover to see the key on the edge of a large puddle. He marched over, dropped to the ground, grabbed it and, as he did so, heard a beep.

Harry stopped, looked up, saw that there were no other cars nearby other than those parked up. Key in hand, and ignoring the rain, he stood up and, with the key pointed at the cars, pressed the button once more. The beep sounded again, but not one light on any of the cars flashed.

Harry looked around, saw nothing, and tried again, this time listening for where the beep came from. He followed the sound, pressing the button again and again until, around the side of one of the old trailers, lights flashed, and he couldn't help but smile.

'There you are,' he said, and headed over to see what he had found.

SIXTEEN

Josh could smell plastic, the heat from the weak flame starting to melt the lighter in his hands. He killed the flame, stopped dead, held his breath. For a moment, the only sound was that of his own heartbeat thundering around inside his skull, a wild beast desperate to escape.

Just like me, he thought. Then, far off, he heard it, a splashing and stumbling of someone coming after him, then a splash of light danced above him, playing a game of shadow puppets as it tried to track him down.

Josh had no idea where he was, what direction to go in, how to get out. All he really knew was that he was underground, but that much was obvious from what he'd seen since making his escape.

His wrists were still tied. He'd tried to cut through the rope holding them together by rubbing it against sharp rocks, but only a few strands had pinged loose so far. So, he tried again, reaching out with his fingers for a sharp edge, but he knew he had to move, or the light would find him, and then its owner. And he didn't want to imagine what might happen then.

Pushing on, the lighter's flame still burning strong, Josh felt his way along the rock wall to his right, forcing himself to keep going, to just keep moving, but then the haste of his pace turned into a tangle of invisible rope around his feet, and he stumbled, fell forwards, dropped the lighter. With a muffled cry, he lashed out, desperate to grab onto something, anything, to stop his fall. His hand found something, and he came to a dead stop, heart in his mouth, breath sharp in his throat.

Josh froze, strained his ears for some sound behind him, of the terror chasing him down. But as he did so, another sensation came to him. His hands, what they were holding onto, it wasn't the hard, cold roughness of rock, but something else, something soft enough to give a little as he gripped it tighter, pulling himself upright. He had no idea what it was, didn't care, because he had lost the lighter, his only hope of getting out of this place. So he let go, fell to his knees, and scrabbled around desperately in the dark, willing his fingers to find it. And when they did, Josh had to stifle the cry of relief he felt bubble up in his throat.

With a flick of his thumb the flame burst forth at his fingertips. Josh leaned against the rock wall, tears in his eyes, staring at it, the warmth of the orange glow drawing him in, comforting him in the darkness. As he did so, he noticed then how the wall behind him felt strange, as though something was between him and the hard rock, something softer, which gave a little as he leaned into it.

Reaching up to knock it away, Josh touched it, felt something cold and rubbery with his fingertips, and as he turned around to see what it was, his fingernails cut into it, pulling some of it away, like flakes of paint, only thicker. As he brought the lighter up in front of his face, he saw at the edge of the halo it afforded him a shape that didn't belong, a shape that was impossible for so many reasons he was sure he was seeing things. Unable to stop himself, Josh leaned closer, his fingers holding the thing tightly, as though to do so was to render it more real than it already was, the light bringing the shape into sharp relief as it emerged from the gloom in all its awful, horrible glory.

It was a foot, bare and pale, the toes curled inwards. The leg it was attached to stretched upwards and Josh was unable to pull himself away from this new vision of horror. The glow from the lighter revealed more and more as he stood up, until the thing that had stayed his fall was before him in stark relief. The body of a man, still fully clothed, half covered by some crystalline skin. Josh saw slashes in the clothing, and pale flesh ripped and torn beneath. The face was wide-eyed, mouth open as though held in an eternal moan.

Josh's mind broke in two. All he knew was that he was moving again, getting away from the thing on the cave wall, its image burned into his brain. How far underground he was, he had no idea, but something deep inside him, something primaeval almost, told him that if he stayed any longer, if he failed to get out, that body on the wall would be him.

He pushed on, determined to get out. To push away the sick thing hanging in the darkness and occupying his thoughts, he forced himself to think about Amber. To attempt to piece together the scattered memories of what had brought them there in the first place.

He had found the cave while out on his bike. He'd been riding for a good while, having not only cycled up Buttertubs Pass, which had seemed like a good idea at the time, but also down into Swaledale, a valley that had seemed haunted by a history that still lived and breathed through the buildings and fields and ruins of mines.

While exploring one of the numerous tracks and trails that crisscrossed the Dales, he had taken a break over by what, at first glance, had looked like a small crag and a large pile of rubble and stone. He thought that it might afford him some shelter while he munched on an energy bar and took in some liquid, but when he'd drawn closer, he'd spotted a small, dark opening at the foot of the low cliff.

Intrigued, he had ventured closer, and what had immediately struck him as odd was how the cliff, and the rock scattered around its feet, looked freshly parted. It was as though it had happened recently, perhaps even during the storm he had been standing in. The face of the crag had fallen away, smashing into untold pieces, to reveal to the world a doorway hidden for eons. Whether or not it was true, he didn't care, but he knew he had to investigate further.

Josh laughed at the memory, thinking how grand and romantic his thoughts had been for what was little more than a hole in the ground. Grabbing the lights from his bike, and unable to still that child-like urge to explore the unknown, he had ducked down into the cave to have a closer look inside.

The beam from his bike lamp had cut through the darkness beyond the entrance, revealing something so spectacular that at first he'd been utterly unable to comprehend it. Where he had expected to see nothing but more crumbling rock and the back wall of a disappointingly shallow cave, he had instead found the bright light of his lamp to be caught and scattered by hundreds of ice-white straws, thin as spaghetti, hanging from the roof.

Sliding himself gingerly down into the cave, he was thankful to still be wearing his bike helmet as his head ricocheted off the cracked and jagged roof. Josh had been careful to avoid knocking into any of the formations, though the ground was covered in them, and he guessed they had been knocked loose when the cliff face had fallen. They littered the floor like broken glass, crunching beneath him as he made his way in.

Once inside, Josh had sat and stared, utterly entranced by the magical kingdom he had chanced upon. He had at first suspected it to be little more than a cave with only one way in or out, but once inside, and having cast the torch beam around the walls, he had seen how the far wall was not actually a dead end at all. Instead, it continued, a narrow tunnel leading off into the hillside above, where it led hidden in a deep pool of forever dark. With no thought beyond finding out where it led, and with no thought at all as to the potential danger of what he was about to do, Josh had been unable to resist exploring it further.

The tunnel from the rear of the cave had twisted and turned, but at no point contracted so tightly as to not let him past, so he had crawled on, soon finding that he could walk, as the ceiling fell away, and sometime later he had ventured into a large chamber.

The darkness, he remembered, had been absolute, almost a physical presence challenging him to dare enter further. His voice had echoed brightly in the unfathomable space, and he had been overcome then by a sense of his own smallness. The thought that a space so huge had lain hidden from human eyes for so long, waiting perhaps, but for what, he didn't want to contemplate.

Josh knew that he would have continued to explore had he not decided it was something he had to share with Amber. Plus, there was safety in numbers, and he knew that she would have a more sensible take on the best way to go snooping around the subterranean vaults he had found. So, he had backtracked, and realised in doing so that other tunnels led off from the one he had come in through. He also remembered deciding that he would have to make sure when he brought Amber that they marked their way clearly so as to not go astray, leave a trail of some kind, of piles of stones or scratches on the wall.

The ride back to the campervan had flown by so quickly that when Josh had arrived, he had been barely able to remember it, just a rush of tyres on wet roads, rain crashing into him as he sped on.

It had taken some persuasion to get Amber to follow him into the rain, but it was amazing what the promise of a good bottle or two of wine would do. She had followed, and once again into the cave he had crept, this time with Amber at his side.

And then ... and then? Josh couldn't remember anything. Well, he could, but the jumble of memories made no sense, marred as they were with bright bursts of pain, the sound of Amber screaming, and then an emptiness so appalling it made him choke.

Josh pushed on, keen now to focus on just getting as far ahead as he could from the one coming after him. The image of that body pushed to the forefront of his mind, those dead eyes staring at him, the feel of that pale skin against his own making his flesh crawl.

He recognised nothing of his surroundings, just great, thick walls of rock rising around him to an unseen roof, the sound of water endlessly dripping, and behind it a black stillness, almost as though it was waiting for the right time to pounce.

Josh slipped, fell forward, managed to catch himself on a rock, but it was too late, and he hammered into the ground, crashing his head hard enough to see stars, and felt the lighter spring from his fingers.

Dazed, Josh lay in dark water, unaware of its chill on his skin. His breath was sharp, uncontrolled, and he could taste adrenaline as it stung the edge of his tongue.

Footsteps. Christ alive, there were footsteps, and they were close! And was that laughter?

Thin, spidery fingers of panic slid around his heart and squeezed.

Josh opened his eyes, blinked, hoping that somehow to do so would either push the darkness away, or give him a sixth sense to see his way through it. But it was a grey thing in front of him, and it wasn't about to let him go.

Grey?

Josh sat up.

The darkness had faded a little. Something was pushing through. And it wasn't the beam of the searchlight chasing him, desperate to find him in the warren of caves. No, this was something else, a pale luminosity that gave him sudden cause to hope.

Pushing himself back up onto his feet, Josh forced himself to calm down, to focus, to seek a way to the greyness drawing him on. It was coming from his left and, narrowing his eyes, he realised then that he could see shapes ahead, ghostly images of a rock-and-boulder strewn channel cut through the ancient geology all around him.

A splash from behind had Josh moving. Half walking, half running, he stumbled on his bare feet, numb with cold and oblivious now to pain, his legs were on autopilot, their one task to get him the hell out, to find help, to find Amber.

The grey grew paler still, then ahead a blade of light cut it through so cleanly that Josh sobbed, fully aware now that this was the doorway he had been searching for.

Josh raced towards the light, broke through it with a yell,

tumbling as he fell, his legs tangled up, his feet unable to find purchase. The fall was a kaleidoscope of bright lights, vivid colours, and sharp pain as he rolled and bounced out of the hillside and into the day beyond. But Josh gave himself no time to recover, to gather his thoughts, to even guess at where he was, as he heaved himself up, using what little strength he had left, and ran.

Grass was at his feet, thick and lush and wet, then heather and bracken, tugging at his ankles like the hands of the dead reaching through the earth to pull him back down. He snatched himself away from their grasp, kept running, could see the valley below now, and far off, rising out of the gloom, the roofs of houses, a church—

Something impossibly hard and fast slammed into Josh with such force that whatever else it was he had seen ahead, that had given him hope beyond hope, was obliterated. One moment he was free, the next he was nothing, a rag doll tossed into the air to come crashing down on limbs broken like reeds in the wind.

As the last sensations of life rippled through his body, as he saw thick clouds and crows tussled by the wind, a terrible blackness barreled its way across his body and crushed him into the ground. The last thing Josh saw, as his life's light blinked out, was the brightest of raindrops, and reflected in its glistening surface was the face of the woman he loved, smiling down at him as he died.

SEVENTEEN

Harry stared at the vehicle to which the key belonged. It was an old and clearly very tired Ford Escort van, sat low on springs that had given up on life a long time ago. The body was sunk low, like it carried the weight of the world inside it and wasn't best pleased about the fact. The pale blue paint was faded, so much so that in places it had turned almost white. Wherever Harry looked he saw patches of orange rust gnawing its way through the bodywork, the bonnet so badly pitted it reminded him of a wildfire eating through a dry forest, and if left untreated, there would soon be no bonnet left. How the van was even road-legal, he had no idea.

With disposable gloves pulled on, he yanked open the driver's door and was immediately met by the strong, pungent reek of something he knew all too well. It was the slightly sweet notes of something that took him back to not only numerous crime scenes, dodgy nightclubs, and dark beer gardens, but also to his own brother's various bedsits and other places of residence, before he'd ended up inside.

Harry had never been tempted to try cannabis himself, and never would, either. He knew that it had its benefits, and that the current approach by the Law in dealing with it was as out of date as it was too heavy-handed. He also knew that he'd met more than his fair share of people who had smoked so much of the stuff that they'd scrambled their brains to mush.

Leaning into the van, Harry did his best to take in what he could see and smell, and none of it filled him with joy. Whoever the owner was, they were clearly not big on taking hygiene seriously. The passenger footwell was so full of rubbish he wondered if it had its own microclimate.

It certainly smells that way, he thought, half expecting to see a rat poke its head out from behind one of the numerous sandwich and chocolate bar wrappers to ask just what the hell he was doing invading its privacy.

The dashboard was unlike any Harry had ever seen before, covered as it was in dozens of Lego figures, all of them stuck down with Blu-Tack.

Both front seats wore a cover made from wooden beads, the varnish long worn off, replaced now by a disturbing amount of grime that Harry was sure would terrify any scientist invited to take a sample for a petri dish or two.

Reaching up, Harry flicked down both sun visors to check to see if the driver had left any details as to their identity. Finding nothing, he then checked the pockets in the doors, and finally the glove compartment. On opening it, however, he immediately wished that he'd left it well alone. It was rammed full with yet more rubbish, and not just food this time either, but old band-aids, random bits of string, CDs without their cases, and a couple of packets of condoms so old Harry guessed they would probably be about as comfortable to wear as an old crisp packet, and not even half as effective.

The rear of the van was cut off from the front by a thick black curtain strung from the roof behind the front seats. Harry reached out to swish it to the side only to find that it was also attached to the van's floor and sides, with only a thin slit down the middle to allow for access. He pushed himself back out of the vehicle and headed around to the rear door.

Once opened, the stench of the cannabis was so strong that

Harry stepped back to allow some air in first before he even considered venturing in there himself. The smell wasn't just cannabis now either, not the normal kind anyway; this was skunk, something specifically grown to have a considerably higher amount of tetrahydrocannabinol. But there were other smells mingled in with it, of sweat and damp clothing, and the sickly sweet reek of junk food left to rot in the dark.

The back of the van was such a vision of lurid squalor that Harry wondered if it might not be best for everyone if he just set fire to the thing where it was parked. The sides and roof were covered in various patches of carpet, all overlapping, some hanging down into the van itself like large, dusty flakes of skin. On the floor was a mattress on top of which lay a sleeping bag shiny with grease and grime, much like the one he had seen resting in the hammock.

It looked like army surplus, Harry thought, then spotted an old mess tin in one corner and a pile of hexamine tablets, which once lit would heat water hot enough to make a brew, so long as you had at least the rest of your life to wait for it to boil.

In another corner was a pile of tins of baked beans and spaghetti hoops, along with a half-eaten loaf of sliced bread, which even from where he was standing Harry could see had started to turn blue. On top of the sleeping bag, however, were two bags that seemed so out of place in their current surroundings they almost glowed. Harry reached in and grabbed them, happy to stand out in the rain to keep himself away from the stench inside the vehicle.

Both bags were padded, and the first contained a serious-looking drone. Most definitely not the kind sold for a few quid to fly around your house and garden. This was specialist-grade, with a camera attached, and looked like it could, if it wanted to, easily lift a small child off the ground.

Harry unzipped the other bag to find it stuffed full of more tech and kit worth thousands. He didn't need a frame of reference to make that judgement either; he had seen plenty of expensive cameras in his time on the force, and the contents of the bag would've put a good deal of it to shame. There was not just one, but three different cameras, half a dozen lenses, a tripod, and various other bits and bobs that he didn't have a clue about.

Considering the value of the van, which Harry would've put between sod all and not worth a damn thing, he couldn't get his head around how the owner would be in possession of anything like this. The two just didn't add up, and yet here they were.

It's a bit of a puzzle, Harry thought, zipping up the bag again, and puzzles were what he, as a detective, was employed to solve. But before he did, he knew he had to finish checking out the rest of the van to see if he could find anything else important.

With a deep breath, Harry had a good rummage around, occasionally having to duck back out of the van to catch a good lungful of clean air. He found more rubbish, some clothes of which not a single piece was close to being clean, half a dozen adult magazines, and then, right at the end of the sleeping bag, where it had been used as a pillow, a green canvas bag, another army surplus purchase, no doubt.

Opening the bag somewhat tentatively, concerned that something might crawl out and introduce itself, Harry found a plastic carrier bag, perhaps acting as a waterproof barrier to whatever it held inside, he thought. Opening this, he peered inside and saw what looked like a couple of notebooks. Separating the carrier bag from the canvas bag it had been stuffed in, he reached in and pulled them out, hoping to find some clue of who the van owner was, and perhaps even where they were now, or at the very least, where they came from. But when he opened the first notebook, that hope died in the wind.

He recognised the faces staring back at him immediately, but then how could he not? Amber and Josh, a young couple he knew not at all, but was becoming increasingly concerned about.

The notebook wasn't a notebook at all, but a photo album, and Harry sat himself down on the rear end of the van, oblivious now to the trash piled up behind him.

He flicked through the pages, each one tracing the lives of two healthy, happy young adults, their eyes alive not just with a love for each other, but with life itself. It was as though the photographs were windows, ones that if Harry tried hard enough, he could reach into, perhaps even grab hold of Amber and Josh and pull them through.

The other book, like the first, was also full of photographs, only this one was markedly different. At first, Harry couldn't work out why, but then, comparing the two side-by-side, the difference was stark; whereas the first was an intimate record put together by the couple themselves, the second was a collection of images in which they seemed utterly unaware that they were being photographed.

Turning through the pages, Harry was struck by a creeping sense of voyeurism. Like, through the lens of whatever camera had been used, he was spying on Amber and Josh, and had somehow become a Peeping Tom.

Though none of the pictures strayed into the young couple's most private moments, their affection was caught on camera. Frozen moments of kisses glanced against cheeks, smiles and laughter shared. Most were taken at a distance, the images blurred, but others were much closer, taken no further away than a few metres at most. Whoever had taken them either knew the couple well, or was very, very good at staying just out of sight, blending into the crowd. Though, judging by the van, that was hard to believe.

Harry moved to lift himself out of the van, the albums in his hand, and was about to pick up the camera bag, when something from the second album caught him sharp. He sat down again, opened it, started turning the pages, searching for whatever it was that had snagged at his mind. He got to the end of the album, and nothing had jumped out at him, but he trusted his gut and had another look, slower this time, more careful, his fingers tracing a path through the pages, trying to identify something. He recognised some of the locations in the photos, scenery he knew so well now that he could close his eyes and walk the fells for hours. And then ...

The eyes were what caught his attention, the way they were

trying to look away, but were clearly drawn to the couple. The figure was that of a man, in his twenties, maybe early thirties, Harry guessed, though it was hard to tell. The face was hidden deep inside a hood, or beneath a woollen hat. Though not in every photo, the man was in enough for Harry to spot him.

Closing the album, Harry stood up, locked the van, and grabbing the camera bag off the ground, walked back to the old Land Rover. There was a clear connection between the man in the photos, who Harry assumed was the owner of the van as well as the rough camp they had discovered, and Josh and Amber.

Whether he had anything to do with their disappearance, Harry had no idea right then, but the photos were more than enough to have him worried. And even if he had nothing to do with what had or hadn't happened, there was a chance that he knew something, so it was imperative that he was found. And luckily, they'd caught a break with the keys. Whoever he was, he'd bolted. He'd abandoned his makeshift camp without his keys, and so far, hadn't returned to his vehicle as far as Harry could tell. They'd be able to trace the registration plate and go from there, though. And he would have someone from the team come up and meet him.

Dave would be a good choice, he thought. He could keep an eye on the van to see if the owner decided to return, and perhaps Jim, Liz, and Jen could get out and about to see if he could spot the man in town, take a photo of him and ask around to see if anyone had seen him; a long shot, true enough, but still one he had to take.

He pulled out his phone, quickly took some snaps of the man in the photos, then went to call the office, only to have his phone buzz in his hand.

'Boss?'

It was Liz, and Harry could hear the thin line of stress in her voice.

'I was just about to call you,' he said.

'I think you need to come to the office,' Liz replied, jumping in before Harry had finished speaking.

'Why? What's happened?'

'Best you come and see for yourself,' said Liz.

'Would I be right in guessing it's not good news?'

'Yes,' Liz said.

'On my way,' Harry said, disconnecting, then brought up Dave Calvert's number and gave him a call.

EIGHTEEN

Having called Dave, and waited for him to make his way to the van so that he could instruct him on what he wanted to do, Harry had then headed off into town, already dreading what he was about to find.

He'd called Liz again before making his way there but had been unable to get any further details out of her due to whatever it was, distracting her so much that she couldn't take the call. And that didn't exactly fill him with glee. Though she had given him some good news, at least. Smudge was with her, and that made him happier than he would ever dare admit. He also called Jim and Jen and sent them the photos he had taken on his phone.

Heading down the hill from Gayle and past the primary school, other than the seemingly continuous god-awful weather, Harry got no hint of what the problem might be. Even when he took a right at the junction to roll into town, everything seemed normal. The Penny Garth Café was busy despite the weather, people walking around in wax jackets and waterproofs doing their shopping, dogs on leads being dragged through the rain, nipping into the old sweetshop to stock up on a few bags of something to remind them of their childhood, like pear drops and sherbet lemons. But then everything changed when he drove past the

Market Hall and looked ahead to where he would usually pull in and park.

The marketplace was rammed with vehicles, the spaces between them filled with people and, Harry noticed, a film crew or two.

He slowed down, not to park, because that was impossible, but to have a closer look, to work out just what the hell was going on. Faces turned, watched him drive past, lifted phones to follow him with their cameras, took selfies. Some seemed utterly unaware that the road wasn't pedestrianized, as they spilled out onto it haphazardly, took more photos, filmed themselves talking to each other excitedly, their words drowned out by the thrum of rain falling on Wensleydale. Though it had abated a little now, the air was still heavy and grey with rain, the drops smaller, but no less wet. A river was running down the street and Harry followed it, leaving the sea of confusion behind him, though he wasn't filled with any sense of relief, knowing that he'd have to head back into it, and on foot.

Parking in the old railway station car park, Harry made his way back into town, every step with feet made of lead, and they only seemed to grow heavier the closer he got to his destination.

Without the protection of being inside a vehicle, Harry was even more aware of just how busy the marketplace was, and how dangerous everything could soon get, particularly if all those waiting outside the community centre continued to ignore the basic rule of not walking in front of vehicles if you wanted to stay alive.

Harry spotted a group of four individuals, all in brightly coloured anoraks, standing in the middle of the road, utterly unaware that behind them a tractor was rolling closer and closer. The driver had spotted them, but even beeping his horn had made no dent in their attention, which was utterly focused on their phones, held out in front of them at arm's length, as they spun around either filming Hawes or taking photos or whatever the hell it was that they were doing. Harry didn't care. He half wondered if the world would be any worse off if they ended up under the monster-sized tyres of the tractor, then waved to the driver and dashed over.

'You lot!' he roared. 'Shift it! Move! Go on, get out of the road! Now!'

The group of four either didn't hear him or were choosing to ignore him. Neither option was the best way of getting on Harry's good side. And he did have one; he just kept it very well hidden. Despite Harry's command, they all continued to point their phones down the cobbles of Main Street, like they were waiting for the arrival of a visiting dignitary.

With teeth clenched and jaw set, Harry walked over, stood in front of them to block their view, thrusting his rain-drenched face up in front of one of the phones.

The person holding the phone yelled in shock, jumped back, and dropped his phone in the process, only to find Harry staring back at him, eyes narrow and dark.

'What the hell are you doing? We're trying to—'

Harry pulled out his ID.

'Police,' he said.

As the one Harry had startled retrieved his phone, the others now turned their own phones on him and threw questions at his grizzled face.

'Do you know where they are?'

'Are they safe?'

'Have they been abducted?'

'Is it true that their camper was found abandoned but like with everything laid out still, like they'd just disappeared?'

'Do you think someone's kidnapped them to hold them ransom for the lottery money they won?'

'Have you had any reports of crop circles in the area?'

'What about lay lines?'

Harry didn't have time for any of this and decided to let them know.

'Shut it,' he said, the words sent through gritted teeth. 'All of you. And get yourselves out of the bloody road. Now!'

'You've not answered our questions.'

'No, I haven't,' Harry said. 'And I'm going to assume that the look on my face is enough to tell you that I'm not about to, either.'

'We have a right to know!'

'Do you, now?' Harry asked, but didn't wait for an answer. 'And on that thorny subject of rights, how are you all on the right to stay alive and breathing?'

Confusion wrote itself in the four pairs of eyes staring at him.

Harry jabbed a finger at the road behind them, watched them all turn and find, barely a metre away from where they were standing, the imposing front of the tractor, the headlights like eyes glaring down at them in rage. The tractor's less-than-impressed driver leaned out of his window.

'Shift it, you daft buggers!' he shouted. 'Get out of the bloody way!'

The group bolted for the pavement and the driver, shaking his head in despair, drove on, the queue of traffic that had formed behind him following on.

Harry gave the driver a wave, then looked over to the lane heading up to the community centre. It was blocked, the crowds so thick he knew he would have to push his way through.

Nothing for it, then. He sighed, and shoving his hands deep into his pockets, started to make his way over, half wishing he had Dave Calvert in front of him to make a path.

As he pushed on, Harry did his best to avoid catching anyone's eye. The only person he wanted to speak to right then was Liz, to find out what she knew about what was going on. He had a feeling that stopping to talk to anyone would have only one result, that being him losing the plot, grabbing someone by their ankles, then swinging them around in front of him like a scythe through wheat to clear the way.

That thought made him grin, but then he heard his name, and the voice uttering it ripped that smile away and ground it into the dirt.

Harry did his best to ignore it, but the voice came again, only this time louder, closer. Then a microphone appeared in front of him and behind it a face he'd done his best to forget. It was Richard Askew, the world's most annoying journalist.

'There you are, Grimm,' Askew said, his voice grating against Harry. 'Got a minute to answer a few questions?'

The man towered over most of the rest of the crowd, but the impression was not so much one of an imposing figure casting a shadow, but more that of a telegraph pole dressed in a collection of clothes blown onto him by the wind. He had wide eyes and a long, thin nose, and when he smiled there were too many teeth, as though he'd been given an extra helping at birth, and they were all tobacco stained.

'Not seen you in a long time,' Harry growled in reply, not letting up in his attempt to push through the crowd. 'Don't see why we should spoil such a good run of it, do you? Tatty-bye!'

Askew kept himself in front of Harry, walking backwards, a cameraman behind him clearing the way.

'You sure about that, Detective?' Askew asked.

'It's Detective Chief Inspector, as you well know,' said Harry. 'You've moved from the papers to the TV, I see,' he added. 'Hard to believe someone like you could go down in the world, but colour me wrong.'

'Actually, I've gone indie,' Askew replied, a thick slice of smugness attempting and failing to give the man's voice an emotional tone beyond that of sly and snide. 'I run my own show now, you see. I search through the lies to find the news for those searching for the truth.'

Harry couldn't help but laugh at that.

'Of course you do,' he said. 'And how's that going for you?'

Askew held up an arm.

Harry saw a gold watch on his wrist and couldn't help rolling his eyes.

'Well enough, I think.' Askew smiled.

Harry paused, leaning in for a closer look.

'Cost you a fair bit then, did it?'

'More than you earn in a month,' Askew replied.

Harry gave an appreciative nod.

'It's a fake,' he said.

Askew's sly smile slid a little.

'Fake? What? No, it isn't.'

Harry ignored Askew's protestations and kept walking, pushing past the journalist, now busy checking his watch, then narrowing his eyes at the cameraman, who sensibly got out of his way.

When he finally made it into the community centre, the hallway was rammed with more bodies, the library and information centre no less busy, the air thick with the noise of chatter and gossip. He spotted the librarian, saw horror and confusion in her eyes, and decided to do something to help.

Once again, Harry reached for his ID, then held it aloft, turning slowly on his heels for all to see.

'On the count of three,' he said, 'I'm going to be arresting each and every one of you for breach of the peace, obstruction, and generally pissing me right the hell off! Understood? Good. One ...'

At first, his voice was met with nothing but silence and numerous pairs of eyes staring at him in bafflement.

'Two ...'

'Wait, you can't do that!'

'What's happened to Jamber? Where are they?'

'Obstruction? Of what?'

Again, Harry pushed on through the crowd and opened the community centre's door. Jumping at the chance to be invited inside, the wind and the rain swept in gleefully, turning the complaints into gasps of shock.

'Three!' Harry roared.

There was a moment of quiet, then everyone was pushing and shoving to get outside and away from the mad policeman who had clearly lost his mind.

Harry shut the door.

'Thanks,' the librarian said, then asked, 'Would you really have arrested them?'

Before Harry could answer, the office door opened, and Liz stepped out.

'You can see why I asked you to come and see it all for yourself,' she said.

'A little,' Harry said. 'Kettle on?'

'Always.'

Harry followed Liz into the office and shut the door, only to be nearly swept off his feet by a black and furry hurricane.

'Missed me, have you?' Harry said, dropping to his haunches to give Smudge a hug.

Smudge pushed herself under his arms, jumped over him, then threw her front paws onto his chest, and sent a wet tongue to clean his ears.

Liz laughed.

'She's been fine,' she said. 'And just so you know, she didn't sleep on the bed at all or nick all of the duvet.'

Harry laughed, playing with Smudge for a while longer, pushing her away as she bounced back at him, tail wagging happily. Then he caught sight of the clock on the wall.

'Bloody hell, it's gone lunchtime,' he said. 'Where's the day gone? Feels like I only woke up an hour ago!'

Harry stood up, only to slump back down into a chair. Smudge came up and rested her heavy head on his thigh.

'Soppy thing,' said Liz.

'She is that,' said Harry.

'I wasn't talking about the dog,' smiled Liz. 'Want me to nip out and grab something for you to eat?'

'No,' Harry said, shaking his head. 'You do that, there's a chance I won't see you again for days.' He tapped his jacket pocket. 'Anyway, I followed Matt's advice and made myself a few sandwiches, enough to see me through, I should think.'

Harry then ran through what was happening up on Cam Road

with the search, the hammock Matt had shown him that morning, and then the van he had managed to find up by Gayle Beck.

'And this is the number plate,' he said, showing his phone's screen to Liz. 'You mind doing a quick check on that? I've got Jen and Jim out seeing if they can spot the owner, but a name would be useful.'

Liz jotted the number down.

'I've spoken with Amber's parents,' she said. 'I called them first thing and then popped round to see them this morning.'

'Where are they?'

'Far enough away from here to not be caught up in the madness,' said Liz. 'Managed to find a little cottage last minute over in Bainbridge. I said I'd head out to see them again later today, that I'd keep them up to date with everything as it was happening, and that our advice was to steer well clear of the marketplace.'

'That's good advice, too,' agreed Harry. 'Don't want them getting caught up in all of that. It's a bloody circus, isn't it?'

'I said you'd be speaking to them as soon as you could, but I passed on everything I knew and they seemed okay.'

'Anything from Josh's parents?'

Liz shook her head.

'I've tried and I keep trying, but nowt yet. I asked Amber's parents, too. They'd heard nothing.'

'Well, keep trying,' Harry said.

'I will,' replied Liz, then she looked over at the office door. 'You going back out into all that?' she asked.

Harry shook his head.

'No point,' he said. 'Sad to say, I left my flamethrower at home.'

Liz laughed.

Harry pulled up a number on his phone.

'But I think it might be time to call in the reinforcements,' he said, and hit *dial*.

NINETEEN

Harry explained everything as quickly and concisely as he could, very aware that Detective Superintendent Walker was no doubt already juggling a dozen other things herself. When he finished talking, he expected her response to be a mix of understanding and well-worded reasons as to why she couldn't simply drop everything and come over to help.

'I can be there by late this afternoon,' Walker said. 'Are you and your team happy to deal with what's going on until then?'

Harry said, 'To be honest, ma'am, I wasn't expecting you to even be able to make it down here this week, never mind later today.'

'Well, it sounds to me like the situation is urgent on a number of levels,' Walker replied.

'So, you've heard of them as well, then?' Harry asked.

'You mean you haven't?'

'All I know is that they won the lottery,' Harry said. 'And that's only because Constable Okri told me that yesterday. But I'm sure it'll come as no surprise to hear that's not something I follow.'

'No, you're right, it's not,' said Walker. 'It wasn't your everyday win though. I'll have to check, as it was one of those rollover ones I believe, but I think it was around fifty.'

Harry was stunned. He may not have been a follower of the lottery, but he knew money, not least because he couldn't think of a single time in his life when he'd ever had much of it.

'Fifty? As in million?'

'Yes.'

Harry let out a whistle.

'I knew it was a lot, but bloody hell, that's ridiculous. Who needs that?'

'No one,' said Walker. 'That kind of money makes people do funny things, and from my experience, and yours too, I'm sure, most of those things are deeply unpleasant.'

'You could say that, yes,' Harry replied, pushing away dark events in his life, investigations where lives had been ruined, brought to a violent end, all for money.

'There's a chance all of this could get out of hand very quickly,' Walker continued. 'I'm not saying that it will, as I've every confidence in you and your team, but situations like this are often beyond our control. Perhaps a sprinkling of extra police seniority might help.'

There was a pause and Harry decided to stay quiet, suspecting that the silence was Walker thinking about something. He was also now doing his level best to stop himself from imagining the kind of unpleasant things people would do for money. He failed, and his concern for the missing couple only grew.

'Do you have anywhere we can do a press conference?' Walker asked, knocking Harry from his thoughts, for which he was relieved. 'Nothing too grand, just something that shows we're on top of things. Give the press a chance to ask a few questions, that kind of thing, and to keep them under control.'

'There's the Market Hall,' Harry said. 'I'm sure I can get that together for early evening.'

'Good. We'll do it at five-thirty. How does that sound? Now, what about all these fans? Any suggestions?'

'A water cannon and a few sacks of potatoes would be useful,' Harry said.

Walker laughed.

'Potatoes? That's a new one.'

'Used to use them back in the Paras to practise dealing with riots, that kind of thing,' Harry explained. 'A fist-sized King Edward on your nose doesn't half make your eyes water, trust me.'

'You're a very complex man, Mr Grimm,' Walker said. 'I'll let you know when I'm on my way.'

Conversation over, Harry turned back to Liz.

'Too soon for you to have had any luck with that number plate, I suppose,' he said.

'Actually no,' said Liz. 'Last registered keeper is a Mr John Robertson. The vehicle hasn't been taxed or insured for over a year.'

'What about a Statutory Off the Road Notification?' Harry asked.

Liz shook her head.

'That stuff's never really checked, though, is it? My guess is that he's had it parked off the road ever since, or just drives it around and risks getting caught.'

'Which there's bugger all chance of,' Harry said.

'Exactly.'

'Address?'

Liz handed Harry a slip of paper.

'Lincolnshire,' she said, as Harry read the name of a village on the paper slip.

'Never heard of it,' he said.

'I doubt anyone has,' Liz said. 'I did a quick search while you were on the phone to the DSup and all the place is famous for— and I use that word very loosely—is an abbey destroyed centuries ago, and a sugar beet factory.'

'Not exactly a tourist destination, then.'

'No.'

'Well, I need you to find out everything you can about Mr Robertson,' Harry said. 'Get on the phone, speak to whoever you can down there, have someone go round his house, door knock his neighbours, whatever you can, understood? I want to know everything about him; who he hangs around with, where he drinks, his favourite takeaway, where he works, who cuts his hair.'

'Already on it,' Liz said. 'What about yourself?'

Harry didn't answer immediately, his thoughts on the gathering media storm outside their front door.

'I'm tempted to go and have a word with a certain journalist.'

Liz's eyes widened.

'If that's a euphemism for a public execution, you do know you're not allowed to burn journalists, don't you? It's frowned upon.'

'I know, I know,' Harry said, but for a reason he couldn't quite fathom, a more moderate approach was already starting to form in his head. Perhaps it was exactly because of the number of people milling around outside that had got him thinking. But there was also what he had spoken about with Walker. Something was telling him that for this he needed the press on his side for once. The thought made his skin crawl, but right now he was starting to see that controlling the information made more sense than antagonizing those so desperate to get their hands on it and twist it into whatever shape or form they wanted. And to do that, he needed a way in ...

TWENTY

Leaving Liz to work on gathering all the intelligence she could about the owner of the van parked up by Gayle Beck, and with Smudge now attached to a lead and at his side, Harry left the office and from the entrance hall stared out into the rain. The lane from the community centre to the marketplace was still rammed with the jostling crowd, but standing a literal head and shoulders above them all like some pale-skinned denizen of foreboding, was Askew.

Harry stepped outside and bellowed the man's name.

Askew turned his head on his wire-thin neck to stare over at Harry.

Harry waved the man over.

'What is it?' Askew asked, having pushed his way through the crowds, his cameraman at his side. 'And just so we're clear, I've already gathered enough information from people to know what's going on here, Detective.'

'Is that so?'

'It is,' Askew said. 'I'm going live in fifteen. The world must know.'

Harry leaned in close to the journalist.

'Must it now?'

'Yes.'

'Good,' Harry said. 'Then perhaps you wouldn't mind stepping into my office for a moment or two?'

Askew fell back a little and Harry saw the man's disturbingly large Adam's apple bob up and down.

'I know enough about police brutality to know that's not a very good idea,' Askew said.

'I thought you were interested in the truth?' Harry asked.

'I am, but I'm guessing we have different ideas about what "truth" means.'

'You're good with words,' Harry said, then reached over and opened the community centre's door. 'I'll give you that. It is your job, after all, isn't it? That's why I want to have a word.'

Askew didn't move.

'I'm not about to drag you inside and beat you around the head with that camera, am I?' said Harry. 'Not saying I'm not tempted, because of course I am, but the one thing that's stopping me is that I'm fairly sure it would do no good.'

Askew glanced at his camera man, then made his way past Harry and into the building.

Harry walked in behind them, then stepped past to lead them down the hallway to the interview room, opening the door he stepped in first.

Harry sat down. Smudge, he noticed, plonked herself next to him but for once sat up rod straight, her dark eyes trained on Askew as he walked slowly into the room.

'Won't take long,' he said as Askew and his cameraman took a seat each.

'What's this about, then?' Askew asked, pulling out a Dictaphone.

'That's a bit old school, isn't it?' Harry said.

'Yes, and it works,' said Askew, then gave a nod to the cameraman, who lifted the camera and pointed it at Harry.

Harry shook his head.

'Not a good idea, not unless you fancy spending the next few days trying to put it back together after I've taken it off you and had a bit of fun with it against this wall over here. And right now, I'm very much in the mood for smashing things.'

'Then we're done before we've even started,' Askew said, and started to get up.

Smudge growled, a sound that even Harry was surprised to hear, not that he was about to let on.

Askew stared at the dog.

'She's already eaten,' Harry said. 'You've nothing to worry about.'

But then he glanced down at Smudge to see her teeth bared and wasn't so sure.

Askew sat back down.

'I want you to be my official liaison,' Harry said.

The journalist turned his eyes on Harry, narrowing them.

'Official liaison? How do you mean? More importantly, *what* do you mean?'

'I mean,' Harry said, trying to work it out himself as he spoke, 'that I've just been on the phone with my senior officer and she will be here later today. I'm going to need someone who understands the media to help run things, let people know what's going on, where the press conference is going to be, that kind of thing. Be a point of contact.'

'Why me?' Askew asked.

'You know the area,' Harry said. 'And you know me.'

A shrug.

'I need someone inside that world I can trust.'

A laugh.

'And you think that person is me?'

'I have to start somewhere, don't I?' Harry said. 'So, why not start at the bottom? You'll be the centre of attention, which is, I'm sure, your favourite place to be. The world's media will be looking to you. How can you resist?'

Askew laughed again, only this time the sound was loud and unpleasant, a cackling thing of high-pitched notes bursting from his throat as though desperate to escape. And who could blame them? Harry thought.

'The world's media? You're bigging this all up a bit, aren't you?'

Harry leaned back, folded his arms, and stared.

'I'm giving you the chance to stand out from the crowd for the right reasons,' he said. 'You know I don't like journalists, so see this as an olive branch if you will, my small attempt to bring them onside.'

'I'll think about it.'

'No, you'll decide now,' said Harry. 'I've an investigation to carry out, a missing couple, and as far as I'm concerned, they're all that matters. Refuse this, and I'm going to spend an awful lot of time and energy making the next few days very difficult for you.'

'What if I say no?'

Smudge growled once again.

Harry stood up, the movement deliberately slow, his hand on the dog's head to give her a scratch.

'You won't,' he said. 'Because I'm playing to that planet-sized ego of yours. All those journalists looking to you for information? Imagine it!'

Harry watched a smile, thin as thread, slip across Askew's face.

'There it is,' he said.

'There it is what?'

'Your ego,' said Harry. 'And right now that's what I'm speaking to.'

'And you think insulting me will persuade me, is that it?'

'Not at all,' said Harry. 'I don't think, I know, because this is something you can't resist. It's too good an opportunity to come out on top, to be seen. And that's what you want, isn't it? To be seen? To be recognised, acknowledged even?'

'Perhaps,' Askew said.

'So, you'll do it?'

Askew rose to his feet, his cameraman doing the same.

'Yes, I'll do it.'

'Do this well,' said Harry, 'and I think this could be the start of a beautiful working relationship.'

He then led the two men back out into the hall and along to the main doors, the words leaving a bad taste in his mouth.

'Press conference will be at five thirty,' he said, holding Askew at the main door. 'I need you to put that together, sort things out with the Market Hall, that kind of thing. I'll keep you abreast of any developments, and you will make sure that you are the absolute centre of attention, not me.'

'That's impossible, Grimm, and you know it. A story like this? It's just too juicy. Everyone will want to try and get a taste of it.'

Harry leaned in close, his voice quiet and all the more threatening because of it.

'They're a young couple,' he said. 'Kids, Askew, that's all. They're what matters. You can see that, can't you? Just Josh and Amber, us finding them, and hopefully getting them home to their families. And right now, all I'm trying to do is reach out to whatever dried-up husk of decency you still have somewhere inside you, in the hope that you can take what I'm offering and come out smelling better than the rest of that flock of vultures out there. Well, can you? Or have I aimed too high, and all things considered, that's barely out of the gutter.'

Askew said nothing for a moment, then said, 'Yes, I can.'

Harry stepped back.

'Good,' he said. 'Then let's get out there and tell them all that you're now my chief liaison with the media, shall we? Time to shine, Askew, time to shine!'

Before Askew could question any of what he had just been told, Harry led both men outside. With a shout, he quickly had the crowd's attention.

'My name is DCI Grimm,' Harry said. 'There will be a press conference this evening at five-thirty.'

Hands lifted into the air, voices called out with questions, insinuations, and much to Harry's dismay, even gave voice to a couple of conspiracy theories, but he ignored them.

'Mr Askew, here, is my chief liaison, so any and all questions will come through him. Until then, if you would be so good as to let me and my team get on with our jobs, it would be much appreciated.'

Then, before anyone could stop him, Harry pushed through the crowd with Smudge by his side. Behind him, as the rain-spattered air erupted in a crescendo of questions and shouts, Askew was swamped.

TWENTY-ONE

Having managed to recruit Askew into dealing with the press, and still hardly able to believe it himself, Harry made his way out of the marketplace and back down to his vehicle at the old railway station carpark. He would then head back up to Josh and Amber's campervan to check on the search with Matt and Jadyn. As he climbed in, he spotted Jim down the road and, with a beep of his horn, called him over.

Jim climbed in.

'Where are you heading?' Harry asked, noticing that Fly wasn't with the PCSO and guessing that the dog was back on the farm helping his dad.

'Back into town again,' said Jim, giving Smudge's head a rub.

'You've not spotted him yet, then?'

'Not yet, no, but with the weather like this, he's probably hiding out somewhere, isn't he? Trying to stay warm and dry? I've already been around all the cafés and shops and pubs, but I figured I'd have another look.'

'It's a long shot, really,' said Harry, 'but it's worth a try. Anything from Dave?'

'Nowt,' Jim said. 'He was good up at the auction mart yester-day, though. Not had a chance to give you my feedback on that, and there's not much to tell, really, but he did good. Most folk know him, so that's a help, and he was fine with any leg-pulling. Expected it, I think. But then he does keep goats, doesn't he?'

'And that's funny, is it?'

Harry saw Jim stare at him in disbelief.

'Are you really asking me that question? He keeps goats, Harry. How can that be anything other than funny?'

'You get anywhere on the fly-tipping thing?' Harry asked, deciding to leave the whole goat thing for now.

'Only that everyone's had it happen to them and they're getting a bit sick of it. There's a fresh pile of goodness-knows-what that has been dumped over the last few days, so I'd like to go over and have a look when I can.'

'Where?'

'Farm lane out by Appersett,' Jim said. 'So, not far.'

'You can pop over if you get a chance later in the week,' Harry said. 'Our priority is to find out who owns that van. Anything from Jen?'

'She's had a couple of sightings, but nothing more,' said Jim.

'How did she get on yesterday with that farmer who keeps having his gates left open?'

'She rang me while she was there to see if I knew anything about him.'

'Well, you do know more of them than the rest of us.'

'True, but I drew a blank with this one. Asked my dad, though, and he knew the name, and his reputation.'

Harry frowned at that.

'That's a very innocent word until I hear it used like that,' he said. 'What reputation, exactly?'

'Not quite sure,' Jim said. 'Dad didn't say much, but what he did say was enough.'

'And what was that, then?'

'He called him Bullshit Brian.'

'Not one for mincing his words, is he, your dad?'

'Apparently, he's always got an excuse or a reason for something not going right,' Jim continued. 'Like it's never his fault if something goes wrong.'

'In what sense?'

Jim said, 'I get the impression my dad thinks Brian always has an excuse no matter what, and that it's never him, like the world's got it in for him, something like that anyway.'

'And what did Jen say about him?'

'She didn't,' said Jim. 'Just asked me the question. I called her back, and she said she was on her way back.'

'I'll have to catch up with her when I can,' Harry said.

'How's things with the search?' Jim asked. 'I bumped into old Mr Fawcett yesterday at the mart, said his son was up there and that Matt had him chasing after someone. You heading back up Cam Road?'

'I need to see how things are going,' said Harry. 'Can't help feeling a little helpless with something like this, but best to just do what we can and let the professionals crack on.'

'They know what they're doing,' said Jim.

Harry said, 'Sorry to push you back out into the weather.'

'It's just rain,' said Jim, and climbed back out into it. Then he looked back at Harry, his face streaked with snail trails of water. 'And like Matt says, it's Yorkshire rain, so it's good for you, isn't it?'

With a laugh, Jim shut the passenger door and headed off.

Yorkshire rain my arse, Harry thought, bemused at times by the likes of Matt and Jim and their staunch belief that if it's Yorkshire, then it's brilliant, no matter what they were referring to. The thing was, though, they probably had a point, Harry thought, as he started the engine.

He wasn't fully convinced that Yorkshire was the centre of the universe, but he could see why so many thought that it was; the Dales especially so. And he wondered if he ended up spending long enough in the Dales, whether he'd eventually feel that way himself. After all, he was a southerner by birth, but now regarded the place as his home. He had friends here, good ones, too, a job he loved, a house, a dog, and a ...

Harry paused, his thoughts catching in his mind like wool on barbed wire, as Grace pushed to the forefront. He tried to shove her away again, but she remained, that smile of hers stubbornly taking centre stage now.

Harry took out his phone, pulled up her number, then shoved the phone back in his pocket again just as quickly. They'd had that quick message exchange, hadn't they, so that was something, surely?

Maybe I'll give her a call later, he thought. No, maybe not call her, but send her another text. Take it gentle, like, and he could almost hear Matt's voice saying exactly that inside his head. Yes, that would be okay, wouldn't it? Or would it?

Bloody hell, he hadn't the faintest idea what was right or wrong, or what he should do next or how he felt. Or did he? Feelings weren't his strong point. He had them, of course he did, but dealing with them, accepting them, talking about them? That's when things got sticky.

Harry's phone rang, and he answered it without checking who was calling, just thankful that someone had interrupted his spiralling confusion.

'Harry, it's Gordy,' said the voice at the other end. 'I see you've a bit of a situation to deal with in Hawes right now. And by see, I mean with my own eyes.'

'That we have,' Harry said, surprised to be speaking to Gordy at all. 'Who told you?'

'Have you tried driving through Hawes?' Gordy asked. 'I only popped in for a few things from Cockett's, one of those fantastic meat pies they do, and it was like pushing through cattle. I parked up behind the school, then headed back in and went for a little chat with Liz. She's just filled me in on everything.'

'How's Anna?' Harry asked, ignoring what Gordy had said. 'All good for the move?'

'Don't you go changing the subject,' said Gordy. 'I'm calling you to tell you that you need my help.'

'You're telling me?'

'I am. Detective Inspector, remember?'

That made Harry laugh, hearing Gordy parrot one of his little catchphrases.

'You're not officially part of the team anymore,' he said. 'You're leaving in a couple of weeks—'

'To go on holiday.'

'Yes, but then—'

'Then we'll be back and will be around a while to pack and sort things through. Then we'll be moving down to Somerset, and inviting that old friend of yours, DCI Jameson, around for dinner plenty often, because I'm sure he's a tale or two to tell about you, hasn't he? But that's not right now, is it? We're still here, we're still part of the community, and you can still call me in.'

'No, I can't,' Harry said.

'Don't talk nonsense,' replied Gordy. 'I'm heading home now to grab my uniform because I think a nice, obvious police presence in town might be useful.'

'Walker's on her way,' Harry said.

'I should hope that she is,' Gordy replied. 'And you've somehow managed to get that Askew chap running around for you? I'm impressed. Those negotiating skills they taught you in the Paras finally proving useful, then?'

'Gordy—'

'I'll keep you posted on things down here,' Gordy said, refusing to give Harry a chance to get a word in edgeways, 'so you focus on finding that young couple, you hear?'

Harry would've replied, but Gordy had already hung up. So, instead, he took a moment to gather his thoughts and decide what to do next.

He'd appreciated Gordy's call and her offer to join in and help. He knew it made sense. He simply hadn't wanted to bother her, what with the life changes she and Anna were now dealing with. He'd not had much of a chance to speak to her about it, but he understood the reasons and supported them.

Where they'd chosen to move had been quite the surprise,

though. Somerset? Really? Anna had done her best to convince him that it was where she had felt called to go, and he'd found himself believing her, too. Something really was pulling her south, and it was more than clear that no one was going to be able to get in the way of it.

Gordy had managed to land herself a role in the small market town of Shepton Mallet, down in Somerset. Harry knew the place well enough, and the area around it. He'd spoken to Jameson about it, too, and the old DCI, having decided against rejoining the force, instead setting himself up as a civilian advisor to the police, was very much looking forward to getting to know them both and offering Gordy a bit of professional support.

The last time Harry had seen Jameson was when they'd bumped into each other from opposite ends of an investigation, Jameson having attended a weekend retreat up beyond Marsett on becoming a private investigator. The weekend had gone pear-shaped very quickly, thanks to being snowed in, the man running the weekend faking his own death only to then actually be murdered, and the arrival of a gang of killers on the run. It had been eventful, to say the least, Harry thought.

Realising that he was relieved to have Gordy involved in everything that was going on with the whirlwind of crazy racing around Hawes, Harry keyed the ignition and pulled out into the road. Instead of heading along the cobbles and through town, he took the long way around instead, driving out of town to turn onto Old Gayle Lane. This also gave him the opportunity to stop and have a word with Dave Calvert, who was sitting in Jim's Land Rover on the opposite side of the ford crossing Gayle Beck.

Harry parked up behind him, then walked over, knocked on the window of the passenger door, and let himself in.

'Now then, Harry,' Dave said. 'Sorry, I mean, Boss. That's right, isn't it? I don't know what to call you. Which is it? Or is it DCI Grimm?'

'Right now, it doesn't matter,' Harry said. 'Nice of Jim to leave you with his vehicle.'

'Thought it made more sense me having it than him,' Dave said. 'He's moving about, whereas I'm on this stakeout, aren't I?'

'It's not a stakeout, Dave,' Harry said. 'You're not in a TV cop show, remember? Have you seen anything?'

Fly popped up from the back of the Land Rover to rest his chin on Dave's shoulder.

'Got myself some company, too,' he said. 'Anyway, so far, I've seen nowt.' He pointed out through the windscreen. 'I've a good view of the van, like, and I figured sitting over here was out of the way enough to not be obvious.'

Harry had to agree.

Just a few metres in front of them, the beck was thundering past, the water so brown from the peat washing off the fells that it looked like melted chocolate. It reminded Harry of a film he'd seen as a kid, something about a chocolate factory. He'd liked that film, and to this day wondered if meting out justice how it had happened in that story to those none-too-pleasant kids wouldn't help a little with reducing the crime rate now and again.

'If you see him and have to rush over and grab him, you'll not make it across that,' Harry said, pointing at the raging torrent.

'I will, because that's how I got over here in the first place,' Dave said. 'Stopped by for a look at the van first. The water's fast, but it's not deep. The wheels skipped a bit, but it was no bother. I've driven across worse.'

'I hear everything went well up at the auction mart?' Harry said, thinking back to his quick chat with Jim.

'Jim mentioned the fly-tipping he wants to have a look at?'

'He did,' said Harry, and was about to ask more about that when movement caught his eye.

At first, he wasn't sure what he was looking at, as a shadow slid itself between vehicles on the other side of the ford. Then it darted out from where it was hiding, looked left and right, then ducked down beside the van.

'You saw that too, right?' Dave asked.

'I'm looking at it right now,' said Harry. 'And you're sure this old thing will make it across?'

Dave grinned, and Harry saw a wildness in his eyes which, if he hadn't known the man as well as he did, would've terrified him.

'Only one way to find out,' Dave said, and twisted the key.

TWENTY-TWO

The Land Rover shot off a hell of a lot quicker than Harry had expected, thrusting him back in his seat before throwing him forward to crack his skull on the windscreen.

'Bloody hell, Dave, I'm not strapped in!'

Ignoring Harry's complaints, Dave swung the vehicle down into the toffee-brown slew of water. Harry, his head stinging from the impact, grabbed the seatbelt and somehow clipped in.

Harry felt the power of the water grab the front wheels and start to push the Land Rover to the left.

'Hold on!' Dave called out.

'What the bloody hell else do you think I'm doing?' Harry shouted back, his hands white-knuckle tight as they gripped the dashboard.

Dave pushed on, steering the vehicle into the current, bringing the rear end in with a thump.

Harry was thankful that the vehicle was four-wheel drive, aware that all four wheels were actively engaged in pulling them across the flooded ford.

'There he is!' Dave said.

Harry saw the figure stand up from the other side of the van. Then he opened the driver's door and jumped in.

'Damn it,' Harry said. 'Must've had a spare key.'

Blue-black smoke blasted out of the van's exhaust pipe and Harry swore.

'Come on Dave, shift it!'

They were halfway across the ford now and Harry was suddenly aware that his feet were getting wet.

'Not exactly watertight, is it?' he said, glancing down to see water spilling in not just from around the bottom of the door, but from the numerous holes in the footwell, too.

'No need to panic,' Dave said, his eyes focused on the other side of the ford. 'We'll catch him.'

Harry was impressed with Dave's confidence, even if it did strike him as being a little misplaced.

The van moved.

'He's off,' Harry said. 'We'll not catch him in this, even if we do make it to the other side. I'll give Gordy a ring, see if she can—'

'No need,' Dave said, cutting Harry off. 'Look ...'

Harry stared at the van to see that instead of racing off, it was crawling forward on wheels that had no interest at all in going the way the driver intended.

'They're flat,' Harry said, looking at the tyres.

'Of course they're flat,' Dave said.

Harry narrowed his eyes at Dave.

'Is there something you need to tell me?' he said.

Dave gave a shrug.

'Told you I stopped for a look at the van, didn't I? Well, I figured I'd give us a bit of a helping hand by letting them down a little.'

'A little?' Harry said. 'As far as I can tell, they're all are pancakes!'

'Best to be sure, right?' Dave said, as the Land Rover pulled itself out of the river. He then steered them over to come to a stop in front of the van, blocking its escape.

Harry jumped out and rushed to the driver's door. On seeing him, the driver leapt across to the passenger seat, only to find that his way was blocked by the imposing bulk of PCSO Dave Calvert.

Dave stooped low enough to stare at the driver and then lifted a hand to give a little wave.

'Now then,' he said. 'Going somewhere, were we, son?'

The driver scrambled between the middle seats, pushing himself through the thin slit in the curtains, His feet trying to find purchase on the dashboard, scattering the Lego figures stuck there left and right.

The back doors opened, but Harry was already there waiting.

'I'll be honest,' he said, 'I'm impressed you even tried.' He then took out his Police ID. 'Mr Robertson? I'm DCI Harry Grimm. Wondered if we could have a little chat?'

DECIDING that driving Mr Robertson into town to march him into the community centre through the throng of journalists and fans wasn't a great idea, Harry went for conducting the interview in the back of the Police Land Rover. Leaving Robertson with Dave, he walked quickly along the road and over the bridge, then back to where he had parked up, to then drive the vehicle over the ford and park up behind Jim's Land Rover. He then had Dave escort Robertson over to the rear of the Police Land Rover, and threw Smudge in the back of Jim's to snuggle up with Fly. Now, as the three of them sat together, he could still hear the two dogs play fighting.

With a quick check of Robertson's contact details, it was time to start asking questions.

'Cosy, isn't it?' Dave said, notebook out and at the ready, in line with Harry's instructions.

With their knees touching, and their heads stooped because of the roof, which, like the rest of the Land Rover, was leaking a little, cosy was not a word Harry would've used. It was cold, too, with blasts of wind shooting through the numerous gaps in the body-work and around the windows. Such a word as cosy implied a level of comfort that the rear of the vehicle was affording none of them, the seats little more than fold-out sheets of metal, the cushioning on them perished and held together with tape. And that was the point, really, because Harry knew just how effective being uncomfortable could be at encouraging people to talk, just to get it all over and done with.

Harry turned his attention to Mr Robertson. The man was sopping wet and reminded Harry of a hare caught in headlights, the fear in his eyes stark. He was dressed in a mishmash of clothes that had a 'charity shop' air about them and, as Matt had suspected when he had first seen him and made chase, army surplus. And there was a rich pong to him as well, an aroma of damp and sweat, of a body unwashed for days, which only served to make their closeness even more uncomfortable.

Harry had opened a window as much as he had dared, trying to get the balance right between being able to breathe and not getting drenched. As to Mr Robertson's breath, that was some-thing that even Harry had found shocking, mainly because he was very pleased to be nowhere near a naked flame, otherwise they would have all gone up like a bonfire drenched in petrol. But despite all of this, he wasn't about to judge. What he needed was answers, facts, an understanding of what the man had been up to, and why, and what connection, if any, he had to Josh and Amber.

'So, John,' Harry said, hoping that using the man's first name might help lubricate the start of their chat, 'perhaps you can tell me where—'

'I don't know where they are!' Robertson blurted out, his words a little rounded at the edges. Probably due to the alcohol still riding his breath, Harry thought, perhaps even a joint or three.

'Point of note,' Harry said, looking at Dave, 'I've not actually mentioned any names yet.'

'But I don't!' Robertson continued. 'I know you think I do, but I don't. And I've been looking, I really have! That's where I've been, looking, you see? I want to find them, to help, that's all.'

Harry remembered Matt mentioning he'd chased someone up on the hill near the campervan.

'You were seen near the campervan yesterday,' he said.

'I know, because I was looking for them!'

'Then you ran away.'

'I was scared, I just panicked, and ...'

Harry gave the man a moment to calm down before speaking again.

'Let's start right at the beginning,' he said. 'But we'll skip over the fact your van isn't taxed or insured, never mind a biohazard that should be burned to a cinder, and move straight on to you telling me what it is you were doing with that little campsite of yours we found up in the hills? And you're a fair way from home, aren't you, John? Lincolnshire, isn't it?'

'But I've not seen them, I really haven't!' Robertson said, his voice strained and desperate, a thin thing pushed through wire, making it sing like the string of a broken guitar. 'I mean, I have, of course I have, but not there, not where the van is now.'

'Wait, so you have seen them, then?' Harry asked.

'Yes, a few days ago,' Robertson said. 'Before all the rain started, that's when I saw them, and a bit after, too, but not since then, I promise. And before that, too. But not now, not up there on the track. I don't know where they are. We have to find them!'

Harry ignored the desperation in Robertson's voice, which seemed to spill from him in a rapid spray of panic and fear, and pulled from his pocket several evidence bags, and also opened the two bags on the floor beside him. He presented them each to Robertson.

'Can you tell me anything about all of this?' he asked. 'I've a pair of binoculars, a camera lens, and some photos, all of which were found at your campsite up on the hill, plus this rather expensive camera set up, and a drone, which right now I'm wondering how it is you managed to afford.'

'I don't know anything!'

Harry held up the camera bag.

'Seriously, John, this is high-end, isn't it? Like the binos. Why would you drive around in a shit tip like that van of yours, yet also have this? You can see how it makes no sense right now, can't you?'

'I'm a photographer, that's all,' John said.

'I could've guessed that,' said Harry. 'But even so, how much is this worth? Ten, maybe twenty grand? I'm just plucking figures out of the air here, but even so.'

'I needed it, for what I do,' said John.

Harry narrowed his eyes.

'And what is that exactly? Because right now, it looks to me like what you do is spy on people and invade their privacy. Is that what you do, John?'

John was quiet.

Harry lifted the bag containing the photos in front of John's face.

'Do you recognise them?'

'Yes,' Robertson said. 'Of course I do.'

'And can you give me their names?'

'Josh and Amber Hill. They were married a couple of months ago, won the lottery four or six months before that. Josh is twenty-five, Amber's twenty-three. They met at university. Josh was studying—'

'That's a lot of detail there,' said Dave, and Harry noticed that the man was busy taking everything down in his notebook.

'Can you tell me where you got them, then? Did you take the photos yourself?'

Robertson fell quiet, but Harry noticed the faint shake of a head.

'Is that a no?'

Another head shake, then Robertson muttered, 'No, I didn't take them.'

'If you didn't take them, then where did you get them?' Harry asked.

Robertson's silence was enough.

Harry now revealed the photo albums he had retrieved from

Robertson's van when he'd first found it, having fetched them from his vehicle while Dave was busy making sure Robertson was comfortable in the back of the Land Rover.

'These, then,' he said, placing the albums on Robertson's lap. 'They look different to me, by which I mean the photos in one don't look like they were taken by the same photographer as those in the other. Are you able to tell me why that is, John?'

Robertson was still quiet, though the fear in his eyes was screaming now, so he pressed on, holding up an album in each hand.

'This one,' he said, shaking the one in his left hand, 'well, it looks to me like these are all photos that Amber and Josh took themselves. But this one?' He presented the album held in his right hand. 'It's different, isn't it, John? So, I'll ask you again; can you tell me why that is?'

Robertson opened his mouth, tried to say something, but no words came out.

Harry flicked through the pages of each album. Slowly, too, to really give Robertson time to see the happy faces of the young couple in each one.

'I'm worried about them, John,' Harry said, his voice quiet, determined. 'Really very worried indeed. And when I get worried about something, I don't think about anything else. I become a little obsessed, you might say. Nothing else matters, you see, John, nothing at all, except for this thing that's worrying me. And when it's people that I'm worried about, people like Josh and Amber here, there's nothing I won't do to help them. Do you understand that, John? Nothing.'

'I'm worried, too,' John said, a ragged knife edge to his voice. 'I am, I promise! That's what I'm trying to say! It's why I've been out looking!'

'I don't know what you're saying, if I'm honest,' Harry replied. 'Neither of us do, do we, Officer Calvert?'

'Not a clue,' said Dave, shaking his head.

'But I don't know where they are!' Robertson said. 'I don't! Why don't you believe me?'

'I didn't say I that didn't believe you,' said Harry, 'it's just that right now, it doesn't make much sense. All we're trying to do here is get to the bottom of what all of this is, and where you fit into it, John, that's all. And I'm hoping, really truly hoping, that you can help.'

'That's what I've been trying to do!' Robertson said. 'I've been looking for them ever since I realised they were gone. That's why I was there, in that camp, and that's why I'm here now! Why won't you listen?'

In an attempt to seem open and relaxed, Harry leaned back as best as he could in the uncomfortable space they were all squashed into.

'Please, John,' he said, 'help us, okay? That's all we're asking.'

'But you think I know where they are. And I don't.'

'What I think,' said Harry, 'is that I have an abandoned campervan, a missing couple, and someone who has been, for want of a better word, spying on them. And with the kind of equipment I'd be more inclined to stumble on being used by a police-sanctioned surveillance team, than someone who lives on boil-in-the-bags and hasn't washed for a week!'

'I'm just ... I'm just a fan, that's all,' John said.

'A fan who camps out in secret, who has binoculars and a camera, who takes photos of them—' Harry lifted the bag containing the photos, then one of the albums. 'and who doesn't mind stopping by to help himself to a few of their things. And then, when he's spotted by the police, does a bloody runner!'

'I'm sorry!' Robertson said, and there were tears in the man's eyes. 'I don't mean to, I really don't, but I ...'

'But you what?' Harry asked. 'What aren't you telling me, John? Because there's something missing from all this, isn't there?' He picked up one of the lenses from the camera bag. 'This doesn't make sense! None of it does!'

John pushed himself away from Harry.

'I don't know where they are, I really don't! I want to help, but—'

'But what?' Harry roared but was interrupted by Dave.

'Wait ...'

Harry looked over at the PCSO.

'What?'

'He said something earlier,' said Dave. 'About when he'd last seen them.'

'What about it?' asked Harry.

Dave was silent for a moment, checked his notes.

'Yes, that was it,' he said, then read from his notebook. 'John here said *not where the van is now*, didn't he?'

Harry was confused.

'Not sure I follow,' he said.

'Where was the van before?' Dave asked. 'At the moment, it's up on Cam Road, right? That's where it was found, and that's where it is. Hasn't moved any that I know of. But he's saying it was somewhere else.' He looked at the man opposite who, Harry noticed, had somehow shrunk in size. 'Aren't you, John?'

'Well, of course it was somewhere else,' Harry said. 'It's a campervan. Josh and Amber, they've been touring the country in it and our friend John here has, I think, been following them around a bit, haven't you, John?'

Harry turned his eyes back to Robertson, who gave a nervous nod.

'Not in a creepy way, though, I promise,' he said. 'I know it looks that way, I do, but it's not, it isn't, it's not what I mean, I'm just a fan, that's all, and ...'

Harry looked back at Dave.

'Read that to me again ...'

Dave complied.

Harry looked back at Robertson.

'What did you mean by that?' he asked. 'Not where the van is now? That's an odd way of putting it, now that Officer Calvert's pointed it out.'

Robertson squeezed his eyes shut, scratched his head, then opened them again and stared at Harry.

'It wasn't parked there the last time I saw them,' he said. 'That's what I mean. It was somewhere else, and then it wasn't, and I had to use my drone to find it, and when I did, I moved camp to be near them, didn't I? That's what I meant when I said that I've not seen them where the van is now. Because I haven't.'

'But it's there, up on the Cam Road,' Harry said. 'They drove it there, they parked it there, they even ate food there; I've seen it myself, John! With my own bloody eyes!'

'And I'm telling you, I've not seen them there, not once in the last two days.'

'And when did you get there, exactly?' Harry asked.

'I just told you that,' Robertson said. 'Two days ago. It took me a whole day to find them, except I haven't, because they're not there. It was the van that I found, but it wasn't right and so I stayed to keep an eye on things, hoping they'd return.'

Harry couldn't get his head around what he was hearing.

'If I've got this correct, then, you're saying that they were parked somewhere else, and you were camped out close by, right?'

'Yes,' Robertson said.

'Then they drove up here without you knowing, but you still managed to find them, and you've not seen them, correct?'

'Yes,' Robertson said. 'And no.'

'And no?' Harry repeated. 'How is any of that *and no*? And where were they parked before? Can you tell me that?'

'Of course I can!' said Robertson. 'There's a little track up out the back of that place with the dragon and the waterfall.'

'Dragon?' said Harry. 'Since when has Wensleydale had a dragon?'

'Hardraw Force, you mean?' said Dave, and Robertson gave a nod. 'The Green Dragon's the pub,' he then added.

'Can you take us there?' Harry asked. 'Show us where they were parked?'

'Yes, but they're not there. They're not anywhere! You have to find them!'

'I know that,' Harry said, 'because it's my bloody job!' Harry heard the growl in his voice, the snarl ripping at the edges of his words, tearing them to shreds. 'But what's bothering me right now, John, is that spying on them seems to be yours, doesn't it?'

'What?'

'A job, John, is that it?' Harry knew he was pushing now, but he had to because he wanted answers. 'You've all of this kit, and you've still not explained how you could afford any of it, when all evidence suggests that you can't. And by evidence, all I need to do is point over to that van of yours, because you either don't care, or you don't have the funds to pay for the tax and insurance, or indeed a decent bed for the night!'

'But I am a fan!'

'But are you just a fan, John? Or is there something else going on?' The idea that there was more to John than met the eye was something Harry couldn't shift, the expensive camera equipment not reconciling with everything else. 'Well? Is there?'

Harry waited for John to speak, but no answer came, the man's mouth bobbing open and closed, no words coming out. He went to say something more, to push John even harder, when he caught sight of the time on his watch.

'Bollocks ...'

'Something up?' Dave asked.

'Press conference,' Harry said, once again amazed by how quickly time was going, and how far away they still were from finding Josh and Amber. 'Starts in half an hour.'

'You best get shifting, then,' Dave said. 'We'll be fine, won't we, John?'

Harry saw Dave's wide smile cause Robertson to shrink even further.

'Call Jen,' he said. 'She's a DC, and when she arrives, I want you all to head out and have a look at this other place they parked up at and where John here set up his other camp. Doubt there's anything useful there, but it'll help us maybe add a bit more to our picture of what's going on, where Amber and Josh might be. And I'll be leaving Smudge with you as well, hope that's okay. Less chance of Fly getting into trouble if she's keeping him company.'

With Dave and Robertson back in Jim's Land Rover, Harry headed back down into Hawes to the press conference. For some reason, he couldn't shake the feeling that he was missing something, that what Robertson both had and hadn't been telling them was important, but that neither he nor Dave, really knew why.

TWENTY-THREE

Harry parked on the road leading down into Hawes from Gayle, the car park behind the primary school, not just full but overflowing. He then walked down into the centre of Hawes to find the crowds he'd pushed through earlier now seemingly larger, and with a great number of them milling around outside the entrance to the Market Hall.

Tempted as he was to just turn around and sneak away, he knew that wasn't an option. Walker would be inside, and Askew would no doubt be in his element. Then there was the small detail that he was the senior investigating officer in the search for Josh and Amber, so he had to show face. He would just be making sure, however, that the face he had on display, one which would turn most people off their dinner as it was, gave a very clear message: let the team get on with their job, and whatever you do, don't ask stupid bloody questions.

It also looked like a good number of those in the crowd had been busy with a little bit of handy craft. Wherever he looked, he saw banners and flags and placards flapping in the wind, some with their ink running, all of them expressing their creator's feelings, from the to-be-expected and numerous *We Love Jamber* signs, and variations on that theme, to a few that were more edgy, demanding *the truth.* There were even a few that were a little more left field, with Harry's eye immediately drawn to one showing a large line drawing of a flying saucer, the words *Jamber Knows We're Not Alone*, and another, clearly belonging to a conspiracy theory nutjob, which somehow managed to tie in the Illuminati, Big Pharma, the moon landing, and even the laughable notion of a hollow Earth, to Josh and Amber's disappearance.

Hunching up his shoulders, in some weak attempt to make himself anonymous, Harry edged through the crowd to the Market Hall. Most people let him through, but one or two stood in his way, demanding to know if he was a fan, why he was there, why he had any more right than they did to get closer to what was going on. A growl and a stare were enough to move them out of the way, and as he drew closer to the front of the building, he saw a couple of people he recognised, both in uniform, keeping the crowds at bay.

Detective Inspector Gordanian Haig, through sheer force of personality alone, had managed to keep everyone back, and when Harry arrived in front of her, he could not have been more pleased to see her. Jim was by her side and taking no crap from anyone, his Yorkshire accent thicker than usual, as he told people to stay back.

'And how are we today, Detective?' Gordy asked, a wry smile on her face.

'Oh, I'm just peachy,' Harry replied. 'A veritable ray of sunshine.'

'No change there, then,' said Jim.

'Change is over-rated.'

'Hey,' a voice barked from behind Harry, 'you can't just push through. We've been here for hours, you know because we're true fans. What makes you so special?'

Harry looked at Gordy, who had to turn her head away to hide her wry smile for a moment, clearly anticipating Harry's response.

Harry turned around to find himself face-to-face, not with a phone this time, but a GoPro camera. It was, for reasons Harry simply couldn't fathom, attached to some kind of elaborate chest rig worn by a young man wearing a jacket better suited to queuing for nightclubs than standing out in the rain. His ice-white hair, the ends of which were all dyed red, hung down in front of his face like thin icicles dipped in blood.

'This does,' Harry said, pulling out his ID.

The young man, who had stumbled back in shock and horror at being confronted by Harry's ruined face, pulled himself together enough to lean in and allow his camera to get a close-up look at the wallet in Harry's hand.

'Probably fake,' he said. 'But that's no surprise, is it? Whatever's going on behind those doors, it'll be fake news, won't it? Every bit of it. And we want the truth!' He then whipped around to the crowd behind him, raised his hands and shouted, 'We want the truth! We want the truth!'

To Harry's dismay, a few people joined in, and soon the chant had spread and was as deafening as it was ridiculous.

'You okay to stay out here and deal with this amount of stupid?' Harry asked, standing beside Gordy. 'There's a lot of it, rather more than I was expecting, actually.'

'What, this?' Gordy said. 'It's child's play. Get yourself inside and do what you need to do. We'll be fine, won't we, Jim?'

'No bother at all,' Jim said. 'I've worked sheep for years, remember? This is child's play.'

Harry gave a nod and turned to go into the hall, but as he did so, Gordy leaned in close, her voice a whisper.

'No news, then?' she asked.

'Oh, there's news,' Harry said. 'I just won't be sharing it with the press, not if I can help it.'

And with that, Harry headed up the steps and into the building, as behind him Gordy revealed her secret weapon, something she'd had hidden behind her back when he had arrived: a megaphone. Then, with Gordy's lilting Highland tones bellowing out across the crowd, he reached for the door in front of him, twisted the handle, and let himself in.

Harry was welcomed by the sound of voices suddenly hushed and chair legs scraping on the floor, as dozens of faces turned to see who was entering the room. He said nothing, gave no sign to indicate who he was or why he was there, and made his way down the side of the sitting masses, towards a table at the front. Sitting behind it was Detective Superintendent Walker, and at her side, Askew.

Walker stood up and met Harry halfway, taking him away to a corner of the hall.

'We need to talk,' she said.

'I know,' Harry replied. 'I've some new information and—'

Walker held up a hand, cutting Harry off.

'PCSO Coates just rang.'

Harry frowned.

'Liz called you rather than me? That's a little worrying.'

'Josh's parents are on their way,' Walker said. 'She mentioned how she had already been in communication with Amber's parents, been over to meet them, but had had no response from Josh's.'

'And now they're here?'

'On their way, as I said, but where exactly, we don't know.'

'You look concerned,' Harry said.

'Apparently, there's some friction between the parents.'

'Divorce you mean?'

Walker shook her head.

'No, not between Josh's parents themselves, but between hers and Josh's.'

'I don't understand.'

When Walker spoke again, her voice was hushed and grave.

'From what I understand with what little Liz told me, Josh's parents have been throwing around various accusations for months. Amber's parents said nothing about it. I think they just prefer to stay quiet, not make things worse, but these things have a habit of becoming that, no matter what you do, don't they?'

'What are these accusations, then?' Harry asked.

'It's all to do with that rather extraordinary lottery win,' Walker explained. 'Liz wasn't able to go into it in much detail, but from what I could gather, Josh's parents don't like Amber much at all. They've also been somewhat vocal about the winnings being Josh's alone, because he bought the ticket. Or so they claim.'

'Well, none of that makes me immediately suspicious at all, does it?' Harry said, sarcasm dripping from his lips. 'But what the hell has any of that to do with anything? Those two kids are out there somewhere, lost and in who knows what kind of trouble; the absolute last thing I care about is who's richer than who. Or is that whom? Never did understand that. I don't take kindly to anyone who thinks that money is what's important here. Because it isn't.'

'I agree,' said Walker. 'But you and I both know that money does funny things to people.'

'And we have no idea where Josh's parents are right now?'

Walker shook her head.

'Anything else?'

'No.'

Harry was quiet for a moment and cast his eyes over to the journalists patiently waiting for something to happen, but who were throwing questions at Askew who, Harry was surprised to see, was batting them away with a degree of professionalism he hadn't really expected.

'Then let's get this over and done with,' he said, and with Walker at his side, he marched over to the table.

TWENTY-FOUR

Harry dropped himself down between Askew and Walker.

'Having fun?' he asked the journalist.

'Is it always like this?' Askew asked.

'No, sometimes it's worse,' said Harry.

'But they won't shut up,' Askew said. 'No matter what I say, they just keep throwing out the most ridiculous questions.'

'Do they, now?' Harry said. 'And this surprises you, does it?'

'I've told them that we will take questions at the right time, that there's nothing else I can say at this time, that they need to be patient, and—'

Harry laughed.

'You told them to be patient? Really?'

'It's not too much to ask, is it?' said Askew.

'No, I've never thought that it was,' Harry said, 'but you know how people are. Now, do you have a sheet of paper I can borrow?'

'What?'

'Paper,' said Harry. 'A4, that kind of thing.'

Askew leant down to grab his bag, pulled out a thin pad, and handed Harry a sheet.

'What do you need it for?' he asked.

'Watch and learn,' Harry replied, turning to the journalists sitting in front of them.

For the first time since entering the hall, he realised just how many of them there were. He'd attended too many press conferences to remember, but this was already one of the biggest he had ever seen. Celebrity would always draw the crowds, for good or ill.

'Right then,' Harry said, standing up, the sheet of paper from Askew is in hand, as though about to read something very important from it. Which it was, because he'd been to enough of these things to know exactly what to say. Plus, he'd hastily prepared it all in his head on the way down from Gayle Beck.

'Is it true that Josh and Amber Hill are being held hostage?'

The question annoyed Harry immediately, and on so many levels, that he immediately wanted to wade through the journalists, find who had asked it, and throw them out the door. Whether he opened said door beforehand was neither here nor there; they'd be on the other side of it regardless.

Then came another question, and another, and soon they were being fired at him like darts.

'How much is the ransom?'

'Are there any other demands?'

'Is any of this linked to what happened in the Peak District?'

Harry hadn't a clue what the Peak District had to do with anything, but didn't have time to ponder on it as more voices called out.

'Do you know who the kidnappers are?'

'Do you know that some are linking this to the sighting of strange lights—?'

Harry held up a hand to quell the storm of questions crashing over him, but also to stop whoever was turning this into a discussion about aliens and UFOs.

'This is going to be short and to the point,' he said, and made a point of rustling the piece of paper in his hands. 'So, my advice is that you listen, because I'm not in the mood to answer questions,

especially such ridiculous ones like you've all just freely demon-
strated ...'

Walker gave a low cough.

Harry glanced down to see the DSup staring up at him with a
look he very much interpreted as *Stick to the script*. That he didn't
really have one was neither here nor there.

Harry turned back towards the journalists, then lowered his
eyes to the blank sheet of paper in his hands.

'As you are all aware, we are currently engaged in an intensive
search operation for Josh and Amber Hill,' he began, working hard
to keep his voice calm and smooth, and to sound as though what he
was saying was something he'd spent a good deal of time preparing
in advance. 'They were last seen five days ago, frequenting several
local pubs in the area. At this time, it remains unknown as to when
they departed from their campervan and their intended destination
is also unclear. Professional search and rescue teams have been
mobilised and are actively involved in the search efforts. At this
stage of the investigation, there is no immediate need for assistance
from the public with the search operation. However, we encourage
anyone who may have information, no matter how insignificant it
may seem, to come forward immediately. Information provided by
the public can play a crucial role in solving this case.'

Harry paused for a breather, then continued, again dropping
his eyes to the blank sheet of paper he was holding.

'We understand the deep concern and anxiety this situation
has caused, not only for the Hills' family, but also for the wider
community. Rest assured, we are committed to leaving no stone
unturned in our efforts to locate Josh and Amber Hill, and to
reunite them with their loved ones. We will provide regular
updates as the investigation progresses. We thank the local community for their cooperation and support during this difficult time.'

Harry sat down.

The journalists were all silent.

'Nice job,' said Walker. 'Very professional. You write that
yourself?'

'Of course.'

Harry handed the sheet of paper back to Askew, who stared at it baffled.

'You made that up?'

'I most certainly did not,' said Harry.

'But ...'

Harry sat back and waited for the questions to come. Hands jumped into the air, arms waved for attention, voices called out.

'You can leave if you want,' Walker said. 'I'll handle this.'

'You sure about that?' Harry asked.

'It's why I'm here, remember?' she said.

Harry wasn't about to wait around for Walker to change her mind, so he pushed his chair back and stood up, just as his phone rang. He answered it.

'Harry? It's Liz, we've just had a call from a walker out on the footpath below Hawes and they've—'

The door at the back of the hall burst open and in rushed a middle-aged couple, quickly followed by Gordy and a crush of people behind her, the noise enough to cut off whatever it was Liz had been about to say.

'What the bloody hell is going on?' Harry roared, as everyone in the room turned to see what was happening.

The man stepped forward, the woman stopping a few steps behind.

'My name is Edward Hill,' he said, 'and this is my wife, Kim.'

Even from a distance, Harry could see that they were both dressed somewhat more expensively than everyone else in the room.

Gordy stepped past Edward and caught Harry's eye.

'They pushed through,' she said. 'Wouldn't listen. Encouraged the crowd to follow them. Jim's still outside doing his best to make sure no one else gets in. He's got quite a bark on him, that lad, way scarier than he looks.'

Walking over to join her, Harry could see stress and barely held back anger, in the DI's eyes.

'Mr Hill,' Harry said. 'Perhaps we should head somewhere more private?'

Mr Hill stared at Harry for a moment, then turned to face the journalists.

'We have reason to believe that Amber has kidnapped our son, and we have come here to find him, to bring him home, and to have her arrested!'

Stunned, Harry remembered then that Liz was still on the phone, so he lifted it to his ear if only to ignore the ruckus that had immediately erupted after the man had spoken.

'Liz, I'll need to call you back,' he said, but Liz cut him off.

'Harry, we've a body ...'

TWENTY-FIVE

Harry's world stopped. He was aware of people around him, lots of shoving, the new arrivals, Mr and Mrs Hill, at the centre of it, as though everything else was spinning around them in a whirlwind, but he was separate to it, detached by what Liz had just said.

'Can you say that again?'

'A body, Harry,' Liz repeated. 'The call came in from a hiker. It's the footpath out the back of Hawes.'

'Which one?'

'The one that heads out over the bridge over the Ure. You can go to Sedbusk that way, or Simonstone Hall, and Hardraw. If you want a good walk out and a swim, you can even make your way over to Cotter Force, but that's a longer trip.'

Liz then provided Harry with the exact location.

As Harry was listening, someone shoved into him, pushing him out of the way to get closer to Mr and Mrs Hill who, Harry thought, seem to be relishing the attention. He saw microphones in the air, cameras, bright lights flashing. And then he heard Gordy's voice bellowing out through the megaphone. But her words were lost to him, his mind only focusing on one thing and imagining who it was, what it could mean ... a body ...

'Where are you?'

'The office,' Liz said.

'Call Matt and Jadyn right now,' Harry instructed. 'Give them the location and tell them to meet me there.'

'Already have,' said Liz. 'Sent them a message anyway; they're already on their way. I knew you were tied up, so thought it best to get someone over there immediately.'

'Well done, Liz,' Harry said. 'Quick thinking.'

'What about Dave and Jen?'

'Busy,' said Harry. 'Is the hiker still at the location?'

'Yes,' Liz said. 'Close by, anyway. Took shelter under a crag and a few trees. You'll see him, I'm sure.'

'Tell him I'm on my way right now.'

Harry hung up to find the room still, and standing beside him, Detective Superintendent Walker.

'She's quite something,' Walker said, gesturing at Gordy.

Gordy was herding everyone who wasn't a journalist, Mr and Mrs Hill, or the police, back out through the door.

'What did she say to them?' Harry asked.

'You mean you didn't hear?'

'No,' Harry said.

'Well, I don't think I caught all of it, mainly because I don't speak Gaelic, but whatever it was, it was certainly enough to have them all shut up sharpish and do what they were told.'

When the hall was finally clear of the crowd, Gordy slammed the door, bracing her back against it for a moment before stepping away.

'Do you need me in here?' she asked.

Harry took her and Walker to one side.

'We've a body,' he said, his voice quiet so that he wouldn't be overheard. 'Out by the river. I'm heading there now.'

'Then we'll deal with this,' Walker said. 'By which I mean, we'll get Mr and Mrs Hill out of the clutches of the press and find out exactly what they mean. Talk about throwing a grenade!'

Harry looked over at the main door and could hear muffled shouts from behind it.

'Don't suppose either of you know a way to get out of here that doesn't involve pushing my way through that lot out there, do you?'

'Actually, yes,' said Gordy. 'There's a door to the car park at the rear of the building. No footpath though, so you'll need to scramble over a wall.'

Leaving Gordy and Walker in charge, Harry wasted no time in exiting the building where Gordy had directed. Making sure no one spotted him from out on the road, he climbed over a wall, dashed across a short area of scrubland, and on into the fields behind. Over another wall, and he was in the car park behind the primary school and running back to the Police Land Rover.

Jumping into the vehicle and slamming the door, Harry noticed that the rain had stopped. The sky was still angry and grey, but nothing was falling out of it. He decided against taking this as a good omen, because experience had told him there was no such thing, and that if at any point you thought things were about to go your way, that was just when life snapped around and bit you on the arse.

Aware that driving a Police Land Rover through town would undoubtedly bring too much attention to what he was doing and where he was going, Harry instead headed out towards Appersett.

The road was wet, and the tyres skipped a little as he took a corner with a little too much enthusiasm, only to then be met by water, his way cut off by a flood. It was something he should have expected, and he felt sure he had heard mention of it at some point, but he also wasn't too concerned, ploughing on into the deep water swilling between the drystone walls lining the road. Harry soon built up a decent bow wave out front, but he made sure to keep the speed constant but not too high.

Driving into Appersett, he headed over the bridge and soon after took a right, throwing him into another flood, though this one was considerably shallower. On he went, arriving in Hardraw, briefly remembering his trip there with Grace, when she had somehow managed to persuade him to go for a swim under the falls. That made him think about their brief text exchange, and then wonder again about giving Grace a call. Now was clearly not the time, but perhaps, later, when he was able to steal a moment, he'd ring her, just to see how she was. Maybe see if they could get together for a pint at the Fountain, that kind of thing? But what if that was the wrong thing to do? What if she needed more space? What if he needed more space? And what was all this space anyway? Harry was sure he had no idea what to do with it; every bit of it was Grace-shaped after all, and that really didn't help.

Leaving Hardraw, Harry soon took a right, the road dropping into a steep hill, to flatten out at the bottom and then cross the river. This was where he knew the road would be flooded, because it always was, and true to form, the river had risen high enough to cover it, the fields now a shimmery, rippling expanse of water, reflecting the drifting clouds above.

Someone was standing in the road.

Harry slowed down, wound down his window, and leaned out.

'Where?' Harry asked.

Matt pointed across the fields.

'Caught up in an eddy,' he said. 'A walker spotted it, behind some bushes. Thought it was an animal, realised it wasn't, called it in immediately.'

'Do I need to ask why they were out walking in the first place when the weather's been as it has?'

'I wouldn't bother,' said Matt. 'As we say round here, there's nowt so strange as folk.'

'And that's what *you* say around here, is it?'

'It is.'

'And by "we," you mean you.'

Matt smiled.

'How's things in town? Liz said it's all gone a bit mad.'

'Let's just say I had to sneak away and that we're best to keep what we're doing nice and quiet for now.'

Harry turned off the engine and climbed out.

'Jadyn's with the person who found the body?'

'He is,' said Matt. 'I'll take you there.'

Harry followed Matt across the road and through a gate, the now vast expanse of the river Ure to his left as he trudged through huge puddles and thick mud. The weather was still holding, the sun even managing to pierce the clouds with bright shards that stabbed into the earth and cast small pools of gold on the water.

Matt led Harry over to a small outcrop of rocks, over which huge trees hung. He saw Jadyn, who waved over to him. At his side was another figure, standing not even up to his shoulders.

'Afternoon, Boss,' said Jadyn. 'This is Mr Williams.'

Mr Williams held up a hand to stop Jadyn from saying anything else.

'It's alright, lad, I can speak for myself. Have been doing for the last eighty-two years, not about to change now.'

Mr Williams was dressed in the kind of outdoor gear Harry was sure he'd only ever seen in documentaries about early explorers attempting mountains with nothing more than hemp rope, hobnail boots, and pluck. He was wearing a faded blue canvas smock covered in patches, knee-length trousers, long thick socks, and hefty leather boots, and was carrying a canvas rucksack that put Harry in mind of the gear carried by the Commandos during World War Two. In his hand was a hefty wooden staff that would've made Gandalf jealous.

'I'm DCI Grimm,' said Harry.

'Best I be taking you straight there, then,' said Mr Williams, not allowing Harry any time to say anything else. 'Come on.'

He then shot off at such a pace that to keep up, Harry was almost at a jog.

'He's like a bloody mountain goat,' Harry muttered to Matt, who was racing along beside him.

'He's doing the Pennine Way,' said Matt. 'Got caught out by the weather, so he's been in Hawes for a few days. He was just out here having a bit of a run apparently. Said he needed to keep his legs in shape and not let them get lazy.'

'Running? Dressed like that?'

Harry was stunned.

'He's actually running the whole of the Pennine Way, would you believe,' said Matt, as Harry stared at Mr Williams, who was carrying the staff over his shoulder. 'Uses that huge stick of his to help him on the steep bits.'

'He's not heard of modern hiking poles, then?'

'Oh, he's heard of them,' said Matt. 'He just thinks they're rubbish.'

Soon, they were standing in another field, staring out across flood water being fed by the burst banks of the Ure. Where the wind was catching it, the surface danced with waves, the spray lifting into the air in swirls. Harry watched a brace of ducks land gracefully, saw a heron standing in the shallows, and above a kite called. It was a scene of pastoral beauty utterly ruined by what was floating only a few metres away from where he stood.

The body, as far as he could tell, was fully clothed, though the feet were bare. Whether it was male or female, he couldn't see with the body floating face down in the water.

'Ambulance is on its way,' Jadyn said. 'You think it's one of them, Amber and Josh?'

'Only one way to find out,' Harry said, pulling out his phone.

TWENTY-SIX

Harry was standing with Margaret Shaw, the district surgeon, and her daughter, Rebecca Sowerby, the pathologist. Darkness was creeping over the tops of the fells to swamp the Dale in its gloom. He looked down at the body lying in front of them, the shape of it brought out in stark, awful relief by the blinding light now flooding the scene from the SOC team's lamps.

There had been no need to call for divers, the body only a walk away through thigh-deep water. On putting the call through to the Scene of Crime team, however, Harry had resisted the urge to go over and make sure it wasn't about to get swept away and sent further downstream. Thankfully, there had been no need, as the branch of a tree hanging over the bushes it was caught in was resting over it, a grey wooden arm protecting it from further harm.

Matt and Jadyn had sealed the area off with tape, with Jadyn setting himself up as Scene Guard, dutifully ticking off everyone who arrived on the site. Matt had quickly driven Mr Williams back to where he was staying, over at the Green Dragon in Hardraw, and given him explicit instructions to say nothing to anyone about what he had found, not until he heard from someone on the team.

The SOC team had arrived an hour or so later, though there had been no sign of an ambulance as yet. Harry didn't mind; it was better that it was used to help the living, than transporting the dead, he thought.

The photographer had been none too keen to wade in and do his job and Harry had delighted in watching the man be ordered to suck it up and just get on with it by Sowerby, who was clearly in no mood for hanging about.

'I'm going to give you a choice,' she'd said. 'Either wade in there yourself, and get wet, or I'll throw you in where it's deeper. And looking at the river, we'll definitely need to call the divers to fetch you out, once we've located you that is, probably three, maybe four miles downstream. You know what, if I throw you in now, you might even make it to Aysgarth Falls before sundown; what do you say?'

The photographer had complained a little and grumbled a lot, but had done his job, then headed off, shivering all the way, and muttering under his breath about sending various medical bills to Sowerby if he ended up with pneumonia and was unable to work. Then his vehicle had died, and after a lot of swearing, he eventually gave in to fate and was now sitting in his vehicle waiting for a breakdown truck to turn up and help him on his way again.

With the photos done, the SOC team got to the task of retrieving the body, and they did so with as much dignity as they could. Unfortunately, one of the team, on taking hold of the body's feet, tripped on something and slipped with the quietest of cries under the surface of the water, returning seconds later in a spray of water and swearing, like the world's most unterrifying underwater monster.

At last, the body reached the shore and was moved carefully away from any further danger from the flood waters and laid on its back. Margaret had then stepped forward.

'Well, I don't think anyone here needs me to tell them that whoever this poor sod is, they're very much dead. But thanks for calling me out in the middle of something.'

'And what was that?' Sowerby asked, looking at her mum, her head cocked to one side.

'Sloe gin, if you really want to know,' answered Margaret. 'I had a freezer drawer full of the things from last year and, being as it's the season, and also because I've not collected any this year, I thought, why not?'

'Why not indeed?' said Matt. 'Don't forget me at Christmas now, will you, Margaret?'

Margaret said, 'I've not just made gin, either. Decided to go a bit off-piste as it were. I've also done vodka, spiced rum, brandy, and bourbon. Bought a load of cheap bottles from the supermarket over in Leyburn. Got some very funny looks, I must say, but I'm used to that.'

'Sloe bourbon?' said Matt. 'Wonder what that tastes like?'

'Me too, actually.' Margaret shrugged. 'I'm going to guess at horrendous, but it'll be fun finding out, won't it?' She turned to Harry. 'How's that girlfriend of yours, then? Not seen you for a while, so I want all the juicy gossip.'

'There's no gossip, juicy or otherwise,' said Harry, his eyes on Sowerby, who had moved over to the body and was kneeling beside it.

'Well, of course there's gossip,' Margaret said. 'There's always gossip, otherwise, what's the point in my even being here? Other than the obvious, but you know what I mean.' She sidled up close and punched Harry on the arm. 'So, come on, out with it, Harry. An old girl like me lives for it, you know.'

'You're not old.'

'And you're not going to get away with keeping shtum.'

'Definitely male,' Sowerby said, her voice cutting the conversation in two. 'Caucasian. I'd say aged anywhere between twenty and thirty, but I'd put him at the lower end. Hard to tell right now with the amount of damage the body has sustained, as well as from being in the water. Doesn't look like he's been in all that long, though.'

'Pretend none of us know what happens to a body left in a river,' said Harry.

Sowerby stood.

'Well, we won't know anything really until we get it back to the mortuary, and you can tell a lot from things like aquatic life found in the body, that kind of thing. Decomposition, though, speeds up or slows down depending on the water's temperature, and I'd hazard a guess at it being cold enough to put the brakes on.'

'There's no way of telling how long he's been in there, then?'

'Well, if you take the water temperature into consideration, the way the weather's been, I don't think it's very long. Looks too fresh. No longer than twenty-four hours, but that's just an observation for now.'

'What about those cuts on his feet?' Matt asked. 'And, well, you know, the rest of it, like.'

The rest of it was one way of describing what they were looking at, Harry thought, and perhaps to be that general about it made the most sense.

When they'd first spotted the body, it had been a thing of candle-white skin in clothes floating in the ebb and flow of water from the river flooding the field. On bringing it closer, however, the true horror of it had been made clear.

Harry had seen a good number of bodies dragged from deep water. Most were those whose lives had become so unbearable they'd gone for the ultimate way out and taken their own lives. Others were accidents, drunks stumbling home after a late night, a trip and a slip and a splash and that was that. Very few had ever looked like this, even the small number that had been dumped in the water on purpose or had suffered a violent death close to the water's edge and fallen in, their last breaths filled with the thick blackness of a canal. This ... this was different.

The body was a mess, the limbs resting at every wrong angle possible. The chest, on which Harry could see deep cuts and gashes, looked strangely flat, like it had been crushed. The face was untouched, but for now, Harry kept himself from looking at it too long, as he listened to what Sowerby had to say.

'Most likely the extensive damage we can see is from being bounced around in the river for a while,' said the Pathologist. 'You see, when a body decomposes, gases build up in the body cavity and it becomes buoyant and can float to the surface, then sink, then bob up again repeatedly.'

'Wouldn't it look a little more swollen, though?' Harry asked.

'Again, that's something that makes me think he's not been in the water for very long,' Sowerby replied. 'Also, he's still fully clothed, isn't he? The shirt he's wearing looks ripped and cut, but it's buttoned up a bit and on him still. Same with his trousers. Clothing can become easily separated from a body over time, like his shoes and socks, for example, which makes it even more difficult to carry out an adequate identification.'

Harry was listening to Sowerby, but at the same time, he was very aware of something else, an evidence bag in his pocket. He didn't want to take it out and look at it, but he knew he had to.

'Is it okay if I come over?' he asked.

In answer, Sowerby waved him over, dropping to a crouch once again, and leaning in for a closer look at the body.

Harry approached the body as carefully as he could, keen to give the poor lad some respect as he did so. Drawing near, he tried to avoid looking at the face, but no matter what he did, his eyes were drawn to it, to the long hair covering it in sodden strands, to the waxy, pale skin of his cheeks and the bloodless lips parted just enough to show the white of his teeth.

Reaching Sowerby, he pulled the evidence bag out.

'Everything okay?' he asked, realising that Sowerby seemed oddly quiet now and was still next to the body, thoughtful.

'His feet,' she said, pointing at them with a gloved hand.

'What about them? Thought you said the damage was from the river, his shoes and socks ripped off by the water? Not much to protect them as the water tumbled him around, is there?'

'I did say that, I know, but ...'

'But what?'

Sowerby was quiet for a moment, then pointed at the body's chest.

'Those cuts there,' she said. 'I'll need a closer look when I get him back to the mortuary, but you can see how they're deep and straight, and that, well, it's not right, is it?'

'You tell me,' said Harry, wondering where Sowerby was going with this, the twist in his stomach giving him a clear idea.

'Could be an anomaly, but I can't see how.'

'What are you trying to say?' Harry asked.

Sowerby rubbed her eyes, yawned.

'If those cuts were done by being knocked against sharp rocks, or something submerged beneath the water's surface, they'd be more jagged, like rips and tears,' Sowerby said. 'By the body crashing into them and being twisted and tumbled around. But those? They don't look like that at all, do they? Like I said, maybe it's an anomaly, the exception to the rule, but ...'

'I don't like it when people leave that word floating,' said Harry. 'But what? Get to the point.'

Sowerby lifted her eyes to stare at Harry, and her look only made the sense of dread in his gut twist even tighter.

'Those cuts to his shirt, they're straight, too,' Sowerby continued, 'like it, and the flesh beneath it, has been sliced open. Now, unless this river here is riddled with razor-sharp rocks capable of doing exactly that, then—'

'They were done deliberately,' said Harry, finishing her sentence. 'But we can't tell that from here, can we? You still need to have a closer look, get the body on the slab, right?'

Sowerby stood slowly, as though it weighed on her terribly.

'You sure about that? Because I've done this job for years, and I'm not, not at all.'

'What about everything else?' Harry asked.

'Anything specific?'

'The fact that his chest looks caved in would be a good place to start,' Harry said. 'Looks like something crushed him.'

'Rivers are violent things,' said Sowerby. 'There's every chance he was trapped under a boulder that then rolled on him, something like that.'

'Maybe,' said Harry, scratching his chin, frowning. 'Doesn't look right though, does it?'

Once again, Sowerby fell silent. When she spoke again, she asked, 'What's in the bag?'

'Photos,' said Harry. 'I know we'll need the parents to carry out a proper identification ...'

He removed one of the photos from the bag and lifted it for both of them to see.

For a moment, neither of them said a word, caught as they were between the photo of a young man, his face cheek-to-cheek with the love of his life, both of them smiling, full of so much hope and happiness, and the pale thing in front of them on the wet ground, an empty shell already rotting.

'That's that, then,' Sowerby said.

Harry shook his head, unable to do anything about the waves of rage and despair crashing over him.

'What a bloody waste,' he said, then turned away from the body and walked back towards Matt.

TWENTY-SEVEN

'So, what do you want to do?'

Matt's question floated in the air just long enough for Harry to realise the silence was getting awkward. He wasn't quite sure what to say, because what they were dealing with was unlike any other investigation he'd ever been a part of. This was a celebrity, this was the press being camped out on their doorstep from the get-go, this was something that could, very soon, spread so far and wide that the implications of it made him shudder.

'We do this as we would do anything else,' he said as, at long last, an ambulance arrived, parking up on the road. 'We follow procedure, stick to it, don't get distracted. We've got a body, and it matches what we know about Josh Hill. Now that the ambulance is here, Sowerby and her team can crack on with getting the poor lad away. We need to speak to Josh's parents, have them carry out a formal identification.'

'It's definitely him, then?' Jadyn said.

'All we can say right now is that we've found a body that matches Josh's description,' Harry said. 'We've all seen the damage caused to it. After talking it through with Sowerby, I have a very strong suspicion that it was deliberate.'

'Not the river, then?' asked Jadyn.

'Some of it, yes, but all of it?' Harry shook his head. 'Not a chance.'

'What do you want to do about the circus in town?' Matt asked.

'I'd like to see if we can't get Josh's parents away from there with as little fuss as possible,' Harry said. 'They can then follow Sowerby back to the mortuary and carry out an identification. There's obviously still the chance it's not Josh, and we need to bear that in mind when we deal with them.'

'Leave that with me,' said Matt.

Harry had other ideas.

'Gordy's at the Market Hall with Walker, doing her best to keep everything under control,' he explained. 'If it's all the same with you, I'd like her to work with the parents on this; she's the most experienced in that area, and that's what we need right now. The rest of the team will be with me on the investigation.'

'We already have one suspect,' said Matt. 'That photographer.'

'He's with Jen and Dave,' said Harry. 'He's taken them to another site that he says he saw Josh and Amber at before they parked up on Cam Road.'

Sowerby came over.

'There's nothing else we can do here,' she said. 'We need to get him back so that I can do the post-mortem. Did I hear mention of parents?'

'Josh Hill's parents are in town,' Harry said. 'Reckon it makes sense to get the identification done sooner rather than later. Only there's a problem with that.'

'There is?'

'Because of what we've found here, we've another crime scene for your team to examine.'

The campervan had drifted out of Harry's mind, the space it had occupied momentarily taken up by the awful sight of the body. It was only when he'd held up the photograph of Josh that he'd then thought about it, but it was the mention of Robertson that had it flash brightly in his mind. Because if those marks on the body's feet and chest were deliberate, then ...

'What other crime scene?' Sowerby asked.

Harry lifted an arm to point a finger across Hawes and up into the fells beyond.

'Actually, there's three,' he said.

Sowerby's face fell.

'And you're telling me this now? Three other sites? Bloody hell, Harry, this is going to be some night.'

'It is,' Harry said, 'but it's a hell of a lot longer for Amber, Josh's wife, who's still missing and, until we know otherwise, alive.

'I'm listening,' said Sowerby.

'Up until a few moments ago, this was a MISPER. Now it isn't. And if that is Josh—and we all know it is—then our search for Amber is even more urgent. You said yourself those marks on him look deliberate.'

'Not exactly,' Sowerby clarified. 'What I actually said was that some of the damage didn't look as though it had occurred through him being submerged in a river and knocked against sharp rocks.'

'As far as I'm concerned, that's enough,' said Harry. 'I'm not about to hang around waiting for confirmation when there's someone else out there that needs finding.'

'But three other crime scenes? How is that even possible?'

Harry looked over to Matt. 'I need you to take Sowerby and her team to the campervan, show them that rough camp we found, and where Robertson parked up. I want his vehicle torn apart.'

Harry saw dismay in Sowerby's eyes, but not at the job, more at the world.

'What the hell's going on, Harry?'

'Right now, I've absolutely no idea,' Harry said. 'But someone knows, don't they? Someone knows why that young lad's life was snuffed out, violently, too, I might add. And my guess is that someone is a hell of a lot closer than any of us may realise.'

'You can't mean local, surely?' Matt said.

'What I mean,' said Harry, 'is that whoever did it, they're here, watching what's happening, fully aware of where we are and what we're doing. This isn't a random act of violence. There's too much going on for it to be that. They killed Josh somewhere out there, and not too far away either, considering how the river's not done much to him. My guess right now is that they dumped him in the water in the hope the flood would sweep him away and that would be that. Maybe they even hoped that when he was eventually found, he'd be in such a state that whatever had happened to him, whatever they'd done to him, would be lost for good, and the whole thing written off as a tragic accident.'

'But why kill him in the first place?' asked Jadyn.

'The hows and the whys are what we're going to do everything within our means to find out,' answered Harry. 'Amber is still out there somewhere. We don't know if she's alive, but until we know otherwise, that's going to be our assumption. That means from here on in, we have two tasks: find Amber, and find Josh's killer. Odds are, we do one, and the other will follow shortly after. Understood?'

No one argued.

'Good,' said Harry. 'Then let's do what we do best.'

'And what's that?' asked Sowerby.

'Find the bastard,' said Harry.

TWENTY-EIGHT

With Sowerby's team duly sent to the various crime scenes, including the photographer who was not best pleased that his vehicle was fixed just in time for him to be sent out with them, Harry was back in the Land Rover and had put a call in to Gordy. Matt and Jadyn were with Sowerby, Liz and Jim were on their way to join them, and the ambulance was already driving down the dale to the mortuary with the body. Now all they had to do was somehow get the parents away from Hawes to go and identify it. Gordy had accepted the task without question, advising Harry to leave it with her, and that taking the parents away from what was happening would be far easier than he suspected.

'How's that, then?' he asked. 'I know I only saw them for the briefest of moments, but they seemed fairly keen to get all the attention they could. They're not going to leave easily, and not without reason, either.'

'I'm going to tell them the truth, Harry, plain and simple.'

'Are you sure that's the best approach?' Harry asked, not entirely convinced.

'They've got a choice,' said Gordy. 'If the body found in the river is their son, they can treat him with the dignity and respect and love that he deserves, and make sure that news of his passing is shared only with close family first.'

'Or?'

'Or they can parade him around like some morbid freak show for the masses. And when I say they've got a choice, I'm not going to give them one. My vehicle is parked round the side of the hall. We'll be out of Hawes before anyone's realised we've gone.'

'What about the crowds?'

Harry heard the faintest of chuckles down the line.

'We've managed to sort out a little distraction.'

'That sounds as cunning as it does worrying.'

Gordy said, 'I wanted to disperse them anyway, and with everything that's going on, I came up with a plan. And this gives me a solid excuse to enact it. Walker approves.'

'And what plan is this?' Harry asked.

'Well, just so that you're aware, there might have been a report of a gas leak in the centre of town. Not a bad one, not so bad that there's a risk of everything blowing up, but certainly bad enough to make it vital that everyone head back to where they're staying, or leave town immediately so that it can be dealt with.'

'No one will believe that.'

'They'll believe the Fire Brigade, though, won't they?' said Gordy. 'They're having a practice night down at the station and positively jumped at the chance to carry out a drill like this. Their job is to minimize the risk to human life, so they'll have to evacuate the area. Think of all those flashing lights, the sirens ... It'll be quite a sight.'

Despite everything, Harry had to smile.

'Did the parents say any more about what they were banging on about Amber kidnapping their son? I mean, I've heard some bollocks in my time, Gordy, but that was something else.'

'They seem to know a fair bit about what's been going on,' Gordy said. 'But then that's social media for you, isn't it? Everyone knows everything, and most of it's nonsense.'

'So, where were they when Liz tried to contact them, then?'

'How do you mean?'

'Amber's parents were here as soon as they could be, but Josh's parents? The first we heard from them at all was when we were about to do the press conference. Liz tried to contact them I don't know how many times, but nothing, and then they just turned up, right in the middle of everything. Dressed like film stars, too, like they'd stopped off for a makeover and a spray tan on the way.'

'Suspicious?'

'Just plain bloody odd,' said Harry. 'If this is their son, then I honestly don't know how they're going to react.'

'I'll keep you posted,' said Gordy.

'Do that,' Harry replied.

Call over, the next thing Harry needed to do was check on Dave and Jen, and how they were getting on with Robertson. Evening had now settled in, the fells no longer visible against the thick tar of night. A quick text with Jen and he had directions and a location, so he did a swift U-turn and headed back up the hill, taking a left towards Hardraw.

Just out of the village, Harry took a right up a thin, rough track, and was immediately reminded of Cam Road. It was obvious that Josh and Amber had a liking for being off the beaten path, and who could blame them? Much better to be out in the open, to really experience the Dales, than surround yourself with crowds.

The lane ran straight for a mile or so, before hanging left along the side of a drystone wall, to then drift away from it gradually, as it crept upwards into the darkness beyond. The headlights of the Land Rover did little to push back the darkness, even on full beam, and Harry was struck by just how lonely the fells and moors could be, even with the twinkling of lights from houses far below.

Following the lane, the one good thing was that the rain was still holding off. So much so in fact, Harry was inclined to think that perhaps it had actually stopped, that the storm had either blown itself out or buggered off somewhere else; either was fine.

The road took several twists and turns, and Harry was acutely aware at one point of a steep ravine dropping off to his left. He took things slower then, concerned that one bad thump of the front wheels and he would tumble down it to land in a mangled heap far below, no doubt upside down in a raging torrent, too, just for good measure.

Just when Harry was beginning to think the lane, which was just a rubble-strewn track, would have him over in Swaledale before he knew where he was, a flash of light caught his attention. He headed for it and found Jen standing in the middle of the track waiting for him.

Harry stopped, and climbed out.

'What've we got?'

'Not much, I'm afraid,' said Jen, 'but it does look like they were here.'

'And you can tell that in this darkness?'

'We've checked the site against their social media posts,' Jen explained. 'They've not geo-located any of the recent ones, and I'm guessing they've done that to stop being followed or harassed by their fans, but this area matches what's on there.'

Jen lifted her phone and Harry looked at the screen as she scrolled through some photos. Harry recognised Amber and Josh, the campervan, but the surroundings didn't seem to have much detail at all.

'There can't be enough in any of those to confirm anything,' he said.

'Rock formations, the track, so there's enough,' said Jen, slipping her phone back into a jacket pocket.

'Dave with Robertson, then?'

'And the dogs,' said Jen, 'who, I have to say, are having the best time together.'

'You mean they've been a pair of idiots?'

'Exactly that.'

'Sometimes I think I should follow your lead and get a lizard instead.'

'Steve's very demanding,' warned Jen. 'And he's still not much of a fan of Jadyn. He's tolerating him now, I think, so that's progress.' Then she added, 'Sounds like it was rough down at the river.'

'Not the best,' said Harry. 'Gordy's sorting things out with the parents, taking them over to identify the body. Matt and Jadyn are with the SOC team at the other sites.'

'Long night for everyone, then.'

Harry walked over to where Jim's Land Rover was parked, and behind it Jen's own vehicle. Dave was in the driving seat with John Robertson next to him.

'How are we all doing, then?' Harry asked, opening the passenger door.

Between Dave and John, two furry heads appeared.

'All good here,' said Dave. 'Learning a lot about our friend here.'

Harry looked at Robertson.

'Really?'

'No,' said Dave. 'He's been quiet as a mouse since we arrived. Hardly said a word. Good with the dogs, though, so that's something.'

Harry stared at Robertson for a moment. He looked rather pathetic, his shoulders slumped, tiredness in his eyes. And as he did so, he brought up the hideously recent memory of what had been found at the river.

Harry pulled the door wide open and stepped back.

'Out,' he said. 'Now.'

TWENTY-NINE

'What?'

'Out,' Harry repeated, ignoring the wild panic he saw in Robertson's eyes. 'Now.'

'Why? What are you going to do?'

'I'm not going to do anything. Out!'

Robertson cowered.

'I've done nothing wrong, I promise. I shouldn't have taken those photos, I know that, but I'm just worried, that's all. I want to help, but I can't. Please don't hurt me!'

'What? Why the hell would I want to hurt you?'

'Because they—' Robertson's voice broke, and he looked up at Harry. 'Have you found them? Is that it? I tried to find them, but I didn't know where they were. They just disappeared!'

Harry said nothing, just waited.

Robertson eased himself out of the Land Rover, almost falling to the ground as he did so.

'We're going to take a little walk,' Harry said.

'You are going to hurt me! You're going to push me over a cliff or into a bog, aren't you? Please, you can't, my dad, he needs me. I can't go missing, please!'

'Your dad?' Harry said. 'Look, John, please, just walk with me for a moment. That's all I'm asking.'

Harry gestured in front of the Land Rover to where the track was lit by the headlights.

At last, Robertson moved.

Harry led him far enough away so that they could talk in private, Jen passing them as she went back to her own vehicle. Harry knew they would all be hungry, but that was the way with this line of work; sometimes, you just had to go without.

'There, you see? Not so difficult, was it?' Harry said.

Robertson shook his head.

'You're not going to beat me up?'

'Bloody hell, John,' said Harry. 'For the last time, no, I'm not. Why would you even think that?'

Robertson looked like he was about to say something but offered no answer.

'You mentioned your dad just then,' Harry said. 'Is he back in Lincolnshire?'

'I live with him,' Robertson said. 'Have done since Mum died a few years ago. He's ill, you see. She used to do everything for him and now he's only got me.'

'And you're up here,' said Harry. 'Spying on a couple of young celebrities who recently came into money. Is that why you're here? To see if they'll give you some of it? They've plenty going spare from what I hear, and my guess is they've had a fair number of begging letters already.'

Harry knew he was pushing buttons here, but he was trying to get a rise out of Robertson. And the mention of his father had given him something to use.

'Why would I beg for money?'

'Beg, steal, doesn't really matter in the end, does it? It's all the same to some people,' Harry said. 'They've got loads of money and, after what you just said, I'm guessing you need some yourself.'

'Of course I do,' said Robertson, 'but I'm not up here to steal anything from them, am I? Why would I do that?'

'You tell me, John,' Harry said. 'You've got all of that expensive gear to spy on them. Maybe you're a photographer looking for a photo or two that you can sell to the papers, maybe use as blackmail, something nice and saucy perhaps?'

Harry did his best to ignore that he'd just used the word *saucy*.

'I'd never do that!'

'You sure about that?'

'Yes!'

At this, Harry decided to push harder, and quickly, still very much focused on finding Amber.

'You're lying, John, I can smell it!'

John protested, but Harry ignored him.

'You're lying about everything. You followed Amber and Josh all the way here, spied on them, and you know where they are because you kidnapped them for their money! How many photos did you take, John? Did you send them to the parents, is that it? A little letter and a ransom demand? How much did you ask for? One, maybe two million? By the looks of things, you need it. And then things went wrong, didn't they, John? Something bad happened, and you had to take action. Josh tried to escape, and you stopped him, but you went too far and now Josh is dead, and you're worried about what to do with Amber.'

John was screaming at Harry to stop, his hands over his ears, but Harry wasn't about to.

'How did you do it, John? Did you kill him first before you dragged him into the river? Did you hope we wouldn't find him? Because we did. And where is Amber? Where have you locked her up? Some old barn out on the moor? Maybe a mine, is that it?'

'I didn't kill Josh! I didn't kill anyone! I couldn't! I just couldn't! Stop! You have to stop!'

'You could've just sold all that camera gear, couldn't you?' said Harry. 'That would've been a start. Sell that, use the money to get yourself cleaned up, help your dad, get a real job, something regular, instead of whatever the hell this is that you're doing.'

'Photography is a real job. It's what I get paid for!'

Harry was about to continue pressing, but what Robertson had just said caught him up sharp, as had the note of indignation in the man's voice.

'What was that?'

'I'm a photographer and a bloody good one,' Robertson said, some real fight in his voice for the first time. And, Harry noticed, perhaps even an echo of the pride he'd once had in himself. 'It's just that the life got to me. I found myself at the bottom of too many bottles, at the end of too many white lines, if you know what I mean. Then Mum died and I had to move home, and everything spiralled.'

'And just what the hell has that got to do with you being here?'

Robertson didn't answer.

'You said ... You said that I killed Josh, that I know where Amber is. I didn't and I don't.'

This time, Harry stayed quiet.

'Why would you say that? Why would you even think ...'

Robertson's voice faded, his face fell, and he stumbled back.

'Oh God ... no ... it can't be true ...'

'We found a body a few hours ago,' Harry said. 'It matches Josh's description. Obviously, the parents will need to carry out a formal identification to be sure, but between you and me, I don't think there's any doubt. We now have a team looking through everything, the campervan, your own little campsite, and that pigsty of a van you own. Everything, John. So, if there's something you need to tell me ...'

Robertson stared up at Harry, tears in his eyes.

'What am I going to tell them? I was supposed to keep an eye on them. That's what they paid me to do!'

'Who paid you to do what? What are you talking about?'

Robertson went quiet again.

'No, I can't tell you. They'll do it again. *He'll* do it again, like he did before, after what happened in the Peak District, only worse. He won't stop, he'll kill me!'

Now Harry really was confused. One minute he was pushing

Robertson on what he already knew, which wasn't much, not much that made sense anyway, trying to get him to say something, anything, that would be of use. And the next, the man was cowering in front of him, seemingly terrified for his life. But why? Who the hell was he so scared of? And why was he mentioning the Peak District? He'd heard that before, Harry realised, trying to remember when. And then he had it. The words shouted at him from the crowd when he had been accosted by Askew outside the community centre.

'Who'll kill you?' Harry asked. 'And what's the Peak District got to do with anything?'

Robertson stared at Harry, his eyes wide with fear.

'I can't say! I can't!'

Harry stepped in front of Robertson, towering over him now.

'Whatever's going on, you have to tell me,' he said. 'We already have one body, Amber is still missing, nothing makes sense, and now you're telling me your life is in danger.' Harry softened his voice. 'John ...'

Robertson looked up at Harry, fear drawing lines in his face.

'If you're worried about your safety, the only way we can protect you is if we know who or what we're protecting you from. If you don't tell me, then there's not much I can do. Do you understand?'

Robertson nodded; Harry waited.

'They paid me,' Robertson said at last, his voice breaking on itself, ripping and tearing on his panic and fear. 'They paid me to watch them, to take photos, and to tell them where they were. Then I lost them and I couldn't find them ...'

'John, you've lost me. You're making no sense. What's this got to do with you thinking someone's going to kill you?'

Robertson stepped away from Harry, his feet scuffing along the ground, kicking up stones. Then he tripped over himself and fell to his knees.

Harry walked over and lifted him as easily as he would've done a small child.

'I don't know what happened,' Robertson said. 'Josh and Amber, they were parked right here, right where we are now, and I was camped out just far enough away to not be seen, but not miss anything. But I was cold, I was tired, I needed a drink. I tried not to, really tried, but I couldn't stop myself. Next thing I know, I woke up, and when I went to get my camera, Amber and Josh were gone.'

'They drove off, you mean?'

'I mean that they were gone,' Robertson said. 'Just that. They were there, then they weren't. I didn't see them leave, only woke to find them no longer here. I panicked, had to find them, used my drone. Took me so long, but then I found them, didn't I? Up on that lane? And I thought everything would be fine, so I followed them, set up my new hideaway, took more photos, but ...'

Harry was growing tired of people speaking to him and not finishing what they were trying to say.

'But what, John?' He asked.

'But I never saw them again,' Robertson said. 'I watched and I waited, but I saw nothing. It got weird, because they never came back, so I went to check, and that's when I took the photos, that album. I don't really know why. It was just that something didn't feel right about any of it. It made no sense.'

'Why?'

'Because where you found their van, up on that lane? They'd already been there,' Robertson said. 'They parked up there before they came here, to this spot, where we are now. They were there for a week, had explored it all, then they moved here, went to Hardraw Force, the Buttertubs. So why would they go back? They had no reason to, no reason at all! It doesn't make sense!'

He's right, Harry thought, it didn't feel right, and it didn't make sense. Why on earth would Josh and Amber go back to Cam Road if they'd already been there?

'You said someone paid you to watch them,' Harry said. 'To take photos. Who, John? Who paid you? And you've still not said who you're so afraid of!'

John stood up, and Harry knew.

'Josh's parents,' Robertson said. 'They paid me to spy on their son and Amber.'

THIRTY

Up on Cam Road, Matt was talking with Helen Dinsdale about the search. They were standing by the Mountain Rescue Land Rover, a map stretched out on the bonnet, trying to work out what to do next.

He had informed her that a body had been found and that it was most likely Josh Hill. Harry had told him to keep the actual details of how the body was found and its injuries to himself. They were all aware that information had a habit of spreading and ending up in the hands of those they would prefer never get hold of it.

'But if he was found where you say, then that's nowhere near here, is it?' Helen said.

'No, it isn't,' said Matt.

Behind them, the campervan was now a flurry of activity, the SOC team in their white paper suits, going through it meticulously, checking the area around the van, examining Robertson's small campsite. They'd also called for reinforcements to deal with his van. They would be arriving at some point soon, and Jim and Jadyn were already there, having cordoned off the area as best they could. Not that anyone was going to go near it now anyway, the night so dark that to walk through it was like wading through soup.

'So, how did he get there?'

'Problem is,' said Matt, 'he could've ended up in the river anywhere, couldn't he? Maybe he wasn't even in it to begin with, just ended up being washed down after what happened to him.'

'You've not actually told me anything about that,' Helen said.

'And I'm not going to either,' said Matt. 'Mainly because we don't know yet, like, but also because I wouldn't want you hearing about any of it.'

'That bad?'

'Worse.'

Helen shone her torch down at the map, then dropped a finger onto the river.

'If it needs searching, then we'll need divers. But there's no way anyone's going in there until the level's dropped. They'll need a location as well. We can't just have them searching at random, makes no sense.'

'Maybe we'll know more once the postmortem's done,' Matt said. 'That might give us a clue.'

'We both know that's a long shot.'

'It is, but it's all we've got.'

A shout caught Matt's attention, and he turned to see Sowerby walking towards him.

'Everything okay?'

'Ignoring the fact that midnight is fast approaching, no, it isn't,' Sowerby said. 'You got a minute?'

Matt was a little taken aback.

'What, me? Why?'

'I need to go over a few things with you,' Sowerby said.

'Aren't you better off doing that with Harry?'

Sowerby looked around, gave a shrug.

'He's not here, is he?'

'No, but—'

Sowerby turned, and Matt followed.

Coming to a standstill, Sowerby pointed at the front of the campervan.

'Notice anything odd?'

'Can't say that I do,' said Matt. 'Van looks in good nick. Expensive, too, I reckon. Parking's a bit off, like, but they don't teach that properly anymore, do they? My dad, he taught me to reverse with my mirrors, said if I was going to learn to drive forwards properly, then I best learn how to go backwards properly, too. Had me reversing trailers round corners for hours.'

'All very interesting, I'm sure,' said Sowerby, 'but you spotted it.'

'Spotted what?'

'The odd thing; the parking.'

Matt remembered when he'd first seen the van with Harry.

'We noticed that when we came to have a look around after a biker had reported it,' he said. 'Harry said something about the angle. How if you parked like that there's no way you'd want to sleep in it.'

'Because you couldn't,' Sowerby said. 'Which is exactly my point.'

'I don't follow.'

'You will.'

Sowerby then moved around so that they were looking at the awning.

'What about that?' she asked.

'Looks worse than the last time I saw it,' said Matt. 'Weather's given it a right proper battering, hasn't it?'

'Have you ever put up an awning?' Sowerby asked. 'I have. Used to go on caravan holidays as a kid. I helped with the awning, all the poles, the ropes, pegging it out. And the one thing I do remember is that you need to be on level ground, and if you weren't, you'd need the caravan level. Dad was a stickler about it, would spend so long getting everything right. And if it wasn't right, then the awning wouldn't hang right, nothing would work.'

'You've lost me again.'

'For a start, why park like that in the first place?' Sowerby said. 'This is a track. It's easy enough to find somewhere flatter than here. In fact, if you walk up about a hundred metres, you'll find a much better place, all flat, perfect really. So, why are they parked here? And the angle, too; the van isn't even straight.'

'So, they can't park, but we've just talked about that,' said Matt.

'This is a campervan,' Sowerby said. 'You have one so that you can park up and sleep well. You don't just dump it, do you? And you don't hang an awning like that, because you can't. This one, it's not done right. There are poles missing, poles in the wrong place, but most of all, the biggest sign that something's not quite right, is the fact that the awning isn't even on the right way round.'

'It's inside out?'

'Yes.'

Matt was baffled.

'Maybe they got confused, putting it up in bad weather or something.'

'There's more,' Sowerby said. 'You've seen inside, yes?'

'I have.'

'It's a mess in there, isn't it? The table's not up properly, there's mess everywhere, like everything was just thrown in there last minute.'

'It's not very inviting, that's for sure,' said Matt. 'That's why we initially thought they might've just given up and gone to hide in a pub for a few days.'

'We've also found gouges in the track and the verge the van's parked on,' Sowerby continued. 'Recent, and nothing to do with any of the other vehicles here now. We've taken photos, measurements, we've checked to be absolutely sure.'

'Of what?'

'Well, whatever it was, it was bigger, heavier, and towing a trailer.'

Matt was stunned.

'But the weather; how can you tell?'

Sowerby pointed at the ground.

'Over there, we've got deep tracks. They're puddles, but they're tracks, and they cross the lane like tramlines, stopping just in front of where the van is now. It's clearer in the photographs, but you can still make it out if you look closely.'

Matt did just that, staring into the darkness, held back by the lights of the SOC team.

'Bloody hell, you're right,' he said. 'But so what? This is a track used by farmers. There's tractors going up here all the time, I should think.'

'And one just so happened to reverse a very heavy trailer right up to the nose of that campervan?' Sowerby said.

Matt frowned, folded his arms.

'You know, right now, you're sounding a little too much like a detective.'

'I'm not,' Sowerby said. 'All I've done is tell you some of what we've found. Obviously, if we find anything else, see something in the photos, whatever, we'll tell you. But what it all means and why, that's down to you.'

Matt wasn't so sure.

'You're leading somewhere with this, though, aren't you?' he said. 'Everything here, it's telling you something, but what? I don't—'

Matt was about to say that he couldn't see what Sowerby was getting at, but then everything she had shown him crashed into him at once.

'But that doesn't make sense!'

'What doesn't?' Sowerby asked.

'What you've just shown me. All of it. None of it. You know what I mean! Why would anyone ...?'

'Why would anyone what, Detective?' Sowerby asked.

Matt's mind was racing now, but to where he hadn't a clue. Nothing made sense, and now even less so.

'Why would anyone put that camper on the back of a trailer?' he asked. 'Why would they do that, tow it up here, and dump it?'

'I've no idea,' Sowerby said. 'But my guess is, we're going to need to find out.'

THIRTY-ONE

When Harry got around to checking the time, it was already morning. He needed his bed, but there had still been a few jobs to do before he could finally get his head down.

With the revelation from Robertson, he'd decided the best thing to do was to put him up somewhere for the night, which would've been a lot easier had Hawes not been rammed with the press and all of Josh and Amber's fans. The Fire Brigade had done an excellent job of clearing the place of journalists and fans alike, but those who hadn't headed for home had soon filled up every bed and breakfast available.

Somehow, though, Harry managed to find a room, and he stumped up the cash to give Robertson a bed for the night. He knew there was no way on Earth that he was a suspect, so had no real concern that the man would do a runner. Not that he could, seeing as his only mode of transport was now on its way back to a large workshop filled with lots of tools, all useful in taking it slowly, and carefully, to pieces.

Harry had then spoken with Gordy, who told him that yes, the parents had confirmed what he already knew, that the body was that of their son, Josh. They were now back at the small hotel they had been staying at for the past week or so, down in Leyburn. That they had been in the area so long simply tied in with what Robertson had told Harry.

As for what Robertson had told him about the beating Josh's dad had given him, the threats, and then the subsequent employment of him to follow their son, Harry would be learning all that and more from them himself when he turned up at their door the next day, a visit he felt very sure they wouldn't be expecting. Except the next day was already here and that only added to Harry's weary head.

Robertson had not been in touch with Josh's parents, so they had no idea where he was, which meant he was safe for now. And all things considered, Harry didn't think Mr Hill would be looking to add to his own pain by seeking out the sneaky little photographer he'd employed as a spy. Or wanting to explain why

After his chat with Gordy, Harry did a quick call around to the rest of the team, sending them all home one by one. He'd already sent Jen and Dave home, leaving himself to deal with Robertson. Jim and Jadyn were next and seeing as Robertson's van had just been towed away on the back of a truck when he called, they were thankful to get away. Harry had met them in town to hand Fly over to Jim, and the dog seemed no less awake than it had hours ago, as it had raced over to Jim and nearly knocked him off his feet.

Gordy had headed back to Anna's, though promised Harry she would be in the office in the morning, and even though he'd tried, there was no telling her otherwise. Which left only Matt. But first Harry decided to head home, parking up on the main road through Gayle, to then walk the last bit of the journey to his house.

'A tractor and trailer?' Harry asked, speaking to Matt on the phone as he slammed the driver's door shut with a dull clang, Smudge waiting patiently by his side on the pavement. He listened to Matt tell him what had been found by the SOC team, and also how the search and rescue was now in the process of trying to work out what to do next, especially with the discovery of Josh's body.

'That's what it looks like,' said Matt.

'But seeing as it's a lane used by farmers,' Harry said, 'wouldn't it be odder if there weren't tracks like that?'

'That's what I sort of said as well,' said Matt, 'but when you look at where the tracks are in relation to the campervan, it makes sense.'

Harry rubbed his eyes as he walked up towards the bridge resting over the dark, rushing waters of Gayle Beck.

'None of this makes sense,' he said. 'I can't tie any of this together, and now you're telling me someone reversed a trailer up to the front end of Josh and Amber's campervan? I mean, why, Matt? Why would anyone do that? Were they trying to nick it while Amber and Josh were away?'

'I'd not thought of that,' said Matt. 'Bit risky, but that would make some sense, I suppose.'

'We're still no clearer as to where Josh and Amber went after they left the camper, though, are we?' continued Harry. 'We've got this other site that our friend John Robertson saw them at, and he says they'd already been up on Cam Road, so why they went back there? There must've been a reason, but what the hell is it?'

Harry had already mentioned Josh's parents and the link between them and Robertson, but Matt had had nothing to say to help him make any sense of it.

'And there's the missing bikes,' said Matt, 'the awning being inside out, the way the van's parked ... No, you're right, it doesn't make sense at all, does it? You home yet?'

'Nearly,' Harry said. 'Walking there right now. And you need to head off now, too, remember?'

'I am,' said Matt. 'Someone's giving me a lift back home.'

Harry noticed movement ahead.

'Now what?'

'Everything okay?' asked Matt.

Harry didn't answer. His focus was on the road just before the bridge, from which the narrow footpath led to the front of his cottage.

He'd seen movement, but that was to be expected. Late though it was, he'd known there was still every chance he might bump into someone, and not just on their way back from the pub, either. Anyone who worked on a farm worked all the hours they had to, and more, and he'd often received a nod from a passerby heading off to fetch the sheep in. But this was different. The movement Harry had seen was furtive, as though they were hanging around somewhere they shouldn't.

'Harry?'

'Give me a minute,' Harry said. 'I'll call you back.'

Harry hung up and took a right turn off the main road down a narrow road towards Gayle Chapel, then took an immediate left before he reached it.

Creeping through the darkest and narrowest of lanes, Harry dodged from shadow to shadow, beside him Smudge was not only being quiet but was perfectly camouflaged, too.

At the other end of the same footpath where he'd seen the movement, Harry paused, hunched up close to a wall, then slipped a little closer along, eventually dipping his head around to see if he could spot anything.

Allowing his eyes to adjust to the small amount of light spilling into the dark from a house or two, Harry saw, hiding in various shadows along the footpath, at least a dozen different shadows. He saw pinpricks of red light; cameras, he thought.

Creeping back the way he'd come, Harry headed back to the Land Rover and climbed in. Now what? he thought.

His phone rang.

'What?'

'Harry? It's Matt.'

'I said I'd ring you.'

'But you didn't.'

'That was only a couple of minutes ago!'

'What's happened? What's wrong?'

God, I'm tired, Harry thought. Maybe he'd just kip in the Land Rover rather than deal with any of this.

'Journalists,' Harry said. 'Don't ask me how, but they've found out where I live. There's a load of them all hiding outside, waiting to pounce.'

'You can't be serious.'

'As you well know, I'm rarely anything else.'

'No, you're right there,' said Matt. 'What are you going to do? Do you want me to come and have a word?'

Harry shook his head, even though he was alone and talking on the phone.

'No point,' he said. 'I'll be fine. I'll sort something out.'

'You'll be nipping over to Grace's then,' said Matt. 'Good plan.'

'No, I'll not be bothering her at this time,' Harry replied.

'What? Don't be daft. You need to sleep. Give her a call. If you want, I can call her now while you just get yourself there and away from those idiots outside your door, save a bit of time.'

'Honestly, I'll be fine.'

Matt was quiet for a second or two, then said, 'So, that's what's been up with you the past couple of weeks, is it?'

Harry wasn't in the mood.

'Get yourself home, Matt,' he said. 'Like I said, I'll be fine. Nothing to worry about.'

'What is it? Have you fallen out?' Matt asked. 'You can't have broken up, surely; that would make no sense at all.'

'Matt ...'

'Where are you?'

'What?'

'You'll be parked up in your usual spot, right? I'll be there in a couple of minutes.'

'Look, no, don't, I'm fine, Matt, I—'

The line went dead.

'Bloody hell!'

Harry stared at his phone, willing it to burst into flames. He considered just driving off and parking in a layby somewhere, but Matt, true to his word, arrived two minutes later, almost on the dot.

Waving his lift off, he then marched around to Harry. 'Right,

shift over; I'm driving. You're staying at ours tonight, and I'll have
no arguing either.'

Harry shook his head.

'No, I'm not imposing on you like that.'

Matt leaned in, stuck a finger in his ear, and wiggled it about.

'Sorry, Harry, didn't quite catch that. Can't hear too well in this
ear.'

Harry said nothing, just stared, hoping Matt would get the
point.

He didn't.

'I said shift,' said Matt.

Before Harry knew where he was, Matt had managed to heave
him out from behind the steering wheel and was now sitting in his
place. Smudge, who was in the back of the vehicle, just stared at
him, her head cocked to one side, almost as though she found all of
this very amusing. Which was a good thing, really, Harry thought,
because he very much didn't.

With no choice in the matter, Harry shuffled around to the
passenger door and climbed in.

'Away, then,' Matt said. 'Let's get you to bed.'

Harry was just about able to manage a grumpy nod and was
soon fast asleep as Matt drove them home.

THIRTY-TWO

Harry stared at the steaming bowl of porridge in front of him as, at his feet, Smudge tucked into a tin of dog food that Matt had nipped out to buy for her before breakfast.

'That's a lot of porridge,' he said, reaching for the mug of tea sat steaming beside it.

'With honey and milk, if you want it,' said Matt, who was holding his daughter Mary-Anne in his arms, and sitting next to Joan, who was at the table in her wheelchair. 'Don't tell Gordy, though.'

'Why?'

'I don't put salt in it.'

Harry grimaced in disgust at the idea.

'Why the hell would you want to?'

'That's exactly what I said,' said Matt. 'Apparently, that's how you're supposed to have it. Or how some grandparent of hers used to have it.'

Joan laughed.

'You do know that not everyone from Scotland lives on a diet of porridge and square sausage, don't you?' she said.

'Actually, Gordy doesn't even like porridge,' said Matt. 'She's more your smoothie-in-the-morning kind of person.'

Harry roared at that.

'Is she bollocks.'

Hearing his own voice boom out and realising that he was in the company of someone considerably younger and more innocent, Harry apologised immediately.

'No, I'm serious,' said Matt. 'For a while, before you turned up, like, we used to do these bi-monthly early morning breakfast meetings, some kind of initiative from above, I think. So, we'd all turn up with our breakfast and chat about what we were doing. Jen was there with her spinach omelettes, which I couldn't even bring myself to look at. Liz and Jim were on with toast mainly, and I turned up with porridge. Which is how we ended up talking about it.'

'And Gordy had a smoothie?'

'Even brought her own whizzy liquidizer food processor whatever thing to plug in,' said Matt. 'Deafening it was. She made this green slurry, all pineapple and spinach and nuts and goodness knows what else.'

Harry added honey and milk to the porridge and tucked in, soon finishing the bowl.

'Thanks for that,' he said.

'No problem,' said Joan. Then she leaned over and asked, 'Come on then, what's going on with you and Grace?'

Harry sighed.

'Nothing is going on.'

Joan leaned back, glanced at Matt.

'Don't like the sound of that at all,' she said.

'Neither do I,' said Matt, and stared hard at Harry. 'Out with it, then, before we have to beat it out of you.'

Harry knew a busy day lay ahead. He did not want to talk about his personal life.

'Whatever's going on, it's private,' he said. 'Not work.'

'What's your point?' Matt asked, then before Harry could answer, said, 'Oh, right, you're confused again, aren't you? That's what this is.'

'I'm not confused.'

'Definitely confused,' Joan agreed.

Harry stood up.

'Sit down,' Joan said.

Harry slumped back into his chair.

'Look, everything's fine,' he said. 'We're just on a bit of a break, that's all.'

Harry saw Joan and Matt's eyes widen.

'What did you do?'

'Me? I didn't do anything! We just decided that we needed a bit of space, that's all. You know what it's like, the job, work-life balance, that kind of stuff. Plus, there's other stuff, like whose turn it is to visit the other. All very boring.'

'And easy to solve,' said Matt.

'You move in together,' said Joan.

Harry took in a breath, then exhaled slowly through his nose.

'It's not that simple, though, is it?' he said. 'Grace has a house, I've just moved into mine, and there's Arthur to think about.'

'What, and your solution to any of this is to go on a break?' said Matt. 'Honestly, Harry, if you weren't my boss, as well as a friend, I'd reach over there right now and give you such a slap.'

'Don't let that stop you,' said Joan. 'I might do it myself.'

Harry didn't like getting attacked with both barrels of the Dinsdale family.

'It was a mutual decision,' he said.

Matt shook his head.

'Can you not hear yourself? A mutual decision? You're being a bloody idiot! And yes, I know I swore in front of my daughter, but she's asleep and I needed to!'

Harry went to speak, but Joan jumped in before he could utter even a single word.

'Whichever one of you suggested it, my advice is that you get off your backside and do something about it,' she said.

'She doesn't want contact for a week or two, that's all,' said Harry, deciding to not mention the texts he had sent.

Joan rolled her eyes.

'The question you have to ask yourself, Harry, is what do you want?'

'I don't know,' Harry replied. 'There's been a lot on my mind and—'

Harry knew he was making excuses.

'And that's never going to change,' said Joan. 'You're a police officer, Harry, a detective, and life is busy because that's what life is! What, you think it's going to suddenly change, and you'll be granted all this time to think? Ridiculous! Pull your head out of your arse and do something!'

'If you think about it, right now you're doing something,' said Matt. 'Nothing. And that's a decision in itself, isn't it? But that's not you, Harry, and it's considerably less than either you or Grace deserve.'

'Call her,' said Joan, and she wheeled herself out from under the table and rolled over to sit in front of Harry. 'If you love the woman, and I'd bet my own legs on it that you do, and yes I know they don't work, but I'm still rather attached to them, but anyway, what I'm saying is, don't blow this! Unless you want to, that is, in which case, do the right thing and just say so. But that isn't what you want, is it, Harry?'

Harry realised he was shaking his head.

Joan smiled and rested a hand on his arm.

'You're a bloody idiot, you know? And goodness knows what Grace sees in you, but whatever it is, I reckon all of that's worth something, don't you?'

'You two should go into therapy or counselling or something,' Harry said, trying to make light of the conversation.

'You wouldn't be able to afford us,' said Matt, his eyes now on his daughter, who was awake and making strange burbling sounds and laughing. 'And besides, we like to help friends for free. We're generous like that.'

A few minutes later, and outside the house with Matt, Harry stared out at the day. The clouds had finally cleared, and he could see the fell tops around them, their silent presence almost comforting. Sunlight was even breaking through, and he could see specks of blue behind the grey wisps dancing in the sky.

'Sorry about all that,' Matt said, as Harry climbed into the Land Rover. 'But sometimes, we both like to speak our minds, you see, can't really help ourselves.'

'And that's exactly what you did.'

'Another long day ahead, then.'

'It is.'

Harry turned the key in the ignition and the engine thrummed into life.

'Jadyn's on his way?'

'Picking me up on the way through,' said Matt. 'And I'll look after Smudge for you until you get back. Gordy's with Josh's parents, doing the family liaison thing, and I'll be speaking with Amber's parents myself this morning.'

'We need a team meeting when I get back,' Harry said. 'And let Gordy know that I'll be stopping off on my way through to have a word with the Hills myself.'

'Well, you head off and have lots of fun at the mortuary, now,' said Matt.

'When is it ever anything else?' Harry replied.

And with that, he slipped the gear stick into first and headed down-dale to meet with Sowerby, all the way thinking about everything Joan and Matt had said, and unable to shift away from the fact that it had all been right.

THIRTY-THREE

Harry stood in the mortuary, wearing over his clothes a long, white coat, rubber boots on his feet, and a face mask. Bright lights presented the room in stark relief, every surface tiled or stainless steel, everywhere sharp angles, and straight lines, except for what lay in front of him beneath the white sheet. Shadows did not exist here, he thought, there was nowhere to hide, and what secrets the dead had to tell, Sowerby would soon out.

'Thanks for the tea and biscuits,' Harry said. 'Just a shame all you had was those bloody awful pink wafers.'

'But they're the best.'

'They most certainly aren't,' Harry replied. 'Have you never tried a Tunnocks caramel wafer? Even something as simple as a Rich Tea is better than filling your mouth with pink dust.'

'You've no taste, have you?' Sowerby said.

'Not even a chocolate digestive, either,' Harry added. 'That's not right at all.'

'I finished those yesterday.'

Harry knew they were both avoiding what they were really there to do.

The conversation paused.

'You ready?' Sowerby asked.

'I don't think anyone's ever ready for this,' Harry said, though at least the body under the sheet wasn't a relative or a friend, he thought. Sowerby had mentioned Josh's parents, who had turned up to identify the body late in the night, one of the other staff dealing with them. They'd been quiet, so in shock over what they saw that there were no tears. Harry knew the tears would have come, though. He knew from experience that they always did.

Sowerby reached over and, gripping the top edge of the white sheet, slowly pulled it down to reveal a face, then the torso.

Josh Hill stared up at Harry, his face still, pale as skimmed milk, eyes closed. Deep purple and black bruising covered his body, like a canvas painted in pain. Harry knew that the lack of blood circulation after death made them seem more pronounced, the body unable to start healing itself.

'So, we've had a positive ID, as you know,' said Sowerby. 'Josh Hill, aged twenty-five, six-foot-one, and a hundred and eighty pounds.'

He had been a fit lad, Harry thought, that much was obvious. Not a shred of fat on him, his physique muscled and lithe, a body that was fast and strong. That made him wonder about what had really happened, if someone was responsible for this, and if so, how they had managed to subdue someone like Josh, taken him by surprise, and then done their worst.

'Is there anything new?' Harry asked. 'Those injuries I saw last night caused by the river, or something else?'

Harry stared at the deep gouges in Josh's chest. He'd seen wounds like that himself, on the living and the dead, on the streets he'd worked as a detective, and in the deserts of Afghanistan. Because sometimes, you ran out of ammunition, and all you had left was your bare hands, a bayonet, your knife. Some of the wounds didn't look quite right, almost as though whoever had done it had been trying to write something, a word perhaps? But he didn't recognise any of it, the cuts just a mess of crisscross angles slicing into each other, and he knew that it was sometimes best to not try and read too much into something.

'You okay?' Sowerby asked.

'Fine,' Harry said, pushing those memories back down, locking them away.

'You're quiet, though.'

'You mean thoughtful.'

The wounds on Josh's chest were particularly deep around his heart, and Harry had the awful image in his mind of the lad fighting someone off as they tried to carve it out.

'Some of the damage is from the river,' Sowerby said. 'The scrapes and so on, and possibly some of the bruising, but not all.'

'Explain,' said Harry.

'Ignoring those cuts for the moment, if you can, as you know, contusions, bruises, they occur because of damage to blood vessels under the skin. After death, circulation stops, so there's no way for the body's natural processes to keep functioning.'

'Are you saying that most of this occurred before he was in the water?'

'Before he was dead,' said Sowerby, 'because it was only then that he ended up in the water.'

'How can you be sure?'

'Not enough water in the lungs, stomach, his air passages for that. Obviously, there's some, because he was tossed around in a river, but if he'd drowned, he'd have chugged the stuff down.'

'Lovely description.'

'Thank you.'

'Also, the injuries he's sustained? There's no way he would have been able to even get to the river in the first place to throw himself in, never mind actually survive them.'

Harry rubbed his eyes, not so much because he was physically tired, which he was, but because the weariness was somehow deeper right then. Faced with what Sowerby was telling him, he knew that Josh's last moments had been horrific and terrifying, and once again he was faced with man's inhumanity to man.

'Take me through it,' he said.

'The cuts,' Sowerby said, 'definitely done by a blade. No way to know how big or anything like that, though. But it was sharp enough to carve him up like a Sunday roast. He would've lost a lot of blood, but not enough to kill him. Then there's this ...'

Sowerby pointed at Josh's wrists, and then rolling away the rest of the white sheet, his ankles.

'Rope marks,' Harry said.

'He was tied at the wrists and the ankles,' Sowerby said. 'From the abrasions, the rope was tight, and he struggled, I think, to free himself.'

'What kind of rope?'

'Synthetic, but not a climbing rope or anything like that. We've found blue as well as orange strands and will be analysing further.'

'There's more, isn't there?'

Sowerby nodded.

'You noticed when we first saw the body how he looked like he had been crushed.'

'And you said it was probably a boulder in the river.'

'Well, it wasn't. Look here ...'

Harry leaned in.

'These marks here, on his torso, and on his legs, they're tyre marks.'

'He was run over?'

'Comprehensively,' said Sowerby. 'If he didn't die immediately, then most certainly just seconds after. His ribs are a mess, his internal organs were mush. Horrendous.'

'So, he was tied up, cut with a knife, and run over?'

'There's more,' said Sowerby. 'There was mud in the cuts on the soles of his feet, maybe from where he was running away from whoever smashed into him with their vehicle, bits of grass, but beneath that was something else, and it matched what we found under his nails.'

'The river didn't wash it away?'

'No, and it's not much, but it's odd.'

'How?'

Sowerby pulled the white sheet back up over Josh, hiding him from view.

'Let's take the first layer of mud,' Sowerby said. 'It contained plenty of organic matter, decaying leaves and grass, that kind of thing, and lots of the kinds of microorganisms you would expect to find living in a surface environment. There was evidence of pollution, animal waste, that kind of thing.'

'And you're saying there was another type of mud?'

'Exactly that,' said Sowerby. 'Deep inside those cuts and gashes in his feet, the mud had a completely different mineral composition. There was no organic material in it for a start, like it was completely sterile. We found some evidence of life in it, but this was all microbial communities adapted to living in dark, nutrient-poor conditions.'

'So, you've found two types of mud,' said Harry. 'Not sure what that's supposed to tell me?'

'It tells you,' said Sowerby, 'that before he ended up in the river, and before he escaped from whoever did this to him, he was in a cave.'

'What?'

'The mud in those wounds would only be found underground, and I don't mean in the kind of cave you'd see at the bottom of a cliff and pop into to get out of the rain, either. This is from deep underground.'

'Which means,' Harry said, 'if Amber's still alive, then that's most likely where she is, too.'

'One more thing,' said Sowerby, 'and this you may well think I'm making up, but I'm not, I assure you.'

She reached for a brown folder on a metal table behind her and opened it to remove a photograph about the size of an A4 sheet of paper. She handed it to Harry.

'This shows the wounds on Josh's chest,' he said. 'They look odd, but I don't see—'

'Now look at this.' Sowerby held out another sheet of paper for Harry. 'One of my colleagues is a bit of a history buff. Started off with his family tree, then got a bit carried away with it all, ended up exploring the legacy of the Vikings in Yorkshire, and seems a little too convinved that he's the heir of some famous warrior. Keeps telling me I should go to the Jorvik Viking Centre in York. Not really my thing, though.'

Harry looked at the sheet of paper in his hand. It was a print out on Norse mythology and belief.

'This is where you tell me why any of that's relevant,' he said.

'That,' Sowerby said, pointing at the paper in Harry's hand, 'is everything you could ever want to know about an old Norse word meaning sacrifice. More specifically, blood sacrifice.'

Harry narrowed his eyes at a word in bold.

'Blót?'

Sowerby said, 'If you compare Josh's body to the photo, you can see that it very much looks like whoever cut into him was trying to write that word.'

Harry shook his head.

'This is already crazy enough as it is,' he said. 'The last thing we want to do is go linking any of this to some weird cult.'

'It's not so much a weird cult,' Sowerby explained. 'It's actually an Old Norse religious practice. Animals, and sometimes humans, were sacrificed.'

'Why?'

'Oh, the usual,' Sowerby said. 'To persuade the gods to look kindly on you, to bless the harvest, that kind of thing.'

'That kind of thing? Look,' said Harry, 'I've dealt with a few crazies in my time, even the odd cult or religious nut here and there, but I've never yet stumbled into anything that involved human sacrifice.'

'Well, there's a first time for everything, isn't there?'

Harry handed the photo and printout back to Sowerby.

'What the hell am I supposed to do with any of this?' he asked. 'I've got a young man who we now think was tied up in a cave, attacked with a knife, run over till dead, then thrown in a river, and if that's not enough, it was all done as a blood sacrifice? You've been to the Dales, right? You know, green fells, sheep and cows, tractors, little chapels here and there, an odd obsession with cheese and cake?'

'Don't forget pies,' said Sowerby. 'And ale.'

'But human sacrifice? In Wensleydale?'

'All I'm doing is telling you what we've found,' said Sowerby. 'Nothing else. Facts. The photos will be sent over later, along with anything we've found at the various other sites you so kindly allowed me to look at.'

'Actually, on that,' said Harry, 'Matt said something about tyre marks on the track by the campervan.'

'We're still analysing all of that,' said Sowerby. 'The team will get back to you as soon as they can, but yes, it was all a bit odd up there, too.'

With nothing else to discuss, Harry was soon led outside and into the fresh air.

'Wish I could provide you with answers instead of more questions,' she said, as Harry climbed into his vehicle.

'So do I,' Harry said, and with a frustrated twist of the key, started the engine, then drove off, back to Wensleydale, taking with him a growing sense of concern for the whereabouts and well-being of Amber Hill.

THIRTY-FOUR

Amber had no tears left to cry. She'd tried to escape, yanked at the ropes so hard and for so long that the pain of them cutting into her, and the strain in her muscles, had made her numb. She didn't even notice the cold now, so thick and heavy and absolute was it that although she shivered, it meant nothing. Even the warmth of her own blood, flowing on her skin, had faded.

She had given in to the darkness, let it swallow her whole. There was nothing to see in it, no shape or form, no sign of hope. Only sounds echoing around her with a freedom she herself didn't have, and she hated them.

There were smells, too, an odd mineral dampness, stagnant and dead. Behind it though, on a faint draft which blew in from she knew not where, and suspected she would never find out, were other odours, both sweet and fetid. It was a mix of decay and something else she couldn't identify or describe. It reminded her a little of the smell of a butcher's counter, of cold meat and blood and bone.

To survive, or to at least keep existing, Amber had turned in on herself, sunk far back into her memories, and wandered free and happy through days near and far but all long gone. On beaches she had played as a child, running across golden sand with a bucket and spade, chased by her father. Then to her room she had escaped, watching it change through the years, from a magic castle filled with stuffed bears, all of them with names, to a teenage cave of dark walls and homework, the air ripped apart by angry music and her own cries of angst. Next had come the university halls, three years studying for a degree she would never use, but completed anyway, because it meant she got to stay with her friends, to have fun, to live a little and explore. But all of it, every single memory she could dredge up from the deepest parts of her mind, was nothing compared to those she shared with Josh.

And Josh wasn't here.

He was gone.

She was alone.

The scream which ripped from Amber's throat shocked her so much that she jumped, terrified by her own fear, yes, but also the rage burning it up. She was angry, needed to lash out, to find who had done this to her, tied her up in the dark, taken her away from Josh, and ...

And what? Why the hell had she been brought here in the first place? It made no sense. Someone had attacked them in the dark, taken them by such sharp surprise that neither of them had been able to respond. The next thing she had known was this, where she was now, the loneliness and the pain of a darkness so absolute that she wondered if perhaps she was already dead, and this was all that came after, a drifting, bitter nothingness, and an eternity of relived memories.

A light flickered in the dark.

Amber stared at it, wondering if it was just a flash in her brain, a neuron misfiring, but it moved, drifted closer, a tiny thing of orange, a tongue tasting the dark.

'Josh?'

No answer, just the light, small and floating in the dark, ever closer.

'Josh, is that you?'

A cough, shuffling feet, a sharp breath.

A creeping sense of horror reached out of the blackness and wrapped its icy fingers around Amber's chest, squeezing so tightly that she gasped. Unable to tear her eyes away from the light, she pushed herself up against the wall of rock behind her, as her mind started to design ten levels of hell coming at her now, such nightmarish creations holding aloft that light, and the awful things they wanted, that she couldn't help but cry out.

In reply, came a laugh, cold and gurgling.

When at last the light was close enough to bring its bearer into faint view, Amber knew then that she would never see anything beyond this darkness, this moment, again. Whoever it was, she couldn't quite tell, their face a reflection of her own in a small window of mirrored glass, their body clothed in black.

Fingers gripped her chin, squeezed hard, pushing her into the rock, scraping the back of her skull.

Amber cried out, but the sound was pinched to nothing by the mean fingers.

'Just you, now, I'm afraid,' said the figure, the voice low and wet, a whispering thing that belonged in caves and deeper places still.

There was a smell in the air, too. It was a scent that, for some reason, reminded her of her grandad; the soft, sweet aroma of burning wood struck through with a note of vanilla.

'Still, you'll do, you'll do. You'll have to.'

The strike that came next, the back of a hand crashing into the side of her head like a wrecking ball, sent stars spinning around Amber's head and she fell backwards, senseless, her world spinning. She was pulled up and hit again, this time even harder, and the violence of it caused her to vomit.

Dazed and in agony, Amber was unable to resist as she felt herself hoisted up onto the shoulder of the shadow that had attacked her. Hanging there, blood rushing to her head, Amber gave in to unconsciousness.

When Amber awoke, her head swimming, her eyes blurry, the first thing she noticed beyond the fact that she was still tied at the wrists and ankles was that the darkness was now being held back. Barely, yes, but enough to allow her eyes to try and pull something from the dimly lit cavern she was now in.

At first, all Amber could see were shapes, lumpen things in shadow, their forms coloured only by numerous candles flickering in the darkness, licking at it hungrily. But as she concentrated, allowed the wooziness in her head to ease, she was soon able to make out what was before her.

She saw great rocks sitting around the cavern floor, like the petrified corpses of ancient creatures trapped beneath the earth. She saw formations, great columns glistening white, stretching up from the ground as though desperate to reach the roof, wherever it was in the darkness above. She also saw not only the candles lighting the space around her, but numerous bowls dotted about, all of them filled with splashes of dark liquid, fresh and glistening in the eerie light.

On the walls, she caught sight of symbols drawn on the rock, except they weren't symbols, but crude drawings, like cave paintings of animals, though what type she couldn't quite make out. Then her eyes were drawn to something else, other shapes in the dark, some hanging from the walls, others leaning against a boulder here, a rock there. At first, she had dismissed them as just odd shadows and strange rock formations, alien shapes formed underground, but then something had scratched at the back of her mind, forcing her to look closer, to see them for what they really were: the dead.

Amber's terror reached such a high pitch that she had no idea whether she was screaming or dying or both. She was trapped, surrounded by things she had only ever seen in horror movies, except that Friday night fear of a good movie and bad food was nothing like this, which stared back at her through eyeless skulls wrapped in skin the colour of parchment tight as a drum.

Amber knew she was alone, that Josh was gone, that no one was coming for her, no one would find her, that this dark hole would be her grave. She knew this so clearly and with such acceptance that in the same moment she also knew something else. She wasn't about to go quietly.

Dragging her eyes away from what she knew—and more certainly than anything she'd ever known in her life—would be her fate, Amber decided, in those last moments bathed in the sepulchral dark, to survive.

THIRTY-FIVE

Harry was sitting at a simple table in a small private dining room Gordy had sorted for them at the hotel in Leyburn, where Josh's parents had been staying for the past seven nights. Beside him was Gordy, and in front of him, Edward and Kim Hill.

Taking a sip from the glass of water he'd just poured, Harry said, 'First of all, Mr and Mrs Hill, may I just say how sorry I am for your loss. I'm not about to sit here and say that I understand how you feel, because I don't. Grief is a very individual thing, and what you're experiencing now can't, and never should be, compared to what someone else has gone through. But you do have my sympathy, and you also have my word that myself, Detective Inspector Haig, and the rest of the team, are working all the hours we can, and plenty of those we can't, to find who did this to your son.'

Harry's words seemed to float in the air for a while, drifting between them, as Edward, and then Kim, each took a sip from their own glasses, before returning them to the table to hold each other's hands.

'It doesn't feel real,' Kim said at last. 'That Josh is gone. I keep looking at my phone, expecting a message, a missed call.'

'That's to be expected,' said Gordy, her voice calm, kind. 'There's no right or wrong way to get through this, only that you will get through it. And by that, I don't mean that you will get used to Josh being gone, because you won't. But what you will do, is grow a little stronger day by day, and gradually, very, very gradually, learn to keep living and to bear the loss.'

'Is that your idea of a comforting speech?' Edward said.

Harry looked across the table and saw a man broken by the events of the night before, his eyes red, tears falling, bitterness and rage, confusion and heartbreak twisting his voice.

'I do need to ask you some questions,' Harry said, drawing Josh's father away from focusing on what Gordy had said. 'It's difficult, I know, but we still don't know where Amber is, and—'

'I don't care where she is,' said Edward. 'Josh is dead, and I bet she's responsible. She has to be, the gold-digging bitch.'

Although Harry wasn't the world's biggest fan of people in general, he usually did his best to not take a dislike to them immediately. Generally, he allowed them a bit of time before deciding whether they were worth his time or not. But there were those rare occasions where just minutes into meeting someone he already knew.

This was one of those occasions.

'Mr Hill,' Harry said, 'I know you're angry, that you're upset, and that you're lashing out, but as far as we are concerned, Amber is alive, she's out there somewhere, and whoever killed your son, has her. Every minute counts if we're to locate her and apprehend the one responsible.'

'You're not listening, are you?' said Edward. 'She's part of it! And whatever it was she had planned, it's gone wrong and she's run off to who knows where, and with all of our money, the thieving shit.'

Harry leaned back in his chair and folded his arms. Edward was making it very difficult indeed for him to move past wanting to reach over and ricochet the man's face off the table. He'd also made a mental note of something the man had just said, but he'd come back to that in a moment.

'Can I ask why it is that you think Amber would have anything to do with what's happened? Seems quite a stretch to me, if I'm honest, that Amber, the young woman I've seen in the photos all over that campervan of theirs, in their photo albums, on their social media whatever, felt anything but love and happiness and excitement around Josh.'

'Well, you would say that, wouldn't you?' said Kim. 'That minx could pull the wool over anyone's eyes.'

Harry swung his gaze over to Josh's mum. He noticed then that they were both dressed well, as indeed they had been when they had turned up unannounced at the Market Hall the night before. Their clothes were not your high street or supermarket purchase, but considerably more exclusive. Edward was wearing expensive jeans, a pale pink cotton shirt with gold cufflinks, and a finely tailored sports jacket, the lining of which Harry had noticed, when Edward had reached inside to deposit his phone in a pocket, was itself a work of art. Kim was wearing an awful lot of tweed, but in the manner of someone whose relationship with the countryside comprised entirely of viewing it through the windscreen of a Range Rover or Aston Martin, or in the pages of Country Living Magazine.

'When was the last time you heard from your son?' Harry asked.

'What day is it now? Wednesday?' said Edward. 'So, Saturday, then, I think.'

'You're sure?'

'Of course he's sure,' Kim said.

'And did Josh tell you where they were, what they were up to?'

'Why would he?' asked Edward. 'We're not the kind of parents who can't let their children go! He's an adult, for god's sake!'

The anger Harry was more than happy to forgive under the circumstances, but it was the venom he was having a problem with.

'Did he mention anything about someone following them, maybe spying on them, perhaps?'

On hearing that question, Harry saw Kim's eyes almost pop out of her head.

'Why would anyone do that?' she asked.

Gordy said, 'If Josh and Amber were kidnapped, then there's a good chance it wasn't a spur-of-the-moment thing. Something like that, it usually takes some planning, and there would be a motivation to do it in the first place.'

'Like the money,' said Harry. 'A ransom, for example.'

'No,' Edward said. 'He never mentioned anything about anyone following them.'

Harry asked, 'Can you tell me what happened in the Peak District?'

He wasn't really sure why he asked the question right then. Perhaps it had been to give himself a bit of a chance to think ahead, to work out where he wanted the conversation to go. He'd remembered hearing mention of it, both by a faceless journalist in the crowd, then later by Robertson. He'd even asked Robertson about it, but the man hadn't answered, and Harry hadn't pressed further. But he knew it was important, that whatever had happened there linked Robertson and Josh's parents somehow, so he'd thrown it in, just to see what would happen.

'What?'

Like his wife, Edward's eyes grew so wide that Harry wondered if he shouldn't actually ask for a bowl from the kitchen so that he had something to catch them in should they pop out.

'The Peak District,' said Harry.

'Yes, I heard what you said, but what do you mean, what happened there? How should we know? We weren't there, were we?'

Now that was an interesting way of answering, Harry thought.

'Did Josh and Amber ever visit the area?' he asked.

'What? Of course they did. Josh was a keen climber, and a bloody good one, too, if you ask me. Loved gritstone, so they went to Stanage Edge.'

'And nothing happened there as far as you are aware?'

Both Kim and Edward shook their heads.

'You see, a journalist asked me about it the other day, asked if

Josh and Amber going missing had anything to do with what happened in the Peak District. And yet you're telling me that you don't know.'

'Well, we don't.'

'Don't know what?'

'What happened,' said Edward.

Harry leaned forward.

'You see, I have a problem with that,' he said, clasping his hands together as he rested his elbows on the table. 'Language is a funny thing, the way we use it, how we turn a phrase. For example, I don't think your answer to my question was born of not knowing what happened. If it was, you'd have actually asked me about it, what we knew, and how it was relevant to what happened to your son and his wife. But instead, you said "*How should we know, we weren't there, were we?*" and that's a little odd, isn't it?'

'But we weren't there,' said Kim.

'No, no, you weren't,' said Harry, 'but you're both more interested in distancing yourselves from it, than finding out what it was. Now, why is that?'

From the corner of his eye, he saw Gordy staring at him with a questioning look on her face, but also one of trust. In absolute contrast to this, from the other side of the table, the Hills were staring daggers at him.

'You're twisting our words,' said Edward. 'We've gone through enough as it is! I want to speak to your superior. I've had enough. Come on, Kim.'

Edward made to stand up, but Harry cut him off with another question.

'Who's John Robertson?'

THIRTY-SIX

Edward and Kim Hill stared at Harry.

'Who?' Edward asked.

'He's a photographer,' said Harry. 'And he mentioned the Peak District.'

'So?'

'So, I would like to know what your relationship is with him.'

'We don't have one.'

'Again,' said Harry, 'a funny way of answering; gives away the fact that you know him.'

'No, it doesn't.'

'As does the fact that Mr Robertson has told me rather a lot,' continued Harry, ignoring Edward's protest. 'Not about the Peak District, which is why I'm asking you about it, but certainly plenty about why he's been following your son and daughter-in-law around for the last couple of months, taking photographs.'

Edward's mouth opened, but he said not a word.

'You see, sometimes, when I ask a question, I already know the answer, more or less, anyway. I just need a little more detail. So, I'll ask you again, and this time my advice is you tell me the truth. Can you tell me what your relationship with John Robertson is?'

Harry watched as Edward glanced at his wife, his lips thin, as though he was hoping that by just staring at her he would be gifted a way out. But none came, and he turned back to face Harry.

'He's a photographer,' said Edward. 'He was following Josh and Amber, trying to take photos to sell to the tabloids, wheedled his way in with some real fans and turned up at a cave they were sleeping in while they were at Stanage. Josh dealt with it, but I found him and had a word.'

'A word?' said Harry. 'My impression is that your fists did the talking.'

'I gave him a bit of slap, that's all, roughed him up a bit.'

'You assaulted him and then you decided to employ his services, correct?'

At this, Kim leapt in.

'How can you sit there and go on about this when we've just lost our son? That man, that photographer, he's nothing, just scum after a story and quick cash!'

'And yet you employed him,' said Harry. 'Blackmailed him, too, I believe? And bribed him, which is impressive. Sort of a carrot and stick, I suppose; threaten to destroy his career by going to the papers and the police with some cooked-up story about him being a stalker, while at the same time providing him with equipment that he would never be able to resist so that he would keep an eye on your Josh and Amber.'

'That's what he told you, is it?'

'Yes,' said Harry. 'So, before you deny it, help me out, if you can, and tell me why?'

'Why what?'

'Why all of this?' Harry asked, lifting his hands into the air. 'Why pursue your own son, your own daughter-in-law? Why hide out up here for days, even after they went missing? Why have someone spying on them?'

'Because we didn't trust her, that's why!' said Kim. 'Never have. They met at university and she's never been good enough for him. We said as much, told him he could do better, but he had to go his own way, didn't he? And then he won all that money and, well, she's made, isn't she?'

Harry stared at both parents for a moment.

'You know, you've referred to the money twice now,' he said. 'First time, you said *our money*, and just now, you said that Josh won it. My understanding is that they won it together.'

'Like hell they did,' said Edward. 'Josh bought that ticket. We know that for a fact. Amber didn't have any cash on her, but then who does nowadays? She'd left her purse with her bank cards in it at home, and her phone was dead.'

Harry gave a shrug.

'And your point is?'

'That ticket was his, that money was his, and she's got her greedy mitts on it.'

'They were married when they won, weren't they?' Gordy asked, joining in for the first time, having allowed Harry full reign so far.

'Yes,' said Kim.

'Would be odd, then, wouldn't it, for Josh to regard a ticket they bought together, the money they won, as his, just because it was his cash they used to buy the ticket?'

'That's Josh's whole problem,' said Edward. 'He's impulsive and generous and she takes advantage of it.'

'Maybe he just thinks that being in a relationship is about sharing,' said Gordy. 'Call me old-fashioned if you want, but I'm inclined to agree with him on that.'

'Same here, actually,' said Harry, and noticed a wry look from Gordy.

Edward was on his feet.

'It's all he's ever done with that woman,' he said. 'Yes, he gave us some money, of course he did, but we're his parents! We didn't ask for it, but he gave us it anyway. But Amber? He's always been too generous. The campervan was his idea, said he wanted to take her on an adventure. He's always taken her to do things, and what's she brought to the relationship?'

'Love?' suggested Gordy, but Harry could see that Edward wasn't listening.

'Oh, she's suggested things I'm sure, but all the photos we get sent by Josh, it's always him taking them to do something new, to see something new. She never climbed before she met Josh, hadn't really travelled, and now here she is travelling with him, rich and famous, having the adventure of a lifetime, mountain biking, swimming in lakes ... Don't believe me? Look!'

Edward reached into his pocket and pulled out his phone. A huge thing, Harry thought, expensive and obvious. He then slid it across the table.

'Photos sent to us by Josh,' he said. 'All of that? It's because of him, not her.'

Harry picked up the phone.

'These are recent?'

'You'll have to scroll through to get to the ones from last week,' said Kim.

Harry did just that.

'Semerwater,' he said, now sharing the phone screen with Gordy. 'And that's Penn Hill.'

'Bolton Castle,' said Gordy, 'the Buttertubs, and that's down by the river in Wharfdale. They've been around.'

Harry was still scrolling, the photos adding to the picture he'd drawn in his mind of this young, happy, vibrant couple, their last moments together.

He came to the last photo. It was a selfie, something he'd so far managed to get through life without taking. Behind Josh and Amber, Harry could make out the front wheel of a mountain bike, the rest of it out of shot. He also saw a cliff face, and at its base, what looked like the entrance to a cave. Must've been their last adventure, he thought, staring now at Josh and Amber, who were smiling at the camera, their faces streaked with rain. God, they looked happy.

Harry handed the phone back to Edward, then paused as the man reached to take it from him, his fingers gripping it tightly.

Edward tried to pull it from his hand, but Harry wouldn't let go.

'You said Josh sent you all of these photos.'

'Yes.'

'Ignoring that you still thought it was in your interests to spy on him and Amber, these would be the last ones he sent you, then, before he disappeared?'

'That's obvious, isn't it?' said Edward. 'Can you imagine how upsetting it is for us to have them? To just see him staring back at us knowing that—'

Harry held up a hand to shush Edward, then snatched the phone back before turning to Gordy.

'This one,' he said, and showed her the final photo. 'Sowerby said something about mud she found when she examined Josh.'

'I'm seeing a photo of a happy couple standing by a cliff,' said Gordy. 'They look soaked through, rather than muddy.'

'Two types of mud were found,' Harry explained. 'Most of it was from outside, you know, from a field or whatever, but beneath that, she found some that was from somewhere else entirely. Underground.'

'That doesn't make any sense at all.'

'No, you're right, it doesn't. Until you look at this photo and see what's on the cliff face behind them.'

Gordy leaned in closer to the phone, narrowing her eyes.

'Bloody hell, Harry that's—'

'A cave,' Harry said, already out of his chair, his own phone to his ear.

Edward leapt to his feet. 'Give me my phone back! You can't just take it!'

Harry snapped around to stare at the man, a finger raised to his face, while he waited for his call to be answered.

Gordy stood up and, slipping herself between Harry and Edward, managed to ease the man back towards the table and into his chair.

'Matt?'

'Harry? What's up?'

'I think I've got something,' Harry said. 'I'm going to have a photo sent to you in a second. It might help us identify a location. It's the last photo Josh sent to his parents.'

Matt swore, then said, 'And they didn't think to show us? What the hell is wrong with them?'

'Not sure I can be bothered to go into that, either now or ever,' said Harry. 'Anyway, behind Amber and Josh is a cliff with a cave entrance. There's a good chance you, or one of the Mountain Rescue Team at least, will recognise it.'

'We should do, yes,' said Matt. 'I know most of the caves in the area, but not all of them. Someone will, though. There's nowt up near Cam Road, though, but there are plenty around and about.'

'Find that, we might find Amber,' said Harry.

'What? How?'

'I'll explain when I get there.'

'Where?'

'The office,' Harry said. 'I want the team there when I arrive.'

'Sounds like the break we need,' said Matt. 'Well done.'

Harry hung up, then stared at Josh's parents, handing Edward back his enormous phone.

'I have good reason to believe that your son and daughter-in-law ended up inside a cave,' Harry said. 'We have no idea what happened after that, but that photo is the best lead we've had all week. I need you to send it to this number right now so that we can get on with identifying and finding it.'

Harry showed Edward Matt's number.

'Now, Edward, if you would be so kind?'

Edward sent the photo.

'Done?' Harry asked.

Edward gave a nod.

'Good.'

Harry looked at Gordy.

'Between you and me, and regardless of what they've been through, I'm tempted to arrest these two right now, for everything from withholding evidence to obstructing the police from doing their duty, and frankly for just being so bloody awful about Amber and Josh.'

Harry heard an audible gasp from Kim.

'You can't say that!' said Edward.

Harry rounded on them both, slamming both hands down on the table as he leaned over, eyes wide.

'Trust me, there's a hell of a lot more I'd like to say, Mr Hill, but thankfully, Detective Inspector Haig is here, which means I won't. She will be looking after you from now on.'

'But—' began Kim. Harry shook his head so sharply at her that her voice caught in her throat, and she gave a strangled cough.

'Josh's wife, your daughter-in-law, is still out there somewhere, and I aim to find her and bring her home,' Harry said. 'You've lost your son, and I can think of no pain worse for a parent than that, so it's my mission now to do everything within my power to make sure that I don't have to go and give the same news you received last night about Josh, to Amber's parents as well.'

Edward and Kim were silent.

'My advice, for what it's worth,' Harry continued, 'is that you both put a match to all that bitterness you're harbouring, the greed that, for whatever reason, you've allowed to eat you up from the inside, and grieve. Think about Josh, think about the times you spent with him, how lucky you were to have shared your life with him in the first place, and the hole he's now left behind, because I'll tell you for nothing, no matter how much money you try and pour in there, it will never, ever fill it.'

His point made, Harry stood back up, nodded a silent farewell to Gordy, then left the room, and headed back outside to drive up the dale to Hawes.

THIRTY-SEVEN

Harry arrived in Hawes, thankful to find the streets quiet. The fake gas leak from the night before had done its job well enough to keep the place clear. It was still busier than normal, but at least he didn't have to wade through influencer wannabes and nosy journalists in need of a slap.

Walking into the community centre, and past a couple of mountain bikes leaning up just inside the door, Harry pushed into the office to be welcomed by Smudge. She bounded over to greet him, throwing her paws high to land on his chest, then immediately slumped onto the carpet for a tummy rub. Harry obliged, only to have Fly come over and want some of that action for himself, too.

'Here,' said Matt as Harry stood up, and held out a Tupperware box. 'I made you some lunch before I left.'

Harry checked his watched and sighed.

'No matter what I do this week, I can't catch up on all the time I seem to keep losing.'

He checked around the office, saw Jim, Liz, Dave, and Jen.

'Where's Jadyn?'

'Interview room,' said Liz, who was sitting at the office computer, scrolling through Josh and Amber's social media again, still trying to find something of use.

238 DAVID J. GATWARD

'What? Why?'

'Those mountain bikes you passed on your way in? They were pushing them through town earlier.'

'That's not a crime so far as I know,' said Harry.

Liz gestured at the computer screen.

'This might change your mind about that,' she said.

Harry leaned over.

'Same bikes,' Liz said. 'But so far, they're not saying where they found them. No, that's not quite true; they're saying they pulled them out of the river, but one look at the bikes and you can tell that story's one they pulled out of their arses. Plus, they had a few other things with them that don't quite fit with that story.'

Harry took a sandwich from the box Matt had given him and placed the box on a table.

'Anything on the cave?'

'No,' said Matt. 'But what you said on the phone about finding that and we'll find Amber?'

Harry then quickly explained what he'd learned from Sowerby.

'What is this, Harry?' Matt asked when Harry had finished talking.

'I really don't know,' Harry replied, then turned back to the office door. He looked over at Liz. 'What are these things that the two lads had with them, then?'

'Might be best if you find out for yourself,' Liz said. 'Let them tell you.'

'I should go along and introduce myself then,' said Harry.

Liz smiled.

'Jadyn was hoping you'd say that.'

Harry left the office and popped back outside to look at the bikes. They were expensive, there was no doubt about that, but they were also pristine. If they'd ended up in the river at any point over the last few days, they would've been bashed around to the point of being unrideable.

Harry walked back into the community centre, down the short corridor to the interview room, knocked on the door, and walked in.

'Now then,' he said. 'Thought I'd come and introduce myself, if that's alright with you, Constable Okri?'

Jadyn was sitting at the table in the middle of the room. Opposite him, two figures were slouched low in their seats, arms folded. They looked to be around sixteen years old, Harry guessed, with scruffy hair and muddy clothes. Neither of them were smiling. And though one was blonde, the other dark, there were enough similarities to make Harry think they were related.

Taking a seat next to Jadyn, Harry said, 'These mountain bikes then ... found them in the river, is that right?'

Both boys stared at Harry for a moment, mouths open.

'The bikes,' Harry prompted. 'In the river, yes?'

At last, the boy on the left spoke.

'That's what we've said, like.' He thrust his chin at Jadyn. 'But he won't listen, will he?'

'And you are?'

'Andrew Blyth.'

'They're brothers,' said Jadyn.

'Twins,' said the boy on the left.

'That's Connor.'

'They're nice bikes,' said Harry. 'How did you get them out of the river?'

'Waded in and dragged them out,' said Andrew.

'Where?'

Connor lifted a hand and pointed at the wall.

'Out there, like, on a bend in the river, where it was shallow.'

'And they were just lying there, were they? And you took them and didn't think at any point that someone might be missing them?'

'Finders keepers, isn't it?' said Andrew.

'No, it very much isn't,' corrected Harry. 'You ever go up Cam Road?'

The boys looked at each other, then back at Harry, shaking their heads.

'You mean the old lane off the road out the back of Hawes?'

asked Connor. 'Lived here all our lives, haven't we? Of course we have.'

'Been up there lately at all?'

'No.'

'You're sure about that?'

'We're not lying,' said Andrew. 'Not been up there in ages. There's nowt to see or do up there, is there?'

'But there was down by the river? Why were you there? What were you doing?'

'Just stuff,' said Connor. 'Nowt much.'

'What kind of stuff?'

'Just stuff,' said Andrew. 'Throwing stones, fishing.'

'Throwing stones and fishing?' said Harry. 'Don't see how that works, do you, Officer Okri?'

'Not really, no,' said Jadyn. 'Throwing stones would scare the fish.'

'Exactly,' said Harry. 'And you can't catch them if you've already scared them away.'

'Doesn't matter anyway, does it?' said Connor. 'Caught ourselves something better, didn't we? Those bikes.'

Andrew laughed at that.

'Yeah,' he said. 'Best catch ever, like.'

Harry gave a thoughtful nod.

'What you're telling me, then, is that you didn't wade in to get them at all, but somehow caught them like a giant trout, yes?'

'I guess,' said Connor.

Harry looked at Jadyn.

'Officer Coates mentioned they had something on them that I might be interested in seeing.'

Jadyn reached down to the floor and lifted a black rucksack, dropping it on the table and unzipping it.

Harry stared at the contents, then reached in and pulled out a couple of the things inside.

'A slingshot,' he said, holding it in his hand, then shook the tin he was holding in the other. 'And my guess is that I don't need to open this to find what's inside, do I? Ball bearings, right?'

'No law against having those,' said Andrew. 'Not illegal, are they?'

'That all depends on what you're doing with them, and where,' Harry said.

'We were fishing,' said Connor, 'like we said.'

Harry rolled his eyes.

'With slingshots, lads? Really?'

'Yes.'

Harry dropped the slingshot back into the bag.

'Probably best then that I tell you I'm fully aware of the effect of water on a projectile like a ball bearing,' Harry said. 'In fact, even a bullet won't get far, usually just a few feet, before it's rendered useless.'

'Been in the army, have you, like?' sneered Andrew. 'You're a copper, not a soldier.'

'Here's what I think,' Harry said. 'I think that you didn't find those bikes anywhere near the river, because if you had, there's no way you'd have been able to ride them into town, what with the storm we've just experienced, the river being so high. So, that's lie one, isn't it? And these slingshots? Never been near a fish, is my guess, which is lie number two.' He turned to Jadyn. 'I assume we have the contact details of their parents?'

'Yes, but we didn't need them; Jim recognised them. They're already on their way over.'

'Good,' said Harry, his attention back on Andrew and Connor. 'Because I'm looking forward to having a little chat with them, to see if we can't get to the bottom of exactly where our friends here have been, and what they've been up to.'

Harry watched a thin veil of fear fall on the faces of the two boys. He was about to press them again when there was a knock at the door and Matt popped his head into the room.

'Sowerby's here.'

'But I was only with her this morning!'

'Said she wanted to have another look at the site up on Cam Road.'

'What about the cave? Anything on that?' Harry asked, rising to his feet.

'Yes and no,' said Matt. 'Yes, because we've located the cliff thanks to Pete recognising it, and no, because there's no cave there, never has been either, as far as anyone's aware.'

'How do you mean?'

'Pete was back at the farm, but he was on the group chat we set up for the search. Said it looked like an old quarry on their land. You find them all over the Dales. Probably not been used since they were putting up all the drystone walls, way back when. But no one's ever seen or heard tell of a cave there.'

'That doesn't make any sense.'

'No, it doesn't,' said Matt. 'We've a couple of lads from the search team heading to the location now. Shouldn't be long before they call.'

Harry looked down at Connor and Andrew, then back at Jadyn.

'They're lying,' he said. 'When their parents arrive, tell them what's happened and see if they can't help you get some sense out of them.' He then stared at the two boys. 'And to answer your question, yes, I was in the Army, the Paras, to be exact. And though I'd love to stay and tell you what it was like, how I ended up looking like this, I don't want to give you nightmares.'

Andrew and Connor fell silent, and Harry left the room.

THIRTY-EIGHT

Harry walked into the office to find Sowerby waiting, a bag hung over her shoulder.

'Didn't expect to see you so soon,' he said.

'You and me both,' Sowerby replied. 'I'm full of surprises.'

'Matt said you've been up Cam Road again,' said Harry, walking over to the kitchen area to make himself a drink. 'Want one?'

'You don't need to ask,' Sowerby replied.

A few minutes later, Harry presented her with a chipped mug of tea the colour of freshly varnished oak and a small plate of snacks.

'Bit strong, I'm afraid,' he said.

'No, it's fine,' said Sowerby, then looked at the plate. 'No pink wafers?'

'They're banned,' said Harry. 'You'll just have to make do with shortbread from Cockett's.'

Dave came over, shaking his head.

'We can do better than that,' he said, then before Harry could stop him, he went to the fridge and returned with another plate. 'Cheese and cake,' he said, then walked back over to talk with Jen.

Sowerby took a sip of her tea, then reached over to the plate Dave had brought over.

'You're spoiling me.'

'No, Dave's spoiling you,' said Harry. 'He's a feeder. Anyway, back to you following me all the way over from the mortuary to head up Cam Road again. What's going on?'

'I'm not sure,' said Sowerby. 'It was after you left. I met with the team and we were looking through a few things, photographs, what we'd collected, and I still wasn't happy, so I thought the best thing to do was to just come over and look for myself.'

'At what?'

Sowerby, Harry noticed, looked weary. But then, when he looked across the room at the rest of the team, there wasn't one of them who didn't look like they could do with at least twenty-four hours in bed.

'First, just after you'd gone, some more results came back from the lab. Now, you know what I said about the mud under his nails? We found something else, too.'

'Like what?'

'Skin, actually,' said Sowerby. 'Obviously, that's entirely normal. Humans scratch themselves, skin flakes get trapped under our nails, it's to be expected. But everything's analysed, and that's where I started asking questions. The DNA we found? Well, for a start, it doesn't belong to our victim.'

'His wife's, then?'

Sowerby shook her head.

'Not unless she's been dead for the last couple of decades, no.'

Harry wasn't sure he'd heard right.

'I'm not following you,' he said.

'That's just a wild guess right now while we do further analysis,' Sowerby explained. 'What we found, it was strange, mummified really. Probably due to the environment it had been left in. If the cave was cold enough, if there was a draft, that might do it. And there was a high concentration of calcium carbonate, too. Water seeps into caves from above, dissolves minerals as it does so, particularly calcium carbonate. It's how stalactites are formed.'

'What you're saying, then, is that at some point, when Josh was in this cave we've not found, he also bumped into a corpse that could be decades old?'

'Yes.'

'And you thought you'd find answers about this up on Cam Road?'

'No.'

'Please, get to the point,' Harry said, reaching for a particularly large square of cake, and a chunk of Wensleydale cheese.

'I am,' said Sowerby, and she quickly finished off her tea. 'You know about the tyre marks we found? How it looked like someone had reversed a trailer up to the front of the campervan?'

'Matt mentioned it, yes,' said Harry. 'There's no reason anyone would do that.'

Sowerby reached for the bag she had with her and pulled out a folder.

'These are photos of the site,' she said, laying out several photographs of the campervan showing where it was parked, the awning, the interior.

'It was a mess,' Harry said. 'I knew something was off about it as soon as I saw it, but I still don't know what.'

'Matt mentioned how, when you first went up there, you'd said it would be impossible to sleep in the van parked at that angle,' said Sowerby. 'And that got me thinking.'

Harry shuffled through the photographs and listened.

'The more I looked, the more it seemed to me that everything was wrong; the way it was parked, the fact that the awning was inside out, everything being such a mess inside.'

'Leaving it like that doesn't seem to match what we know about Josh and Amber,' said Harry. 'It all just looked like it had been dumped there.'

'Exactly!' said Sowerby. 'And that's the word I'd use, too. I knew you'd agree with me.'

Harry frowned.

'About what?'

Sowerby took one of the photos from Harry and lifted it up in front of him.

'You were right, I think,' she said. 'There's no way anyone could sleep in it like this. And you know why? Because they were never meant to.'

'This is very rapidly turning into a headache,' Harry said. 'What do you mean, they were never meant to?'

'Like Josh's nails, tyres also carry with them evidence of where they've been, don't they? It can look like thin layers in rock, all squashed together, nice and flat.'

Harry could hear the excitement in Sowerby's voice.

'I never studied geology. If I'm honest, I never really studied, not at school, anyway.'

'The van was found on Cam Road,' she said, 'but there's a problem with that.'

'There is?'

'What we've found in the tyres shows something else, something completely different. There's no doubt that Josh and Amber were on Cam Road. The trouble is, they were somewhere else as well. There's no evidence to show that they drove up Cam Road to park where their campervan was found. The dirt and grit and everything else in the tyres doesn't show that at all.'

'But you just said they were there.'

'They were, but that was probably a week ago at least,' said Sowerby. 'After that, they drove somewhere else.'

Harry took a moment, trying to work out what Sowerby was saying.

'You look confused.'

'I am.'

'Think of it like layers in a cake,' said Sowerby. 'We've one layer showing them up on Cam Road, yes? Then on top of that there's another layer, showing they drove somewhere else to park up.

What we don't then have is another layer on top of that, to support them driving back to Cam Road once again.'

'That makes more sense,' said Harry. 'So how did they get there, then?'

Sowerby went to answer, but Harry jumped in before she could.

'A trailer!' he said. 'Bloody hell, Rebecca, someone took the campervan up there on the back of a trailer and dumped it!'

'Someone who probably didn't know too much about how to set it all up, but wanted to make it look like it had been there for a few days. Which it had, just not when we thought.'

'That explains the awning,' said Harry, on his feet now. 'The mess inside, the angle it was parked at, everything! Bloody hell, we've been searching in the bloody wrong place all this time! We've been using where we found the campervan as the epicentre of all this, but it's wrong, everything is wrong, the whole damned investigation, and now Josh is dead and Amber is still missing and—'

Matt called over and Harry swung around to face him.

'What?'

'Just had a call from the two lads we had heading over to check on that quarry. Their vehicle's broken down. I'll head out myself, have a look.'

'I'll come with you,' Harry said.

Jadyn popped his head around the door.

'Boss, you got a minute?'

Harry wasn't one for screaming, but right now, he was close to considering it.

'What? Why?'

'Andrew and Connor, they've changed their story a little.'

'Well, excuse me while I grab a trombone and play out a fanfare!'

'A trombone?' said Sowerby. 'Who does a fanfare with a trombone?'

'First brass instrument I could think of,' said Harry.

Jadyn said, 'They didn't find those bikes in the river.'

Harry was very keen for Jadyn to get to the point.

'Well, they didn't just fall from the sky, either, did they?'

'They found them in an old barn out on the fells. And I've got the location.'

Harry took a moment to collect himself.

'Are their parents here yet?'

'They've just turned up.'

'Right then,' Harry said, now talking to the whole team, 'Jen, Dave, I'm going to leave those two lads, and their parents, in your hands. Liz? I need you to check in with Gordy and Josh's parents, and with Amber's parents, too. Matt, I want you to head off and do what you just suggested. Jadyn? I'm with you.' He glanced over at Sowerby. 'And Rebecca?'

Sowerby was finishing off a second piece of the cake Dave had given them.

'Yes?'

'You're spilling crumbs all over the floor,' said Harry, and with that, he walked out of the office.

THIRTY-NINE

Having checked on the two lads from the rescue team and found their vehicle to be spilling oil all over the road, it was clear to Matt that there was nothing he could do to help. Grabbing the caving equipment they'd taken with them in case they found the cave they'd been sent to look for, and leaving them to wait for the breakdown truck to come and sort them out, Matt headed off to the location of the old quarry himself.

The journey was an easy one, taking him over Buttertubs Pass and into Swaledale, through Thwaite, and then finally up onto Shunner Fell. The wilderness here was spectacular, Matt thought as he drove along an old track, the gravel and stone beneath the wheels giving his slow ride out a hypnotic thrum, punctuated now and then with a loose stone flicking up to bounce off the underside of the vehicle with a dull clang or ping.

Shunner Fell was a vast thing, an expanse of grass and heather, of bracken and moor, and Matt wondered why he'd not explored up here more over the years. But how many corners of the Dales were there that he had yet to visit? How many other valleys and fells, fields and streams waiting for him to discover them?

Soon, a collection of low, rocky outcrops came into view and, as he drew close, he saw a lone figure standing beside a tractor. He pulled up next to it and was immediately impressed with just how shiny it was.

Pete walked over to greet Matt as he climbed out of his vehicle and was hit by a gust of wind, which brought with it the damp smell of peat and the chilly hint of snow. Not that any would fall yet, but Matt couldn't help feeling excited at the thought.

'Now then, Pete,' he said. 'This it, then?'

'It is,' said Pete, and turned to lead Matt up to the rocky outcrop. 'Like I said on the phone after you'd sent that photograph through, there's no cave here and never has been so far as I can remember. And I'm thinking that a cave's not something anyone would be likely to forget!'

Matt looked at the photograph on his phone and compared it with where they now were. It's definitely the place, he thought. Amber and Josh had been here, and then they had disappeared. But as Harry had said himself, people don't disappear, and finding Josh had proved him right on that, sadly.

'I need to be getting off,' Pete said. 'Harvest is always a busy time.'

'Harvest on a sheep farm?' said Matt. 'Never really thought about that.'

'Lambs have to go to slaughter at around eight months,' said Pete. 'And that's about now. We keep some on as hoggets, like, sell them at around eighteen months. I prefer it myself. The meat's got a stronger flavour to it, but not like mutton.'

Pete walked over to the tractor.

'Don't see many like that around here,' said Matt, admiring the machine, the green paintwork gleaming, though the front loader looked like it had seen a bit of work. 'Not unless they belong to one of the large contracting firms, anyway.'

Pete smiled and patted one of the tractor's huge rear tyres.

'Bought her this year,' he said, then climbed up into the cab. 'Anyway, best of luck with the search. Let me know if I can be of any help.'

'You've been of plenty enough help already,' said Matt, and waved Pete off as he headed on down the track.

Alone now, Matt decided that he may as well have a look around to see if he could find anything that might link the place to Amber and Josh. Not that he had high hopes of finding anything, but he knew he'd not be doing his job properly if he didn't have a good scout about.

The cliffs themselves, weathered faces quarried by those who had lived in the area so long ago, afforded Matt some protection from the wind, and as he drew closer, the place grew quiet. Beneath the cliffs were rubble, rock, and stone chipped away by chisel and the weather, to form a hard pillow at their feet.

Matt scrambled up the scree until he was at the foot of the cliffs themselves. He looked up, leaning back to take in the rugged beauty of the exposed geology, its surface damp, and lit by the glint of crystal. He spent a while scrambling around, constantly checking the photograph on his phone, trying to spot something, anything, in the rocks at his feet, but he found nothing. And soon, with daylight now fading, he decided it was time to call it a day.

It was then, as Matt made his way out of the shelter of the small crag, that the change in sound made him stop and turn to look back at where he had spent the last while ferreting around for some sign of the missing couple. But what was it he had noticed? Where he was standing now, the wind filled his ears with whispers, but closer to the quarry, all had been quiet. Or had it?

Intrigued, Matt walked slowly back towards the cliffs. The wind died, and the silence fell again, except now he realised that it was so quiet as to have no sound at all. Just at the back of it, faint but no less clear because of it, he heard running water.

Walking carefully now, the lengthening shadows starting to turn the rocky slope into a shifting thing intent on tripping him up, Matt followed the sound, stopping frequently as he worked to locate it. When he did, he found himself again at the foot of the cliff, but he could see no stream. And yet he could hear it, water bubbling away happily, so it had to be close.

Matt took out his phone once again, stared at the photograph, then back at the cliff. This was where Josh and Amber had been, and where he was standing now, if he wasn't mistaken, was where the hole in the cliff face had been.

An idea then struck him. The rubble he was on, what if it wasn't as old as he thought? What if the face had collapsed on itself, the storm working its way into cracks to pull it free?

Matt knew it was a long shot, but he didn't care, so he stooped down to pull at the rocks at his feet. The heavier ones he had to heave with both hands, rolling them down the slope, the smaller ones he lobbed free to clatter behind him, all the while the sound of the water growing louder as he worked. Then a smell rose to meet him, the cold mineral-rich air he knew well from the numerous caving trips he'd taken himself. Spurred on, Matt dug further until, at last, and with a hefty kick, a large boulder toppled forward into darkness.

Matt stood back, around him the evening gloom was thick as treacle. But he didn't care. Here, at his feet, was a cave, the one in the photograph behind Josh and Amber. Without a second thought, he made his way back to his vehicle, pulled on a set of tough overalls, grabbed a helmet, head torch, spare batteries, and a small waterproof bag filled with emergency food and first aid, then tried to call Harry. After the third call and still no answer, he sent a message, then pushed on, knowing time was critical. Then, with his helmet on, and a bright beam leading the way, Matt slipped beneath the moors.

FORTY

With Jadyn driving, and Smudge buckled in the back, Harry headed out of Hawes towards Hardraw. The road was no longer flooded, and they were soon zipping along a thin lane beyond the village itself and heading up into the moors beyond.

Harry had never been out this way before and was struck by how bleak the place seemed despite being so close to civilisation, the emptiness almost lunar, and broken only by the angular shapes of small patches of forest planted here and there like make-and-mend patches on an old blanket. Light was fading and Jadyn had already switched on his headlights, shadows chasing them along the lane, dashing between spiky tufts to throw themselves into hidden holes.

Harry wondered how the rest of the team was getting on with the tasks he'd set them. Before leaving, he'd instructed them all to keep in touch, so he wasn't about to start chasing them for progress reports.

'There it is,' said Jadyn, and Harry saw, rising out of the fading light of day, a low building, squat and isolated, just ahead.

Jadyn slowed down, rolling them to a stop just off the track.

'Odd looking barn,' said Harry, climbing out.

Smudge whined, but soon hushed with a scratch from Harry on her snout.

'Got a torch?' Harry asked as Jadyn climbed out as well.

Jadyn walked around to the back of the vehicle and opened the boot. From it, he removed a rucksack, pulled out two head torches, then swung it onto his back. He handed a torch to Harry.

'A little over-prepared, aren't you?' Harry asked, flicking on the torch.

The beam threw itself before him, turning their little part of the moors from evening almost to daylight again.

'I just leave it in there all the time now,' Jadyn said. 'All part of being in the Mountain Rescue Team, you see? Never know when I might be called out.'

'I'm impressed.'

'Actually, so am I.' Jadyn laughed, and flicked on his torch to double the brightness ahead.

Harry led the way towards the barn, and it was only when they drew close enough to see it clearly that he knew what it was.

'That's an old railway carriage,' he said. 'And by old, I mean decades.'

'How did it get up here?' Jadyn asked, as their torch beams licked at the flaking walls of the structure.

'Probably a remnant of the death of the railways,' Harry said, struck by how the carriage looked at once both alien and an integral part of the world around it, as though it had somehow always been here, a thing of rusting iron and painted wood, pushed up through the soggy ground beneath it.

Walking around it, Harry took a minute or two to find the door, the carriage having no windows and no obvious way in. But then he found a rusting iron handle and with a sharp yank was able to wrench it free.

The door slid to his right, complaining all the way, the scream and moan of iron against iron, despite the thick, black grease he saw in the runners that held it in place.

From the murkiness inside, a dry breath of air slipped out, bringing with it notes of hay and fleece.

Harry lifted his torch to shine the beam inside and then stepped over the threshold.

Jadyn followed.

Inside, Harry found sheep pens stacked up against the far wall, the floor covered in straw, and a couple of bales of hay at the other end, the blue and orange twine, which had once held them together, cut to let the dry strands fall loose. A large coil of thick hemp rope lay in a corner like a snake sleeping off a meal, and beside it lay a yard brush, the bristles half worn to nothing.

Harry walked around the carriage, looking for he knew not what, the wooden floor dull beneath his feet, then briefly soft and hollow in the centre, the wood no doubt rotten, he thought.

'And this is where they found the bikes?' he asked, as Jadyn poked around in a corner, sifting noisily through a bucket containing a hammer and nails, a torch, a pair of sheep sheers, and yet more of the twine, twisted into tight bundles, all of it nothing more than oddments collected by a farmer, used for one job or another, and stowed away for another day.

'Apparently so,' said Jadyn, now sifting through a couple of wooden boxes that had been tipped on their sides, one on top of the other, like makeshift shelves. 'Finally admitted that they were out here after rabbits,' he said, pushing a couple of faded hard hats to one side. 'Said they ducked in here for a bite to eat.' He lifted something up for Harry to see. 'I'm guessing they're not fully signed up to the idea of taking their rubbish home with them, either.'

In Jadyn's hand was a plastic carrier bag.

'Anything in there of interest?'

'Couple of cans of cider, crisp packets, that's about all.'

A sudden cough sent a shock of adrenaline through Harry, and he turned to see a tall silhouette standing in the carriage door.

'Grimm?'

Harry lifted his torch beam to see Pete Fawcett in front of him.

'I saw lights and thought I'd come and see what my old dad was up to,' Pete said.

'This is his?'

'It's been on the farm since before I was born,' Pete said. 'I always thought we should burn the thing, replace it, but Dad's a bit sentimental like that, especially when it comes to Mum.'

'Sentimental about a shed?' Jadyn asked.

Pete laughed.

'Him and my mum, they used to meet in it back when they were courting, like, if you know what I mean.'

Harry's laugh joined Pete's.

'The sly old dog,' he said.

'It used to be down in one of the lower fields,' Pete said. 'You could move it around if you needed to. It's been up here for decades, though. Dad dragged it up here after we lost Mum.'

'Dragged it?' said Harry. 'How?'

'It's on wooden runners,' Pete explained. 'They've nigh on completely rotted away now.'

'Sorry about just turning up,' Harry said. 'Didn't mean to worry you. Just following up on something. Two local lads said they found a couple of bikes in here and decided to help themselves. The bikes match the descriptions of those we believe belonged to Amber and Josh Hill.'

'And the bikes were in here?' Pete said.

'Maybe they spent the night in here,' Harry said. 'It's dry enough.'

'But then why would they leave their bikes?' said Jadyn.

'There's a lot I don't understand,' Harry said, shaking his head as he cast another fruitless look around the inside of the carriage. 'If they were here, how did Josh end up in a cave and then in the river? And where the hell is Amber?'

'That's a lot of questions,' said Pete.

'Just a few.' Harry sighed.

Pete said, 'I showed Matt around the old quarry. There's nowt there, either, though, like I said. He's probably on his way home by now, I should think.'

Harry checked his phone to see if there was a message from the DS.

'No signal,' he said. 'Well, we'd best be heading back.'

'I'll keep an eye out,' Pete said, swishing the carriage door shut behind them as they walked back outside. 'If I see anything, I'll give you a call.'

In the car, and all the way back to the office, Harry did his best to run through everything again in his mind. He knew Amber was out there somewhere, but in what state he didn't dare imagine. He felt as though he had all the pieces of the puzzle, but no idea what the picture was he was trying to make, so he had no idea where to begin.

Back at the office, with his phone on the charger, and night now fully in, Harry was staring at a map of the Dales on the wall. It had been there since the day he'd arrived, so much a part of the furniture that he never really took any notice of it. Now, though, he was trying to work out, well, everything really, and hoping for inspiration.

None came.

Jadyn came to stand alongside.

'What are you thinking?' he asked.

'I'm thinking that somewhere under all of that is Amber,' Harry said. 'We just don't know where. Everything we've looked at this week has been nothing more than a wild goose chase.'

'Does feel like that, doesn't it?' Jadyn agreed. 'What now, then?'

'That's the problem,' said Harry. 'I don't know.'

A ping sounded from the other side of the building, and Harry walked over to look at his phone, pulling up a message from Matt.

'Bloody hell,' he said. 'He's found it!'

'Found what?' Jadyn asked.

'The cave,' said Harry, and dashed over to the map. 'Where is it?'

Jadyn leaned in close, then dropped a finger onto it.

'There,' he said. 'Not far from where we were ourselves, actually, back at the carriage.'

Harry showed Jadyn his phone screen.

'Matt sent you a selfie?' the constable said.

'Look at what he's pointing at though,' said Harry. 'That's a cave entrance, isn't it?'

Jadyn narrowed his eyes at Harry's phone.

'I guess so,' he said.

'We need to get there now,' Harry said. 'What time is it? No, don't answer, I'd rather not know. Shift it!'

The journey over to where Matt had headed off underground was a blur, with no thought in Harry's mind beyond the fact that at last, some of the threads of the investigation were now coming together.

Arriving to find the old Police Land Rover parked alone in the dark, Harry leapt out of Jadyn's vehicle, leaving Smudge happily asleep on the back seat. He ran past the Land Rover and up to where, in the beam of his torch, he had spotted a small cliff sunk in the hill, Jadyn at his heels.

'This is it,' Harry said, a moment or two later standing at the foot of the rolling mounds of rubble, above which rose the black rock of an old quarry.

With a scramble, he made his way up the slope. He cast the beam of his torch left, then right, then left again, before chasing it along the base of the cliff, checking the photo Matt had sent him as he searched for the entrance to the cave Matt was in.

Except it wasn't there.

Harry searched again, zigzagging left and right, unable to still the frantic burn of worry he could feel growing in his mind.

'This makes no sense, Jadyn,' Harry said, coming to a stop. 'This is where Matt was, right? This is where he was when he sent us the message. And look at the photo he sent; the cave entrance is supposed to be right bloody well here! But it isn't, is it? So, where is it? Where?'

Jadyn's answer was to look at the photo, then back at the cliff face.

'Maybe it's somewhere else,' he said. 'I know it's not, but I can't see what else could've happened.'

Harry walked away from the cliff, kicked at a stone, and roared into the night. Then he turned around and stared back at the rocky outcrop, painting it with the beam of his torch, comparing it again with the photo Matt had sent him.

Then he saw it.

'No ...'

Jadyn came over.

'Boss? What's wrong? What've you seen?'

Harry checked again. It couldn't be. It wasn't fair. But then, when is life ever fair? he thought.

'The cliff,' he said. 'All this rubble? I think there's been a fall. The entrance, it's gone.'

'What do you mean, gone?' asked Jadyn.

'Matt,' Harry said, 'is trapped.'

FORTY-ONE

When Matt had heard the dull rumble somewhere far off behind him, he had known immediately what it was. He'd heard rocks falling in caves before, though mostly in old mines. They were notoriously dangerous places to explore, especially the old tin mines where tunnels crisscrossed each other, and the vast weight of rock was stacked high on wooden floors, ready to give way at any moment. And what he had just heard had most definitely been a lot worse.

He had remembered the cliff face above the cave entrance he had uncovered, the rubble beneath it, and he'd known immediately what had happened, because it was something that had clearly happened before; the face had given way, slumping over the entrance he had uncovered, and now he was trapped, in a cave he'd never been in before, without a map, and with no idea where another exit might be, or if one even existed.

Matt had never been one for panicking. It was something he prided himself on. There had been many a time when his unflappable nature, his absolute inability to get wound up and stressed no matter what kind of crazy was whirling around him at the time, had got on people's nerves. But for a moment, though, when he'd heard that distant sound, his heart, he was sure, had stopped.

I'm entombed, he'd thought, buried alive, lost to the under-world. Then he'd had a quick word and steeled himself for the task ahead. He had come here to find Amber, and he wasn't about to let having no way out of the cave stop him.

But that was then, before something heavy had crashed into the side of his head hard enough to knock him unconscious.He woke to absolute darkness. This was not how he had expected things to go. He had found the cave, slipped down into the darkness almost excited at the prospect, and pushed on, sure as he could have ever been, that soon he would find Amber and bring her home to her parents.

But no.

Instead, the world had caved in, quite literally too, it seemed, and not just back at the entrance he'd come in by, either, but right here and now.

His head throbbed, he was cold, and above all, he was angry.

Matt didn't do angry. He did happy, he did thoughtful, he did careful. He did grateful and confident and enthusiastic. What he did not do was the kind of rage now scorching a hole so hot in his gut that he felt sure it would burn through his skin and, should he ever get out, give him a dicky stomach for at least a week.

Matt quickly took stock of where he was, and by feeling around as best he could, had quickly discovered that things were bad. The cave entrance being blocked by a rockfall seemed the least of his worries, tied as he was by his wrists to the wall of rock behind him, with elephants doing the foxtrot inside his head. He had eventually noticed a faint orange glow in the cave, but it was far off, a distant thing that was useless to him right then.

Matt tugged at the twine wrapped around his wrists, then turned to brace his feet against the rock he was tied to and heaved.

'Snap, you bastard!' he spat, the words launching from him with a venom he had never known existed. 'Come on, just bloody well snap!'

Matt pushed and pulled, his muscles straining, his teeth grit-ted, but they held fast.

'Shit! Shit-shit-shit-shit-shit!'

Matt sagged, sucked in a breath. After a break, he'd give it another go.

Then, from somewhere in the cave, a voice.

'Hello?'

Matt sat statue still, holding his breath, willing every bit of his body to be quiet.

He listened again, sure he was hearing things, but it came again.

'Hello? Who's there?'

The voice was female, and it curled around in the dark, bouncing around on the edge of its own echo.

Matt decided to reply.

'This is Detective Sergeant Matthew Dinsdale,' he said, somewhat surprised by the formality in his voice.

'You're the police?'

'Not all of them, no,' Matt said. 'But yes, I'm a police officer. Is that you, Amber?'

'What? How do you know my name? Where's Josh? Have you seen him? There's someone else down here with us. And ...'

Amber's voice crumbled.

'Amber?'

Nothing.

'Amber!'

Matt tried again with the twine around his wrists, willing the rock to give way, to crumble.

It didn't.

'I'm here,' Amber said.

'Good,' said Matt, now searching for the right turn of phrase, something that would let Amber know they were going to get through this.

'We were exploring the cave,' Amber said. 'Josh found it and couldn't wait to show me. Then someone attacked us. I don't know where Josh is. I don't know how long I've been down here.'

'We'll be out soon,' Matt said. 'People are coming. They know we're here.'

Well, that much is true at least, he thought, because they did know where he was, and he felt sure Harry would be on his way if he wasn't already. And the rescue team would know what to do. They'd be through the rockfall in minutes, scrambling along the serpentine tunnels he had ventured through himself to rescue them both.

'He's going to come back,' Amber said. 'He's going to come back, and he's going to do to me what he's done to all the others.'

Others? thought Matt. What others? There was only Josh, and he wasn't in the cave, not anymore.

'Who is it?' Matt asked. 'Have you seen him? Can you describe what he looks like?'

'It was too dark,' Amber said. 'I couldn't see. Smelled like my grandad.'

'Your grandad? How do you mean?'

Amber was silent again. Then, far off, Matt heard something, faint footfalls shuffling through the dark.

When Amber spoke again, her voice had changed. It was flat, calm, accepting, and cold.

'I won't let him.'

Matt yanked his wrists away from the wall, numb to the pain.

'Amber? Stay calm, okay? The police, the rescue team, they're on their way.'

'I've got a weapon,' Amber said.

'A weapon? What? How? Amber? Amber!'

When Matt called again, Amber was silent, and the stillness of the dark was deafening.

FORTY-TWO

Harry was on the phone.

'Rope, pickaxes, hell, I don't know, do I, Helen?' he said. 'Just bring whatever you've got. All I know is that the cliff face has collapsed somehow, but the cave entrance is here somewhere. It has to be. Matt sent me a photo of it, we're here, and he isn't. Hurry!'

Harry hung up, stuffed his phone in his pocket, then rubbed his face wearily.

'Bloody hell, Matt,' he said. 'Why didn't you just wait?'

'He wouldn't think to,' said Jadyn. 'All he'd be focused on is Amber. He's probably looking for her right now, might even have found her and is right this minute trying to find another way out.'

That thought made Harry laugh.

'He'll be feeding her, then,' he said. Then, in a very poor attempt to mimic Matt's voice, said, 'Now then, Amber, best you get some food in you. Here, have this pie.'

Jadyn laughed, then had a go himself.

'I've only bought two cold roast chickens, but they'll have to do, won't they? Now, how's about a nice mug of tea?'

'That wasn't bad,' said Harry, impressed not just with Jadyn's willingness to join in, but also his ability to laugh when things weren't actually that great. He'd have made a good soldier, he thought.

'We just wait then, I guess,' Jadyn said. 'How long is the rescue team going to be?'

'No idea,' said Harry. 'They've moved the search teams in light of where we found Josh, but they're all spread out and on foot. Helen's doing her best to get a team together with all their kit and will have them head over here as soon as she can.'

'She'll have them moving alright,' said Jadyn. 'She's very good at motivating people.'

'You mean shouting, don't you?'

'Yes.' Jadyn nodded. 'I do.'

For the next couple of minutes, there was no conversation. Harry stood staring into nothingness, thinking about Matt crawling around in the dark somewhere under the hill, trying to find Amber and bring her out again.

He tracked back over the last few days: the discovery of the campervan, John Robertson, the tragic and awful death of Josh. Then what Sowerby had found out about how the campervan had been moved, and how that had seemed like a revelation at the time, but Harry still felt no closer to uncovering who was behind it all, or why. And as for the bikes being found in that old carriage? That was sticking in his mind like a thorn, and he had no idea why.

'That carriage,' he said, breaking the silence, deciding that two minds thinking about something were better than him tying himself in knots.

'What about it?' said Jadyn.

'I don't know,' said Harry. 'Something, though, don't you think? Josh and Amber's bikes were found there and there has to be a reason as to why.'

'Does there? Maybe someone found them and left them there and then those two lads stumbled on them.'

'Plausible,' said Harry.

'It was just an old farm shed,' said Jadyn. 'Just sheep pens and farming junk, that's all.'

Jadyn had a point, Harry thought. That's exactly what they'd found; sheep pens and hay, a bucket with a hammer in it, some old rope, a couple of old hard hats, a pair of sheep shears.

Harry cast his mind back to the carriage, remembered walking around inside, the air dry, rich with the scent of hay and straw.

'Boss? You okay?' Jadyn asked.

Harry ignored the question as he continued going over what they had found. He saw the thick, grey coil of rope in the corner, a torch, the hollow sound of the floor, rotten he had thought, though Pete had mentioned runners, the carriage being dragged to where it now sat, sinking into the hill.

Harry's eyes went wide.

'There's another exit,' he said, turning to face Jadyn, who stared back at him, face screwed up in confusion.

'What? Where?'

'Think,' Harry said. 'Think back to the carriage. There was rope, right? A couple of hard hats, a torch. What if—'

'What if what?' Jadyn asked, but Harry didn't answer. He was already moving, phone to his ear.

'Helen?'

'We're on our way,' Helen replied. 'Fifteen minutes, max.'

'We won't be here when you arrive,' Harry said.

'What? Why?'

'I think I've got something. I need to go.'

'But—'

Harry hung up and was already back at Jadyn's vehicle.

'Where are we going now?' Jadyn asked.

'Back to the carriage,' Harry said. 'We're following a hunch.'

'A hunch? Really?'

Harry jumped into the passenger seat, Jadyn beside him at the wheel.

'Blues and twos, then?' Jadyn asked.

'Absolutely,' said Harry.

Heading over the Buttertubs Pass, they passed the rescue team coming the other way. Jadyn flashed the headlights and beeped the horn as they flew past, though Harry noticed he was gripping the door handle tighter than he expected, all too aware of the heaving chasm that fell away to his left.

Through Hardraw they sped, past the Green Dragon pub, its windows dripping golden light into the night, then out of the village and soon they were back on the lane they had already driven up once before that evening, only this time Jadyn wasn't hanging around, and grit shot out from under the tyres like the spray of waves crashing on a beach.

Jadyn brought them to a sharp stop, and Harry was out, torch in hand, amazed that Smudge was snoring away in the back of the vehicle as though nothing was wrong, utterly undisturbed by the journey.

At the carriage, Harry grabbed the rusting handle of the door and swept it open with a grunt, then he dived inside, whipping the torch beam around to see the rope, the hard hats, the torch.

Jadyn stumbled in behind him, almost tripping over, his ruck-sack in his hands. He jogged over to the torch and grabbed it, then flicked the switch. A bright beam of light burst from the lens.

'Works, then,' he said.

'Why would it need to?' Harry asked. 'Why have it here at all?'

Jadyn picked up the hard hats as Harry turned his attention to the floor.

He walked around, stamping his feet hard, and noticed the tone deepen.

'You hear that?'

'But it's on runners, isn't it?' asked Jadyn. 'It's not resting on a solid foundation or anything.'

Harry grabbed the brush, swept the floor clean, stepped back to stare at what he had uncovered.

'Bloody hell, Boss,' said Jadyn.

There, in the middle of the floor, was a trapdoor, a small iron hoop bolted close to one of its edges.

'There's no lock on that,' said Jadyn.

'No, there isn't,' Harry said. 'My guess is whatever's down there, was never expected to get out.'

He grabbed the hoop and pulled.

The door lifted easily, but Harry stumbled back away from what was beneath it, a rich stink hiding in the darkness. It transported him back to caves in the desert, the sound of his heartbeat thumping like a drum in his ears, and the awful sounds of death echoing around him.

Jadyn brought the torch over the edge of the trapdoor, sending the beam downwards to cut through the black.

'I know I'm stating the obvious here, Boss,' he said. 'But ... that's a cave, isn't it?'

Harry walked over to the rope in the corner of the shed to lift it over to the hole in the floor. He was about to tell Jadyn to fetch the vehicle closer so that they'd have something to tie it to, but he was jarred to a stop. Thinking the rope was caught on something, he turned to give it a sharp yank and saw that it was tied to another iron ring, this one larger, and attached to the metal frame of the old carriage.

Harry tossed the rope down into the dark.

Jadyn handed him one of the hard hats.

Harry slipped the head torch onto it, then placed the hat on his head.

'You know, the last time I did this, it was Matt who took me,' he said. 'I swore I'd never do it again, no matter how much fun he thought it was to make me think the stream in Crackpot was waist-deep.'

Jadyn smiled.

'That was properly funny, though,' he said. 'You have to admit.'

'Ready?' Harry asked.

In answer, Jadyn swung his rucksack onto his back.

'Good,' said Harry. 'Then let's get this over with.'

FORTY-THREE

Grabbing the rope, Harry shone his torch down into the hole. The sides were rough to begin with, but further down they were smoother, and he could see the bottom clearly.

'Looks to be about ten, maybe fifteen metres,' he said. 'We're abseiling in.'

Harry stepped over the rope, placing it between his legs, the loose end behind him and down the hole. He then took hold of the loose end, looped it around his left hip, then up and across his chest, before finally letting it fall back over his right shoulder and down into the hole.

'Do exactly as I'm doing now,' he instructed, holding the loose end of the rope in his left hand, his right holding the end of the rope tied to the carriage. 'Watch your footing, go carefully, do not rush. And wait until I'm at the bottom. I'll guide you down.'

'Got it,' said Jadyn.

Harry leaned back, the rope taking his weight easily, the iron ring it was attached to making no complaint. Then he shuffled backwards to the edge of the hole, and with his torch beam guiding the way, started to shuffle down into the unknown.

The going was easier than he expected, the sides of the hole providing numerous footholds, many like steps, and soon he was on the cave floor. Looking back up, he watched as Jadyn followed on, taking it steady, and requiring only a shout or two to find a foothold he had missed.

With them both down in the cave, Harry paused for a moment. They were standing in a tunnel, the walls smooth from being carved out over millennia by water. He could just imagine how much fun Matt would've been having, had the seriousness of their reason for being there in the first place not been so acute.

'Which way?' Jadyn asked. 'And that smell, it's not gone away, has it?'

There was a faint breeze, Harry noticed, the air moving just enough to bring with it a hint of something unpleasant. It wasn't overpowering, and mostly it was drifting on the chill mineral scent the cave itself had, but it was there, a mix of rot and decay, but also the familiar note of something burning.

Harry led Jadyn along the tunnel, deciding to follow his nose as best he could.

The tunnel was narrow, and in places so skinny they walked like crabs. At one point, the floor of the tunnel disappeared, and they were forced to jam their feet into a narrow channel in one wall and brace themselves against the other, shuffling along as beneath them a chasm yawned. When the floor came up to meet them again, the roof of the tunnel disappeared, a vast crack in the earth, draped with calcite formations like curtains.

'And Matt does this for fun,' muttered Harry as they pushed on, around corners and over boulders polished smooth by waters now long-drained away.

'There's light ahead,' Jadyn said.

Harry brought them to a stop.

'Lights out,' he said.

Darkness fell, and it was absolute, a thick velvet that fell on them in the silence. Then he saw a faint orange glow ahead, flickering in the dark, thin fingers of it stretching out across the rock as though searching for something.

Harry went to switch on his torch when he heard a voice, the sound of it warped by the funnels and caverns of the cave.

'I heard that, too,' Jadyn whispered.

Harry pressed on around another corner.

AMBER WAS TRYING to stay calm, but her heart was beating so fast she was sure it would soon break free. Her breath was rapid, and she felt faint from it, though she had no doubt that the hunger and thirst she felt was as much to blame. Clamped tightly to her chest she held the thing she'd found in the dark, covered by stones, forgotten, a bone, snapped at the end to form a point.

Initially, the voice of the police officer had filled her with hope, the sensation of it so overwhelming tears had welled up unbidden, as her mind had filled with thoughts of freedom, of light, of her parents, of Josh. But then that other sound had joined them, those awful footfalls drawing closer from some other place in the darkness, and what hope she'd had just died.

'Amber?'

The police officer had called her name three times now, but she couldn't answer, not now, not when she knew what she had to do.

Amber knew that whoever the officer was, like her, he was tied somehow, unable to get to her, otherwise he would have been at her side already, and they would have been able to face their kidnapper together. Instead, he had called to her in the dark, trying to give her hope on promises of rescue.

There would be no rescue, Amber thought, because no one was coming. Except him.

The footfalls were closer now, and she narrowed her eyes in the dim light of the cavern, forced herself to ignore the stares of the dead, the numerous eyeless skulls glaring at her from the walls, the floor, mocking her, and waiting to welcome her as one of their own.

She saw movement in the inky murkiness skulking at the other side of the chamber, a hunched shape emerging out of shadow to stand before her.

The bone in my hand is a sword, she thought, and I will wield it terribly.

The shape came across the cavern, and dead eyes followed it.

It paused, standing in front of one of the shapes Amber had tried so hard to avoid looking at. Then it knelt, leaned over, and rested a kiss on its head.

Amber gripped the bone tighter still.

The shape rose and turned to stare down at Amber, and she saw a metalic glint in his hand.

HARRY DUCKED under a thick formation of calcite stretching across the tunnel like a crystal shelf, then squeezed around a sharp bend to find himself in a small cavern, staring at Matt.

'Bloody hell!' said Jadyn. 'That's the Sarge!'

Harry raced over, almost tripping as he ran.

'Amber,' Matt said, and Harry saw that his ankles were tied together with twine, his wrists bound the same way and attached to the wall behind him.

'Here, Boss,' said Jadyn, and handed Harry a pocketknife.

Harry cut Matt's wrists and ankles free, recognising the twine from what they had found in the carriage. At the same time, he remembered the marks on Josh's body showing where he, too, had been tied, and Sowerby's description of the fragments they had found of what had bound him.

'She's over there,' Matt said, his voice frantic. 'Amber! Someone's coming! We have to hurry!'

He pointed further into the cave and Harry saw the odd light he and Jadyn had noticed a few minutes before flickering on the walls.

Matt tried to stand, but his legs gave way.

Harry looked at Jadyn.

'Stay with Matt,' he said. 'Help him get some circulation back in his legs.'

'I'm fine,' Matt said, but Harry wasn't listening. He was

moving, dodging rocks and puddles as he ran, heading towards the light.

A scream lit the dark, the sound piercing as an arrow through flesh. Then a bellowing cry came after it, the sound raked by shock and rage.

'Police!' Harry roared, thundering to a wall at the end of the room they'd found Matt in to follow a short tunnel into a place considerably larger.

Harry found himself in a cavern lit by candlelight like a church at Christmas. Amber was lying on the floor just a few metres ahead of him, face down, her hair splayed out like it was floating on water. Standing over her was a figure, clothed in shimmering shadow. It was clasping something greyish-white that was rammed into their thigh.

The figure heaved the thing from its leg and threw it at Harry, then turned and ran.

Harry sped over to Amber and dropped to the floor.

'Amber?' he said, reaching down gently. 'Amber? I'm Harry ...'

Harry placed his hands on Amber's shoulders, refusing to accept that they were too late.

She gave cry, weak at first, but rising then, growing to an animalistic screech that rent the moment in two.

'Jadyn!' Harry called. 'Matt! Get in here! Now!'

They both appeared at that same instant, dropping down beside Harry as he helped Amber sit up.

Jadyn swung his rucksack off his back and then gasped, his gaze caught by the space they were now in.

'Don't look at it,' Harry said. 'Right now, we deal with Amber and we get the hell out. Understood?'

'What about who did this?' Jadyn asked. 'Did you see them? Who was it? Where did they go?'

Yes, Harry had seen them, but only as a shadow in the dark.

'Right now, I don't care,' he said. 'Amber's alive. We get her out.'

'I can go after them,' Jadyn said, jumping to his feet. 'You and Matt can get Amber out and I'll—'

'You'll do nothing of the sort,' Harry said. 'This place is a warren. For all we know, there are other ways in and out, tunnels all over the place. Trust me, an ambush somewhere like this is easy to create and a nightmare to avoid.'

'But you've only ever been in Crackpot,' said Jadyn.

Harry ignored Jadyn's confusion and looked at Matt.

'You good?'

'No, I'm not,' Matt replied. 'But nothing's going to stop me from getting out of here and taking Amber with me. How is she?'

Harry looked at Amber now. She was alert, her eyes wide, terrified, and they flitted between them.

'You're bleeding,' he said, seeing blood oozing from a thin line on the side of her neck.

'He attacked me,' Amber said. 'A knife. But I stabbed him. I think I got him. I don't know. Who are you? Where am I? Where's Josh?'

Before Harry could answer, Jadyn was speaking to Amber, first aid kit pulled from his rucksack as he quickly dealt with the wound.

'It's not deep,' he said, 'but it'll probably need stitches. This might sting a bit ...'

Amber winced.

Jadyn patched up the wound.

'Can you walk?' Harry asked Amber, and he stood up, reaching down to help her to her feet.

At first, she stumbled, her legs weak and floppy like a new foal learning to walk, but she recovered quickly, her jaw set firm, determination in her eyes.

'Yes,' Amber said.

'Good,' said Harry. 'Let's move.'

FORTY-FOUR

Harry led the way, retracing their steps back through the cave to find the rope still attached to the carriage above. At one point, a thought had struck him that Amber's attacker would return there themselves, climb the rope, and pull it up after them, leaving them trapped. But when he saw it still hanging in the darkness ahead, he guessed that his assumption about other ways in and out of the cave had been correct. That the killer had escaped made his blood boil, but Amber's safe return home had been his priority, and chasing someone through a cave system would have only led to trouble.

Jadyn was first up the rope, and he scaled it quickly, hand over hand, almost running up the walls of the hole.

'You're next, Matt,' he said.

Matt tried to protest.

'I need you there to help Jadyn lift Amber,' he said. 'Once you're out, I'll tie the rope around Amber under her shoulders, then you can pull her up, and she can guide herself up easily with her hands and feet, but without having to take her own weight. Understood?'

Matt gave a nod, grabbed the rope, and started to climb.

Harry looked at Amber. She was a mess, and not just on the outside either. What she had gone through over the last few days would haunt her. She would need a lot of help to face up to what had happened, to overcome it, and to live again. And there was still the weight of what she didn't know about Josh. But for now, Harry decided it was best that only he carry that for now.

A call from Matt above and Harry lifted the rope, tying it around Amber.

'They've got you,' he said. 'Frankly, Jadyn could probably heave you up there on his own without breaking a sweat, but one is none and two is one, right?'

Harry saw a flicker of confusion in her eyes.

'Two is better than one,' he said, and she gave a nod.

Harry guided her over to the wall.

'All you have to do is just stop yourself from banging against the walls,' he said. 'They've got you, they'll pull you up, and before you know it, you'll be out.'

'Where's Josh?' Amber asked. 'We were in the cave together. Have you already got him?'

'Remember,' Harry said, avoiding the questions, 'just stop yourself from banging into the wall. That's it.'

He called up to Jadyn and Matt to take in the slack, then saw something in Amber's eyes. At first, he thought it was her seeing through his avoidance of her questions, that somehow she'd read his mind and the horror she saw there was the knowledge of Josh's death. But as Jadyn and Matt lifted Amber to the surface and she started to climb, a yell tore from her throat.

Harry never saw it coming. Something slammed into him, knocking him to the ground, sending his helmet and torch skittering through the dark.

Harry rolled to his left, saw a boot launch towards his head, rolled right, and hit the wall of the tunnel.

'Get her out of here!' he roared.

The boot came at him again, this time connecting with his gut, winding him violently, sending bile to burn the back of his throat.

'I won't let you ruin it! I won't! I can't! Not now, not after all these years and everything we've achieved! No!'

The voice was rasped with pain and came at him on a spray of spittle.

In came the boot once more, but Harry was ready this time. He dodged it and jumped up onto his feet.

The rope fell back down the hole.

'Harry? Amber's out! You there?'

Harry didn't answer. He was focused on his attacker who was caught in the broken gleam of his torch lying up against a rock on the floor. A man he'd never seen before stared back at him with fire in his eyes.

'Harry?' Jadyn called again. 'What's wrong? What's happening? What's going on?' Jadyn shouted, his voice sounding far off.

Amber was out, thought Harry, and raised his arms in front of him, hands open, palms facing outwards.

'Giving up, is that it?' the man said, stumbling as he approached, passing into the bright light of the torch.

Harry saw a large swell of blood on the man's right thigh, remembered seeing him yank whatever had been embedded there free to throw at him.

'It's over,' Harry said, arms still up, hands still out. 'Whatever this is, it's finished and you're under arrest.'

The man hobbled forward, the wound in his leg making him weak.

'You don't know what you're talking about,' he said. 'You can't. Not in a place like this. You saw, didn't you? Back in the cave? All those others who came before, gave their blood to the soil? That's why, you see? That's what you must understand! If I'd not done it, it would have been in vain, wouldn't it? And I couldn't have that, not after she'd done so much, given so much.'

Harry hadn't the faintest idea what the man was talking about, so ignored it, focusing instead on somehow getting them both out of there, preferably alive.

'I can't let you go,' the man said. 'I can't let any of you go.'

'Hate to break it to you,' Harry said, 'but they're already out. It's just you and me, and the way your leg's looking, if we don't do something about that soon, the only way you'll be getting out of here is in a body bag.'

He knew he was exaggerating, but the loss of blood would have the man unconscious soon, or at the very least unable to put up any fight as they tied him to the end of the rope and got him out of the cave.

'She was first,' the man said, stepping out of the light from the torch and back into darkness, shadows covering his face like a mask. 'Gave herself to the land, she did. Never told me that's why she left that day, but when I found her, down here, I knew.'

Something in what the man was saying had hooked itself into something he'd heard before, but what was it, and who'd said it?

'You won't be able to walk on that much longer,' Harry said, racking his brain.

The man moved, stumbled, fell into the tunnel wall, but when Harry moved to try and incapacitate him, a blade caught the light in mean relief.

'Old I may be,' the man said, 'but I could gut you where you stand before you'd taken your next breath, trust me.'

The blade was long and thin and curved slightly towards the end. A butcher's tool, Harry thought.

Then a voice came to Harry, and he remembered.

'You're Pete's dad,' he said.

'William Fawcett,' the man said. 'The Fawcetts have farmed at Faer Fjallr for generations. I've never known anywhere else, neither's our lad.'

'I thought the farm was called Fairfield,' said Harry, not understanding.

'That's what it is now,' said William. 'But like so many of the old names, they change over time, don't they? And their old meanings get lost. Faer Fyallr became Fairfield; it means Sheep Hill, in the old Norse.'

Harry remembered standing in the mortuary, looking at the wounds to Josh's body.

'You carved a Norse word into the body of the lad you killed,' he said. 'Blót.'

'Blood sacrifice,' said William. 'Like my wife, Elsie, and all the others. Had to give blood to the soil, you see? The land needs it, demands it, and that's all there is to it.'

Without warning, William lunged at Harry, the knife flailing wildly.

Harry stepped back, the blade cutting the air in front of his throat. Was the old man really responsible for everything that had happened, everything he'd seen beneath the ground?

The knife came in again, but Harry was ready for it, dodging it easily.

'You're making this hard for yourself,' said William. 'Just accept your fate, lad. Let the land take you.'

He lifted the arm holding the knife, and that was enough.

Harry burst forward, closing the distance between them with ferocious speed, slamming his raised left arm hard into that of his attacker. William roared in pain as Harry's attacking defence sent an agonising jolt through his body. But Harry hadn't finished. He was committed now and had to keep going, to make sure he was at no further risk. As he blocked William's arm, he slammed his right elbow into the side of his face, once, twice, three times, all the while pushing forwards, forcing him to stumble backwards, until he heard the knife fall to the ground.

William dropped to his knees.

Harry kicked the knife away and heard it clatter down the passageway.

'Enough,' he said. 'You're injured. Stay down.'

He removed a set of handcuffs from one of his pockets, and secured William's wrists in front of him. He'd read him his rights in a minute once he'd got his breath back.

'Harry?'

Jadyn again.

Harry walked over to the hole and looked up to see the constable looking down at him.

'How's Amber?' Harry asked.

'She's okay,' Jadyn replied. 'Pete's just arrived.'

Harry glanced down at William.

'Tell him I have his father down here with me and he's under arrest. But before that, he's going to need medical attention, so we need an ambulance, sharpish.' Harry looked over at the old man, who was now staring up at him. His nose was bloody from Harry's attack. 'Can you walk?'

William nodded.

'I'm going to tie the rope around him,' Harry called up to Jadyn, 'then you do the same as you did with Amber, but he's in handcuffs, so I'll climb up with him and give him a hand.'

Harry saw Pete Fawcett's face appear over the edge of the hole above.

'What's happened? Is he okay? Dad? What've you done?'

'I'll explain when I get up there,' Harry said.

For the next few minutes, Harry helped William get enough life into his good leg so that he could be pulled up out of the hole with as little discomfort as possible. He checked the leg wound, judged it to be superficial, and was happy that it wouldn't need to be dealt with until they were topside.

The climb out was slow and careful, with Jadyn and Matt pulling the rope, and Harry gently guiding the old man up to the surface. As they climbed up, he ran through everything again, trying to work out how they'd got to where they were now. William was responsible, that much was clear, but there was still something not quite adding up.

At the top, Jadyn grabbed William and hauled him away from the hole, as Matt came over to make sure Harry didn't just topple backwards.

'A little more interesting than either of us expected, I think,' said Matt.

Harry saw Amber sitting on the bales in the corner, wrapped in a survival blanket and nibbling on a bar of chocolate, no doubt pulled from Jadyn's rucksack.

'Where's Pete?' he asked, seeing that the man wasn't in the carriage as he'd expected.

'He just nipped back to his vehicle,' Matt said.

Harry headed over to check on Amber, and Pete arrived at the door, a lit pipe in his mouth.

'Pete,' Harry said, heading over to speak to him. 'Mind if we have a quick chat?'

Pete stared at Harry.

'Sorry about this,' he said.

Harry caught the scent of Pete's pipe tobacco, and for the second time that week he was reminded of an old officer he'd known, back in his soldiering days.

'The biker in the office,' said Harry. 'The one who originally reported the abandoned campervan.'

Pete gave a shrug.

'It's like my dad's always said, the land needs the blood.'

In his hand was a shotgun, and it was pointed at Harry's chest.

FORTY-FIVE

'So, you're Jeff, then,' said Harry, catching Pete off guard.

'What?'

'The biker. I thought it was cigars because the smell reminded me of an old officer, back in my army days, but it was that pipe you're smoking now; you brought the smell into the office with you when you reported the campervan.'

Pete puffed out a thick, blue-grey plume of smoke, but said nothing.

'Don't suppose you'd care to explain the reason behind your little charade?' Harry asked. 'Why you went to the effort to draw our attention to the campervan?'

'It were him,' answered Pete, nodding his head in the direction of his dad. 'He'd taken them, taken them both. But it wasn't until I looked at their phones that I realized who they were, that they'd be missed. Bloody fool. We'd always been so careful, but now I had to do something to throw the scent off. Draw your attention away from our land.'

As this last piece of the puzzle fell into place, Harry couldn't help but yawn, despite the adrenaline flowing through his veins.

'We're tired, Pete,' he said. 'And if you don't mind me saying so, you're making a fool of yourself.'

'Is that right?' Pete asked. 'Looks like I'm the one holding the shotgun, doesn't it, Detective?'

Harry noticed that Pete's warm persona was gone and, in its place, something cold and hard had slipped behind the man's eyes.

'So, you're a part of all this, then?'

'The farm's a family business,' said Pete.

'What are you going to do?' Harry asked. 'Shoot all of us? How? That's a semiautomatic, right? One cartridge in the chamber, two in the magazine?'

Pete shook his head.

'I've got a section-1 firearms licence,' he said, 'so this holds five.'

Harry almost laughed at the notion that Pete had bothered to sort the legal side out of the weapon he was holding, but at the same time was responsible for kidnapping and murder. For a moment, no one moved, no one said a word, which gave Harry a chance to get his breath back and to get his thoughts in order.

'Well done, lad,' William said.

'Shut it, Dad,' said Pete. 'I'm tired of clearing up your messes. If you'd not let that other one escape, then we wouldn't be here now, would we?'

'I didn't let him escape!'

'Then why did I have to run him over and dump him in the river, then, eh?' Pete snapped back. 'I went to all that trouble, moving that ridiculous campervan of theirs, even joined in the search, and you still made a mess of it! You're too old for this, Dad. It's mine now, you hear? Once we've cleaned up this mess, I'm taking over.'

Harry saw Pete's words creep into Amber's mind. Her hands fell from her face and the chocolate bar dropped to the floor.

She stared at Pete, her eyes hollow.

'What do you mean? What other one?'

Pete swung the barrel of the shotgun around to point it at her.

'Shut it,' he said. 'You've caused too much trouble already.'

'Where is he? Where's Josh?'

'Your boyfriend, was he?' Pete said.

'My husband,' said Amber.

Pete shrugged and stepped further into the carriage.

'And that smell, I recognise it, too,' Amber said, her eyes wide like twin billiard balls. 'It was you in the cave.'

'Both of us, actually,' said Pete. 'The pipe's a habit I picked up from my dad. Can't beat a bowl of tobacco when the weather's cold, or to relax. Anyway, fun though this all is, best we get this over and done with. Dad?'

William shuffled over to his son.

Pete asked, 'Which one do you want to do first?'

The old man lifted his hands, still handcuffed together, and pointed a bony finger at Amber.

'She's ready,' he said. 'Your mum blessed her. And she'd have blessed that other one, too, if he hadn't run off.'

Pete gestured with the barrel of his shotgun towards the hole in the floor.

'Away then,' he said. 'Move.'

'I'm not climbing back down there,' Amber said.

Pete laughed, the sound cold, rattling around the carriage like a steel ball in a biscuit tin.

'Who said anything about climbing? Move!'

Harry stepped forward to draw Pete's attention.

The man swept the shotgun around.

'No rush,' he said. 'You'll have your turn soon enough.'

'You can't do this,' Harry said.

Pete frowned.

'I'm struggling to see what you can do about it.'

'I'm fairly sure I can do a better job of it than you've done with any of this,' said Harry, his words catching Pete's attention. 'It's been balls-up from the off, really, hasn't it?'

'How's that, then?' Pete asked, his dad now looking at Harry as well.

Behind them, Harry saw Jadyn moving slowly in front of Amber. Brave, he thought.

'I've seen what's down there,' Harry said. 'The bodies. I didn't count them, had other things on my mind at the time, but my guess is, they all have names found on fading lists of missing persons. The homeless, well, no one misses them, do they? And a hitchhiker's easy enough to pick up, or certainly used to be before we had all that CCTV put in everywhere. But this time, you went rogue, ended up with a couple of celebrities on your hands, people who would be missed, filled Hawes with their fans and journalists, all wanting to find out what had happened. It was a shitshow, Pete, and you know it.'

'That wasn't me, it was Dad,' said Pete. 'We only found out about the campervan because the lad's phone was unlocked when he found them wandering around in the cave. I made the best of a bad job.'

'No, you made a bad job a whole lot worse,' said Harry. 'I mean, credit where credit's due, you obviously had a good try, making it look like the van had been there awhile, but who parks a campervan at that angle? And the awning; you know you put it on inside out, don't you? Left the door open as well.'

William stared at his son.

'You idiot,' he said. 'Can't get anything right, can you? And you want me to hand the farm over to you? Are you mad?'

Matt spoke next, and when he did, Harry saw raw anger on his face.

'The search team trusted you,' he said, the words hissed through gritted teeth. 'And the whole time you knew where Josh and Amber were, what your dad was going to do.'

'As far as I knew, they were already dead,' said Pete.

'What the hell is wrong with you?' Matt snapped back. 'What kind of person—'

Amber screamed. Pete swung the barrel of his gun around to bear on her, but Harry was already in the air, and before the weapon came to rest on where she was, he had connected with Pete.

Harry's shoulder drove into Pete with enough force to send the startled man flying, the gun bouncing out of his hands. There was a scramble as bodies threw themselves everywhere, Matt diving into the bales, Jadyn in front of Amber. The gun hit the deck and blasted a hole in the ceiling.

Harry was up on his feet in a beat. He raced over to the shotgun and threw it out into the night. Turning, he saw Pete charging towards him, fury in his eyes.

'You bastard!'

Harry met the man's charge, grabbed him, and with a twist, sent him flying into the carriage wall.

As Pete struggled to get to his feet, Harry ran out through the carriage door, found the shotgun, and in quick succession fired off the rest of the cartridges, before smashing the gun against a rock with such force that the barrel broke away in his hands.

Dashing back into the carriage, Harry saw Pete staggering to his feet. William was standing in the middle of the floor, the hole directly behind him.

'What have you done?' he yelled. 'What the hell have you done?'

Then Harry saw Amber. She was standing, facing William, tears streaking her face.

She stepped towards him, and he took a step back, his foot catching only air.

William turned, saw the hole waiting to swallow him, looked back at Amber in panic, and reached out for her with his cuffed hands.

Amber held out her arm, almost caught hold of his fingers ...

Then he fell.

Everyone heard the sickening, life-ending thud.

Harry walked over to Pete, flipped him over onto his chest, and pinned him to the ground with his knee hard in the man's back.

Jadyn came over.

'Here you go, Boss,' he said, handing Harry a set of handcuffs.

Behind Jadyn, Harry saw Matt guiding Amber away from the hole in the floor.

Above them, moonlight broke through the clouds, and from somewhere far off, Harry heard an owl.

'I hate caving,' he said.

FORTY-SIX

The next twenty-four hours were a blur, though that wasn't helped by another late night and an exhaustion Harry felt deep in the marrow of his bones.

Having called the SOC team to inform them about the cave, he'd headed home and, once again, found journalists outside his house. This time, however, instead of running away, he'd made it very clear to all of them that they weren't welcome. To really send the message home, he'd pushed on into his house, then a couple of minutes later, returned to the front door with a washing-up bowl full of icy cold water.

'If you're going to behave like nosy bloody cats, then I'm going to treat you like them,' he'd said, and threw the water over them, slamming the door to a pleasing crescendo of shocked gasps.

When he'd then looked out of his window upstairs, he'd watched them wander off, bedraggled and shivering.

Smudge, seemingly untouched by any of the week's events, had slumped herself down on his bed before he'd even had a chance to do so himself. And with barely enough energy to get himself under the duvet, he'd left the dog where she was, the warmth of her body better than any hot water bottle.

The next day, the first thing Harry did was drop in at the office to check up on the rest of the team, and have a quick chat about the past few days, give everyone a chance to talk it all through, and to know what they were on with for the next few days. There would be plenty, but then there were numerous other police involved now, so the team would be able to check in on a few other local jobs, too.

Jadyn and Dave were to pop over for a chat with the hobby farmer Jim had helped round the sheep up for at the mart, and Liz and Jim planned to follow up on the fly-tipping. Jen was liasing with both Josh's parents, and Amber and her parents as well. Harry would be speaking to all parties later on, as well as checking up on Robertson, the photographer, who was still at the bed and breakfast he had put him up at. As for Matt, after being given a thorough checkover by the paramedics, Harry had sent him home with strict instructions to stay there for a few days until he was rested.

With that done, Harry then drove out to the cave, stopping by at both the entrance at the quarry and the one in the field beneath the old railway carriage.

Sowerby, her eyes bloodshot with tiredness, was at the quarry.

'You look how I feel,' she said, as Harry walked over.

'Same,' Harry replied, unable to stifle a yawn.

'I've never seen anything like this,' said Sowerby.

Harry let out a long, weary breath.

'I don't think anyone has. How many bodies?'

'Human or animal?'

That answer surprised Harry.

'Didn't realise there was a choice.'

'Right now, I'm not sure we'll ever know,' Sowerby said. 'They're all in different stages of decay, and it's not just that main cavern, either; they're scattered about the tunnels as well.'

'Explains what you found under Josh's nails,' said Harry.

'No idea which body it was from, though,' Sowerby said. 'Where do you think they're all from?'

Harry shook his head.

'Every force has a list of people who have gone missing.

Nationally, you're talking not far off four hundred thousand every year in the UK alone. Some return, some are found, but too many just end up a statistic.'

'How is that even possible?' Sowerby asked.

'Politicians will tell you that Missing Persons is a crisis,' Harry said. 'I'd be more inclined to say it's a national bloody disgrace.'

'We've identified one, though,' Sowerby said, and took Harry over to one of the SOC team's vans.

She handed him something in an evidence bag. It was a black-and-white photograph of a man and woman, and behind them was the carriage, though in slightly better repair.

'Mr and Mrs Fawcett,' Harry said. 'Pete's parents.'

'There was one body in the centre of it all,' Sowerby said. 'Surrounded by photographs, little scraps of paper covered in poems. It was wearing the clothes you see in the photograph. Some of the jewellery matches, too.'

'All we know is that she went missing,' Harry said, thinking back to what William Fawcett had told him, and what he'd learned from Matt, who had relayed what Pete had said about his mother. 'Walked off into the moors one night. Don't know why. Maybe we'll never know. Could be she went after a dog that ran off, or maybe she'd just had enough of living with a husband who turned out not to be what she'd been expecting when they got married.'

'A leaning towards old Norse ways and a bit of blood sacrifice, you mean?'

'That would certainly do it,' Harry said. 'Pete swears she fell into the cave by accident, or that's what his dad told him, anyway. Said the ground must've just opened up beneath her and she fell to her death. Not that we'll ever know for sure, with William dead.'

'And you think he somehow made a connection between that happening, and the farm prospering?'

'Death and grief affect everyone differently,' said Harry.

'How's the girl?' Sowerby asked.

'With her parents.'

'How can anyone come back from an experience like that?'

'Trauma isn't something you ever really get over,' Harry said. 'You just learn to cope with it a little bit better each day. Somedays, you just congratulate yourself for getting through them at all. Others, you'll see a gap in the clouds as sunshine breaks through. But coming back? You can't, not really; you're too changed by it, and the only way to live is to embrace the change and become something new.'

Sowerby stared up at Harry for a moment.

'You're a complex man, Harry Grimm,' she said.

'No, I'm not,' he said. 'Everyone has scars.'

There was more Harry could've said, but he wasn't really in the mood. He'd seen enough darkness this past week, and now he needed to hope that Amber would soon be blessed with a little light, however weak.

Sowerby walked Harry back to his Rav4. She opened the rear door and reached in to give Smudge a scratch. The dog, Harry was sure, almost purred.

'How are you going to cope without DI Haig?' she asked.

'I'm trying not to think about it,' said Harry. 'Though that does remind me that I need to give her a call and thank her for stepping in like she did.'

'You'll miss her.'

'We all will,' said Harry, and opened the driver's door to drop himself in behind the steering wheel.

'Any plans for the weekend?' he asked, slipping the key into the ignition.

'Actually, yes,' said Sowerby, and a smiled slipped across her face.

'Well, whatever it is, you look happy about it.'

'I've been seeing someone for the last few weeks, that's all. We're going away.'

'You are? Where?'

'Haven't a clue. Apparently, it's a surprise.'

'You've never really struck me as the kind of person who likes surprises.'

'I don't, but sometimes you just have to roll with it, don't you? What about yourself?'

'Nothing much,' said Harry, and went to pull the door shut, but Sowerby stopped him.

'Something wrong?' Harry asked.

'I forgot something,' Sowerby said, reaching into a pocket.

Harry expected to see another evidence bag. Instead, he saw purple and yellow wool in her hands.

'One of the mountain rescue team left it for you,' Sowerby said, then before Harry had a chance to react, she jammed it down onto his head.

'Suits you.'

'I have a face for hats,' Harry said, then headed back down the track and away from the cliff, catching sight of a laughing Sowerby in his wing mirror.

Before reaching the main road, he parked up for a moment, pulled off the bobble hat, took out his phone, and called Grace.

'Hi,' he said.

'I hear you've had a busy week.'

'You could say that. What about yourself?'

'No more than usual.'

'How's Arthur?'

'Dad's okay,' Grace said. 'Is there a reason for the call?'

Harry reached over to his glovebox and, opening it, pulled out a paper file.

'Yes,' he said, shuffling through the papers.

'Well, I'm busy myself, so—'

'I've been having a think,' Harry said, now staring at what he'd thrown into his vehicle that morning but hadn't had a chance to look through.

'About what?'

Harry quickly told Grace what he'd been thinking, all the time staring at the particulars of the house he'd bought in Gayle.

'Are you sure?' she asked.

'I know it'll take a while to sort out, and there's no rush,' Harry said, 'but we can't keep on like this indefinitely, can we, driving all over the place, living out of each other's wardrobes and fridges? It makes no sense.'

Harry heard a laugh down the phone.

'Are you sure you didn't knock your head this morning?' Grace asked.

'Very sure.'

'It's a lot for me to take in. You know that, don't you?'

'I've missed you,' Harry said. 'Smudge has, too, I might add. And I don't want to go back to how it was.'

'And how was it?'

'Busy,' Harry said.

'That's one way to describe it.'

Harry's phone buzzed, and he saw that Walker was trying to call him.

'I have to go,' he said. 'You'll think about it?'

'I'll think about it,' Grace said.

Conversation over, Harry answered the other call, and had a quick chat with Walker about where they were with everything and what was happening next. Thanking her for her help, he hung up, and was about to drive off, when his phone pinged.

It was a text from Grace.

I've thought about it.

Harry went to type a reply when another message flashed up. He didn't want to read it, felt his gut twist as the words floated in front of him.

It's a yes.

And Harry grinned.

What are you waiting for? Jump into the next thrilling investigation in the dales in See No Evil

JOIN THE VIP CLUB!

IF YOU'D LIKE to read my original first chapter for Dark Harvest, where you'll meet Amber and Josh in their camper van, before they head off to explore the cave, then download the eBook and audiobook here and sign up to my VIP Club! You will also receive the exclusive short origin story, 'Homecoming', to find out where it all began, and how Harry decided to join the police. By joining the VIP Club, you'll receive regular updates on the series, plus VIP access to a photo gallery of locations from the books, and the chance to win amazing free stuff in some fantastic competitions.

You can also connect with other fans of DCI Grimm and his team by joining The Official DCI Harry Grimm Reader Group.

Enjoyed this book? Then please tell others!

The best thing about reviews is they help people like you: other readers. So, if you can spare a few seconds and leave a review, that would be fantastic. I love hearing what readers think about my books, so you can also email me the link to your review at dave@davidjgatward.com.

ABOUT DAVID J. GATWARD

David had his first book published when he was 18 and has written extensively for children and young adults. *Dark Harvest* is his sixteenth DCI Harry Grimm crime thriller.

Visit David's website to find out more about him and the DCI Harry Grimm books.

 facebook.com/davidjgatwardauthor

ALSO BY DAVID J. GATWARD

THE DCI HARRY GRIMM SERIES

Welcome to Yorkshire. Where the beer is warm, the scenery beautiful, and the locals have murder on their minds.

Printed in Great Britain
by Amazon

34138189R00170